The

"Anyone who has suffered from the agonies of romantic obsession and unrequited love will empathize with Nevis, the protagonist of David Leddick's new novel *The Millionaire of Love.* In Nevis's beloved Radomir, Leddick accurately depicts the charming, selfish, beautiful young men who lend so many of our lives both delight and despair. Composed of shifting viewpoints and tones, set in locales as varied as Paris, Crete, the Loire Valley, Turin, Miami, and Sandusky, Ohio, this novel is infused with the deep regret we all must face, sooner or later, when the object of our passions proves unattainable."

—Jeff Mann, MA
Assistant Professor of Creative Writing,
Virginia Tech

"This moody and introspective novel of obsession follows the intertwined not-quite relationship between the wealthy patron Nevis and his would-be charge Radomir, an unconventional beauty thirty years younger.

But this is no modern-day *Death in Venice*; Nevis is far too self-aware of his history with men, and that history forms part of this contemplative novel. Radomir, on the other hand, becomes more than the unattainable prize, the heartbreaker, the 'millionaire of love,' as we see how he has carefully constructed himself over time.

Nevis and Radomir spend the years spinning through each other's orbits, changing each other's lives as they dissect their own. Leddick deftly characterizes each of them as well as minor characters, and gives Nevis and Radomir the authentic voices that carry the book."

—Jonathan Cohen
Author of *Bear Like Me*

"Leddick deftly chronicles the inexhaustible love Nevis has for Radomir, the object of his obsession—complete with hot back massages and erotic fantasies. Readers will find this book much like Nevis finds Radomir—sexy, fascinating, and utterly irresistible."

—Gary M. Kramer
Author of *Independent Queer Cinema: Reviews and Interviews*

"The millionaire of love is richly loved and desired, yet he is unable or unwilling to return the favor. That doesn't stop him from taking advantage of the one who unselfishly loves and cares for him the most.

In his most recent novel, David Leddick creates a tapestry of feeling and unfilled desires that is unsettlingly familiar, a mosaic of introspection and inner conflict that is compelling and stunningly beautiful. Leddick aptly explores the overlapping contours of undying passion and never-ending obsession, of heroic persistence and dreaded folly that any of us can fall victim to when faced with unrequited love.

Passionate, unrelenting, obsessive, and beautiful, *The Millionaire of Love* will capture your heart."

—David M. Pierce
Author of *Elf Child*

NOTES FOR PROFESSIONAL LIBRARIANS AND LIBRARY USERS

This book is published by Southern Tier Editions™, Harrington Park Press®, an imprint of The Haworth Press, Inc. Unless otherwise noted in specific chapters with attribution, materials in this book have not been previously published elsewhere in any format or language.

CONSERVATION AND PRESERVATION NOTES

All books published by The Haworth Press, Inc., and its imprints are printed on certified pH neutral, acid-free book grade paper. This paper meets the minimum requirements of American National Standard for Information Sciences-Permanence of Paper for Printed Material, ANSI Z39.48-1984.

The Millionaire of Love

HARRINGTON PARK PRESS®
Southern Tier Editions™
Gay Men's Fiction

Elf Child by David M. Pierce
Huddle by Dan Boyle
The Man Pilot by James W. Ridout IV
Shadows of the Night: Queer Tales of the Uncanny and Unusual edited by Greg Herren
Van Allen's Ecstasy by Jim Tushinski
Beyond the Wind by Rob N. Hood
The Handsomest Man in the World by David Leddick
The Song of a Manchild by Durrell Owens
The Ice Sculptures: A Novel of Hollywood by Michael D. Craig
Between the Palms: A Collection of Gay Travel Erotica edited by Michael T. Luongo
Aura by Gary Glickman
Love Under Foot: An Erotic Celebration of Feet edited by Greg Wharton and M. Christian
The Tenth Man by E. William Podojil
Upon a Midnight Clear: Queer Christmas Tales edited by Greg Herren
Dryland's End by Felice Picano
Whose Eye Is on Which Sparrow? by Robert Taylor
Deep Water: A Sailor's Passage by E. M. Kahn
The Boys in the Brownstone by Kevin Scott
The Best of Both Worlds: Bisexual Erotica edited by Sage Vivant and M. Christian
Some Dance to Remember: A Memoir-Novel of San Francisco, 1970-1982 by Jack Fritscher
Confessions of a Male Nurse by Richard S. Ferri
The Millionaire of Love by David Leddick
Transgender Erotica: Trans Figures edited by M. Christian
Skip Macalester by J. E. Robinson
Chemistry by Lewis DeSimone
Friends, Lovers, and Roses by Vernon Clay
Beyond Machu by William Maltese
Virginia Bedfellows by Gavin Morris
Seventy Times Seven by Salvatore Sapienza
Going Down in La-La Land by Andy Zeffer
Independent Queer Cinema: Reviews and Interviews by Gary M. Kramer
Planting Eli by Jeff Black
Tales from the Levee by Martha Miller

The Millionaire of Love

David Leddick

Southern Tier Editions™
Harrington Park Press®
An Imprint of The Haworth Press, Inc.
New York • London • Oxford

For more information on this book or to order, visit
http://www.haworthpress.com/store/product.asp?sku=5535

or call 1-800-HAWORTH (800-429-6784) in the United States and Canada
or (607) 722-5857 outside the United States and Canada

or contact orders@HaworthPress.com

Published by

Southern Tier Editions™, Harrington Park Press®, an imprint of The Haworth Press, Inc., 10 Alice Street, Binghamton, NY 13904-1580.

PUBLISHER'S NOTE
This is a work of fiction. Names, characters, places, and incidents either are the products of the author's imagination or are used fictitiously, and any resemblance to actual persons, living or dead, business establishments, events, or locales is entirely coincidental.

Cover design by Kerry E. Mack.
Cover design concept by David Leddick.
Photography copyright 2005 by David Vance.
Cover model is Eduardo Goicolea.

Library of Congress Cataloging-in-Publication Data

Leddick, David.
The millionaire of love / David Leddick.
p. cm.
ISBN-13: 978-1-56023-563-7 (pbk. : alk. paper)
ISBN-10: 1-56023-563-2 (pbk. : alk. paper)
1. Gay men—Fiction. 2. Young men—Fiction. 3. Unrequited love—Fiction. 4. Middle aged men—Fiction. 5. Americans—France—Fiction. 6 France—Fiction. I. Title.

PS3562.E28444M55 2005
813'.54—dc22

2005009125

"My dear, do not give your love to one of those millionaires of love. Give it to someone who really needs it."

Quentin Crisp

~Chapters~

~1~ Going to Crete

It was storming in Heraklion, although it was May. The Athens airport, where passengers sat in large stalls ready to embark for Rhodes or Cyprus or Kios or Samothrace, lay low in a steadily dripping curtain of rain. So far the flight to Heraklion had not been canceled, although the loudspeaker voice, always so loud as to be broken and incoherent, kept referring to possibilities of delay.

To the left the Mykonos flight was canceled. The shoal of stranded passengers rose, milled, drifted, and then a few guide fish headed back through luggage inspection toward the ticket counters. The rest of the shoal followed.

Nevis had arrived from Paris at noon with a long afternoon to spend. He watched the rainy roulette of the skies disappoint some stalls full of passengers, while others slipped away through the steady drip in their plane-bound coaches across the tarmac.

Nevis remembered coming to Athens long before on a flight from Rome that also carried Melina Mercouri, then on the upswell of her international rise to blonde stardom. Melina and her mini-starmaker husband rode in first class, while her secretary sat not far from Nevis in tourist class. When they descended from the plane, Melina shrugged off suggestions that she take ground transport and strode off toward the airport, two blond dogs on a leash, blond furs on her shoulder, blonde hair flying, husband and secretary and airline officials dangling about behind. She headed intuitively toward a mob of reporters and photographers, who had broken loose to rush toward their very own blonde Greek goddess of a star. Finally, Greece was in the twentieth century.

God, thought Nevis. *Can this be the same place?* All these Greek widows in black, these gray-suited tavern owners snoring in the corners, these red-legged backpackers all looking half-grown, half-awake, half-attractive. Nevis graded travel routes on the basis of the number of passengers aboard the plane he'd be willing to sleep with. So far, the Miami-Los Angeles run had been the low ranker. Athens-Heraklion was not down at the bottom yet. Nevis rated cities the same way and preferred living in Paris because it maintained a steady one-or-two-people-per-block of sexual potential. New York City rated very low. One a day perhaps, and anyone you'd consider sleeping with you already had.

The 7:00 departure for Heraklion inched closer. Nevis had finished reading *The Last Picture Show.* He had also brought Kundera's *Laughable Loves* for the flight back.

He was beginning to want this trip to be over. It was a long way to the village of Mythios on Crete, a village on the obscure south shore where Radomir had a summer job in a hotel. Who is Radomir? A lost friend? A lost love? A laughable love? Nevis wasn't sure, but ever since his cards had been read two months ago, he had been looking for Radomir. Whether the cards had been laid out in rows, circles, or straight lines, the piercing Russian eyes of his card-reading friend kept underlining, "There is a young man in trouble here." Both she and he knew the cards usually reported, "You are going to earn more money. There is money here. There is money waiting." But this time there was no money, just a lost boy.

Radomir had departed suddenly from Nevis's life some months before. He had originally been a friend of a friend at a Christmas house party at Nevis's country place in the Loire Valley. There had been an unmistakable sexual pull. The hunched shoulders with the hands in the pockets. The slightly rolling American athlete walk, as though the soles of the feet were slightly sore. The always slightly furrowed brow. It was not an uncommon type. Nevis defined it as the "I may not be much on conversation but I'll fuck your brains out if I get the chance" type.

Then one evening, as everyone was going to their rooms, Radomir raised his arms and his sweatshirt pulled up and exposed his very hard, flat stomach. *I'm going to get into a lot of trouble here if I'm not careful,* registered Nevis, and then wiped his brain clear of the memory.

On a sunny day walking through the streets below the chateau at Amboise Radomir had gone ahead with Nevis's niece and her boyfriend, Randy. They wanted to look over the gates of a townhouse and Radomir reached up to the gate pillar and leaped high onto a jutting portion of wall. The unsuspected strength of his arms pulled him higher than his perch and he almost floated into place beside the pillar. Nevis saw a large-shouldered, leather-jacketed Cocteau angel floating down to Earth. An Orpheus messenger. Or an eighteenth-century-ceiling Apollo, surrounded with the drifting sculpture of his draperies, the sun behind. Or a Mercury alighting. The moment flashed and was gone, but it had been there. Nevis pushed this thought away, too.

Nevis's niece Amanda cut Radomir's hair one evening in the bathroom that lay between two bedrooms. Radomir took off his shirt, and his powerful shoulders and arms gleamed in the overhead light. *This is not fair,* thought Nevis as he passed through the room, but he managed to force the image into the "Forget It" file along with the others.

Radomir was visiting with an advertising friend Nevis knew from New York. One morning Nevis noticed his houseguest's eyes shining as he came down the stairs from the attic guest room. It was the look you have when you've just had sex—pleasure, victory, being wanted. He found out only later that it was the last time the friend and Radomir had slept together.

When Radomir left after the holiday, he had never really spoken to Nevis directly. Radomir was not big on dinner table conversation, which made it all the more surprising at the New Year's Eve dinner when Nevis overheard Radomir at the young people's table in another room doing black comic dialect and hoots of laughter rising around him. The taciturn athlete was parodying the stuffy manner of a neighbor's daughter by repeating it as a black stand-up comedy routine. *Who do we have there under those football shoulders?* Nevis had wondered. But he never found out before the holiday was over.

Now the plane was boarding. The intercom had announced storms, but landing was considered possible. The stewardess at the door had long blonde hair and made Nevis remember Melina Mercouri again.

What is it about blondes? Nevis wondered. Even the Congo and Tokyo prefer them. As a blond, he had gotten a lot of mileage out of it, without ever finding an answer to the question.

The plane quickly fled over the rain and the cloud of gray nimbus below. The pilot spoke Americanese and pointed out an island to the left. Was it Lesbos? At the time they were to land the pilot cheerily announced that in fact gale winds would make it impossible to land at Heraklion after all. They were turning back to Athens.

The American couple next to Nevis were controlling their concern. "What's going to happen?" they asked.

"Either they'll put us up for the night or they'll try later," Nevis said. "I'd guess they'll try later. It's a lot cheaper than paying hotel bills for this mob."

Babies cried. Greek widows tightened their black babushkas and their seat belts. The plane landed and the blonde stewardess said on the intercom in what was possibly the only English she knew, "We have arrived at the airport of Athens. Thank you for flying Olympic Airlines. We hope you enjoyed your flight and will fly with us again." *Christ,* thought Nevis. The passengers were not polite to the blonde stewardess as they filed out and down to the buses standing in the rain.

As soon as he was back in the terminal Nevis found a telephone exchange and told the clerk he wanted to call Mythios in Crete. The clerk claimed there was no such place, obviously hoping this would be enough to discourage further effort. Nevis said, "That's okay. I've got the number. Can you give me a line?" The call went through quickly, and when the hotel in Mythios answered they recognized Nevis's voice and put him through to the dining room. Radomir was called to the phone and Nevis shouted through the buzz and rattle of the line that he was held up by storms but if he didn't call again he'd be there in the night. Radomir's voice seemed to sound both concerned and unconcerned.

In the airport the passengers wandered aimlessly and knotted and untied in clusters, trying to find out if anyone had any information. Nevis went to the ticket window and bought an additional ticket for the 5:45 flight the following morning just in case he needed it.

Shortly before ten o'clock the intercom squawked and the Heraklion flight assembled again. The passengers bolted for the ground transport as though once they were aboard the bus they had as good as left the ground. The flight unfolded itself once again. The Melina Mercouri stewardess greeted them once again, the American-voiced pilot once more pointed out Lesbos, this time the lights only. And this time the plane came down in a wet, dark place called Heraklion.

Nevis knew he would have to take a taxi for two hours through the mountains and the night to Plakias. He'd called the Heraklion Tourist Bureau from Paris earlier in the week and was told a price of 10,000 drachmas would be usual for the trip.

He was having the feeling that the closer he came to Radomir, the more he was receding from him. The sensation, with the fatigue of the trip, was that of operating on two channels. Channel One was the trip to Crete to see a friend who was working in a hotel in a small seashore village. Channel Two was the mythic channel, and on this channel there was a voyage to find someone who perhaps didn't really exist. Nevis, while on this channel, began to wonder if he had hallucinated Radomir's entire existence and was wandering off aimlessly into the Cretan night looking for a fiction deep within himself.

The Sunday before he had left for Crete he had crossed the Tuileries Gardens to visit the Pavillon de Flore at the Louvre. He'd passed a statue of Theseus struggling with the Minotaur. The Minotaur had a beautifully muscled male body; only the bull's head made it a monster. Theseus's own beautiful body was thrusting the Minotaur to the ground. Sensuality, if not sexuality, wove the two beautiful bodies together more than their struggle. The Pavillon de Flore was closed because of "a situation beyond their control" the small sign said in English. They offered their apologies.

Was he pursuing a beautiful mythic monster, he wondered? He got into the taxi in the windy, rainy night. Once underway he scrupulously turned off the myth channel, Channel Two.

Radomir had written him from Germany several months after the Christmas holiday, with the suggestion that he come to the Loire Valley and renovate Nevis's house there. At Christmas time Nevis had talked about renovating, and tentatively planned to get it done the following summer. In his letter Radomir said that he had renovated his family's home in Ohio with his father and felt he was skilled to do this work, and offered to do it for only room and board.

Nevis called his friend in Germany to see if he thought Radomir was capable of all the wallpaper stripping, replastering, painting, and woodwork scraping that would be necessary, and if he was really serious in his offer.

The friend said, "He's very capable. He's done a lot of things for me here. He could come next week. I'll be done with him then." Nevis thought, *Once a cunt, always a cunt,* and wrote Radomir that he could come. He offered to pay him modestly in addition to the room and board. And he told him that perhaps living alone in an old house in a small French town might be more isolating and less amusing than he anticipated. And that any time he felt he wanted to call it quits, he should feel free to say so and not feel any qualms about walking out on the project.

An acquaintance from Germany dropped Radomir off at the house in the Loire Valley on a weekend. Nevis and Radomir went to buy supplies together. He let him drive the old Peugeot that was kept in the country, and on Sunday evening Radomir took him to catch his train at Blois. Radomir seemed very confident about the project. Nevis himself had rarely stayed alone in the rambling seventeenth-century stone house and felt misgivings. He called several evenings during the week to check, and Radomir always seemed cheerful and bustling. He had a particular manner of answering the telephone with an upnote on his "hello" which made the caller feel he was delighted to be speaking to him, even if he didn't know who was calling.

Nevis decided to go down to the country the following weekend to keep Radomir company. He wasn't sure his sang-froid wasn't covering up some trepidation. He had discovered that Radomir was only twenty-two, although he looked and acted several years older than that.

As Nevis came into the train station at Blois, Radomir was waiting by the outer door. He was wearing his big-shouldered leather jacket, his thumbs hooked in the pockets of his jeans, and he was scowling. *Oh, God,* thought Nevis. *Oh, God. Oh, God.* And he knew he would only be able to keep the brakes on. There was no question of stopping and getting out of this situation. "Heartbreak, here I come," he sang mentally.

Nevis took to going to the country most weekends to keep Radomir company. One Saturday morning Radomir said at the breakfast table, "I dreamed about you last night. I dreamed I was looking all though the house for you. I went upstairs and I went through the attic, which in my dream was a dangerous place. I could have been attacked there. I couldn't find you anywhere. And then I went into Amanda's room, the tower room, and when I looked out the window I saw you down below, coming back from the village with croissants and things for breakfast. And I was so relieved. I knew you hadn't really gone."

Nevis felt something pull up on the handbrake in his heart. The telling of the dream was so guileless. And it certainly needed no interpretation.

He got up and went behind Radomir and started massaging his shoulders and neck. He told Radomir that it was a touching dream, but he didn't say how much. Radomir sagged into his chair and said, "You can give me a massage any time." Nevis felt another defensive piece move inside himself. He felt on thin ice. As he stood there with his hands massaging Radomir's strong neck and shoulders his American friend Fritz, who lived down the street, walked into the house unannounced and gave them a reflective look. Nevis knew better than to spring away from Radomir, seated before him. Looking at Fritz he said, "When I'm done here, you're next."

The cab raced through the wet night of Crete. From the map Nevis knew the coast road was excellent and the taxi could make good time. He felt the sea off to the side of the winding, rising, sinking road, but the night was black. He could see nothing. The driver offered Nevis a cigarette. He was glad to take it.

~2~ The First Night on Crete

The cab turned at random through the gloomy, yellow-lit streets of Rethymnon, the only major town on the way to the south coast of Crete. Then they turned uphill. In the mountain town branches littered the road. Nevis peered though the car windows at the trees still tossing in the high winds.

Entering a village beyond Rethymnon, the taxi stopped in front of a restaurant. Inside well-dressed Greeks reveled in the final stages of their dinners. At a large table near the entrance the driver joined a group of men. *It's midnight,* thought Nevis. *How do I explain to this man I'm in a hurry? That someone is waiting?* The driver pointed to a chair and, gesturing to the remnants of dinner on the table, said, "You want?"

"A tea?" Nevis asked. The owner went behind a counter while the driver put bits of shish kebab and fragments of fish from the other men's platters directly into his mouth.

Pouring himself a large glass of red wine he again said to Nevis, "You want?" The owner slipped a large glass of tea in front of Nevis so he could shake his head and smile. The driver said, "I drink this. No coffee. Never coffee. This keeps me awake." *Oh, great,* thought Nevis, knowing the route wound through mountains, along cliffs, and through gorges.

Young Greek men were wandering through the village streets under the grape vines as they left the taverns. The night wind still moved gustily and felt damp as they took the road again.

At regular intervals the driver turned off onto side roads. Nevis had considered renting a car if necessary and now realized how impossible it would have been to find his way. He mulled, not seriously, about being robbed and abandoned on the highway as the road wound on and on. The only other traffic was an occasional taxi heading in the opposite direction. One stopped and backed up to chat with his driver. His occupants, a couple, peered curiously at Nevis, who tried to look mysterious and distinguished. *My God,* he thought. *How much weirder could it get than to be stopped beside another taxi in the dead of night deep in a gorge in the mountains of Crete?* They had been descending through narrow looming gorges for some time. Nevis vaguely remembered reading about them in a guidebook.

Suddenly rushing out between blowing green fields, the driver said, "Plakias just three kilometers." Nevis dug into his bag and squeezed eyedrops into his eyes and combed his hair. Down a hill toward a suddenly appearing shore they plunged, and at the first large, white building under a street light the driver stopped. He seemed confused. Beyond the building more street lights glimmered along the curve of the bay.

"Is this the hotel?" Nevis asked.

"Don't know," the driver said.

A small sign read HYDRANTHOS BEACH on the building, which was part of a complex that reached back toward the hills. Inside harsh overhead lights fell over a table of four people. A man stood and approached Nevis as he entered the door. "Is this the Hydranthos Beach Hotel?" Nevis asked. The man seemed numb. He was short and faintly oriental looking. He didn't answer. "Does Radomir Pulkanovic work here?" Nevis asked, trying not to sound hysterical.

"Radomir, Radomir. Yes. He work here."

"Where is he?"

"Maybe in town with friends. Maybe asleep. You want room?"

"Yes," said Nevis. "Do you have my reservation?" "Reservation" seemed to be stretching the man's vocabulary. He reached behind the counter at one side and handed Nevis a key.

"Number Five," he said. "Upstairs." The other three people at the table watched Nevis carefully. *Two ugly German women tourists,* Nevis thought, *and Greek guys trying to get laid. This is some place.*

He climbed a marble stair in a small entryway beyond the restaurant and went down the bleak hall that leads to third-rate hotel rooms everywhere. The equally bleak room stared back at him. He looked out the window at a semifinished building across the street under the street light. *I've got to find him,* he thought and went out into the night.

The restaurant was attached to a larger complex of buildings, revealing themselves to be somewhat stylish with a pool and flower-filled balconies. A larger lobby showed beyond the pool. *This is the real hotel,* thought Nevis. *I've been euchered.* An older man was washing the lobby floor and a bartender stood behind the bar counting receipts.

"Is Radomir Pulkanovic here?" asked Nevis. The older man stared and muttered, "No, no." The bartender said, "Radomir? That American guy that works at the taverna? No, he's in town."

Nevis walked back out into the tossing night air and headed around the taverna toward the distant lights. There were smaller hotels, a bridge, then more tavernas with terraces, all facing a street that ran along the water's edge. A few people loitered inside each one. Nevis could easily see none were Radomir. *Curious,* he thought. *He knew I was coming. Will he be here, joking around with his friends, just to show me he doesn't really care? Just to make the voyage into the labyrinth ever harder?*

A toylike disco popped up, unreal looking as the stormy winds blew and waves crashed in the darkness. Young itinerants lounged on the steps, looking nonchalant, bored, available. It was hard to define the new international manner. They made having no money and nothing to do look interesting.

Nevis forced himself to go into the disco and peer about. When he was sure Radomir wasn't the guy in the back with his arm hung around the neck of a frizzy blonde at the end of the bar, he left.

Walking back through the wind and crash under the pools of light along the quay, Nevis thought of trying to find Radomir's room and canceled the idea. He went back up the empty marble stairs and when he put on the light in the equally barren room he thought, *This is the true bottom. This may not even be the right town. Or the right hotel.* He knew it was, and somewhere, probably close by, Radomir lay sleeping.

In the night the nearby waves continued pounding. The motorbikes of the homeward-bound discothequers roared under the window at regular intervals. Each time one stopped and pulsated below, Nevis got up and opened the blind to see if it was Radomir, returning with his girlfriend on the pillion. Radomir had told Nevis on the phone that he went to a nude beach, so Nevis imagined he might have a motorbike to do so. Then Nevis came to believe that the partially finished motel-type building across the way was where the staff lived. And that he was going to see Radomir going there each time he heard a motorbike stop. Again with girlfriend in tow. As he lay there his heart pounded painfully. He removed the rock-hard pillow from under his head and tried to control his breathing in order to slow down his heartbeat. It was really hurting as it thudded on and on against his ribcage. Through the hysteria he could observe his mind constructing scenarios with some interest.

Nevis thought of Radomir traveling through Italy with the couple from California with whom he had left Paris. *He's probably sleeping with her,* he thought. *They were hugging each other rather intensely in the street after we all had dinner together in Pigalle.* Nevis didn't like her because she exposed a wide expanse of her gums when she smiled. And was very serious about ecology. *They're probably catching quick ones in a youth hostel double-decker while her husband is out shopping for vegetables and wine in plastic containers.*

They're probably all three getting it on together. Beside a campfire among the Etruscan ruins somewhere. He knew this was rather farfetched, but the male of the couple looked like one of those sort of sexy guys who don't know anything, until suddenly you find them throwing back your covers in the middle of the night in someone's cold guest room.

No, he thought, *Radomir's probably fucking his way through a long string of German and Scandinavian backpackers. All with frizzy hair and half-formed features.*

~3~ The First Day on Crete

When Nevis woke up in his room at the Hydranthos Beach Hotel it was eight o'clock. He knew Radomir went on duty at eight. Somewhere inside him a voice said hysterically, "Is he there? Is he there? Is he there?" Another voice said, "You are not going downstairs until nine o'clock. Under any circumstances." He laid on the hard bed and stared at the ceiling, the sun leaking through the shutters for ten minutes. Then he got up and cranked up the rolling shutter. Below in the early light a woman jogged by in shorts. And a trio of very young American girls came down the road and curved around in front of the hotel. *These are the kinds of little girls he sees every day. Who think he's very sexy. Who all have crushes on him the few days or weeks they're here. What am I doing?* Nevis thought. He laid down on the bed again until eight-thirty and then slowly went through the process of showering, shaving, dressing. As he left the room he looked in the mirror. *Not too bad for a superannuated old fool who got two hours sleep last night,* he thought, and went down the dim hall and echoing marble steps.

As he came into the dining room where the proprietor had given him the key the previous night he looked about. Several tables were occupied. No waiters were apparent anywhere. He braced himself for the final shock: "He left this morning early." "He never worked here." "We don't know where he is." "We never heard of him." All the possibilities rattled like hail through his brain. And he turned to the counter full of shish kebab and baklava to look into the kitchen to see Radomir standing sideways in the shadows looking at him. Radomir said, "You're up early." Nevis thought, *I don't remember his eyes being so very, very gray.* Then said, "I got in about one o'clock." They shook hands across the counter.

"Oh," said Radomir, "I asked them at the desk when they thought you'd get here and they told me you couldn't possibly be here before three. So I went to bed."

Nevis asked if he could have a tea and went to a table near a window. Radomir brought him a tray with pot and cup, toast and jam, and a plate filled with little lozenge-shaped cookies. "I gave you a lot of cookies because I know you like sweet things," he said as he unloaded the tray in front of Nevis. Nevis asked him where his room was, and he explained it was right behind the restaurant. Nevis realized that his guess that Radomir had been somewhere nearby sleeping soundly as he wandered the night had been right.

After Radomir had been working on the country house about a month, Nevis called him and suggested he come up to Paris for the weekend, instead of Nevis coming to the country. He was feeling guilty that Radomir was working hard and well at the house. He wanted him to have some good times, and he also wanted to see him in the context of friends, rather than employer and employee. And he was wondering where the long massages he had been giving Radomir might eventually lead. Radomir was taking on a more and more baroque character as Nevis got to know him better! During one massage as he sat atop Radomir working on his chest and the heavy upper arms thrown back over the pillow he said, "What's this below your nipple, a mole?" From under his slightly opened lids Radomir glanced at him. "It's an extra nipple. I have an extra vertebrae, too. That's why I have trouble with my back." Every time Nevis gave him a massage he examined the miniature nipple and began to think of Radomir as a kind of magical changeling. Someone out of that time when Central Europe was fascinated with alchemy, when kings believed in magic and charlatans and scientists alike provided it.

When Radomir came to Paris for the weekend Nevis told him to take a taxi the twenty miles to the train station, to come first class, and that he'd repay him. Nevis always traveled first class and always paid the fares of those who traveled with him. He found it too embarrassing to explain to his guests that they should buy first class tickets if they wanted to be with him. And he didn't want to force them to spend more money than they had planned to. He always paid for any dinner he shared with friends. In his mind the idea of discussing who had the moussaka and who had the shrimp salad placed him with a class of people he had never been in and had no plans to join.

Through the spring they took turns. Radomir would come to Paris one weekend. Nevis would go down to the country the next. Radomir began studying French with the wife of the mayor's assistant in the village. Nevis suspected she had a bit of a crush on her student.

Nevis realized he really was falling in love with Radomir one June evening walking back to the flat on the Boulevard Haussmann after having seen a film on the Champs-Elysées. It was the kind of evening of which Nevis had often said, "You'd fall in love with whoever happened to be walking with you." The sky was still light, the chestnut trees, with their unusual ability to conceal very black shadows among their leaves loomed overhead. No one else walked the wide avenue, and the stop signs sent out their green and red signals blocks ahead to the handful of cars sliding by. The dusk was the exact "Deep Purple" of the song, and they were lost in it as they moved slowly along under the trees. Nevis looked at the sulky boy walking beside him, heavy shoulders hunched forward, looking slowly downward under his heavy brows. He seemed unaware of the evening around him, but Nevis had come to know that the unawareness often signaled being very aware and not wanting anyone to sense it. He felt an old familiar lurch inside. It was like seeing a dish falling. The crash, the breaking apart, the irrevocable thing hasn't happened yet but cannot be avoided. Those moments when everything is still all right but where there is no road back, the smashing that changes everything cannot be avoided—the moment before death must be like that. That was the moment on the Boulevard Haussmann. The falling toward the bad thing.

On the weekends that Nevis went to the country they began making day trips. Trips Nevis had talked of making for many seasons. He gave Radomir *Le Grand Meaulnes* to read in English, and one weekend they traveled into the Sologne to visit the village where that magical, romantic story had taken place. The *Grand Meaulnes* village itself was dead of any magic, but the long, straight roads through the flat, pine-burdened land, the glimmer of tiny lakes flashing through the trees, the red-brick eighteenth-century chateaux standing straight and lonely in this noncommital Scandinavian-looking countryside had the effect of throwing them more closely into each other's companionship. The difference in their ages and lives began to wear away. Radomir did all the driving of the ancient Peugeot and at the wheel as he stared over the road he talked more openly about himself. The fact that in the old car the passenger's seat was so dilapidated that Nevis, a good bit taller, could look directly into Radomir's eyes leveled their relation even more.

"I felt very strongly I had been here before and I wanted to come back. That's why I wrote you," Radomir said. Nevis had very limited feelings about past lives. He had been educated and done military service before the 1960s had arrived, and at Radomir's age he had moved with a brittle, hard-drinking witty set who would have thought the hereafter was something their kind of people never discussed. They believed that serious people acted silly, and only silly people acted serious. It was the final fading of the "entre les guerres" attitude that ended in their generation. Radomir had come to Europe from California where the 1960s determination to explore oneself quickly and with the least possible effort lives on eternally.

"You know there's a ghost in your house, don't you?" he said as the car hurtled between the pines in the fading light of the early spring day. Nevis said that many people had felt that in the house, but unfortunately he had never had any sense of it. Nevis felt all large empty houses were spooky and was reluctant to even stay in his own alone. But he blamed this on being brought up in a large house full of people, a house that was heavy with their absence when it was empty.

He asked Radomir about it. "I hear his footsteps over-head." Nevis reported that a number of others who slept in the bedroom Radomir was using had said the same thing. He wasn't sure it wasn't the elderly couple next door whom he knew cavorted about greatly in the night. His own imaginings ran more to black lace underwear and dildos and "You chase me, then I'll chase you."

"He's young," Radomir went on. "Or was young once. He doesn't frighten me. Well, he did once. He touched me and I probably would have seen him if I hadn't acted like a fish out of water. I think he likes me. I think he likes my company."

As the day grew darker Radomir put on the slightly wall-eyed headlights of the Peugeot and Nevis pondered on the ghost. He didn't discount it. Radomir had earlier told him that when he was young their family home had been invaded by poltergeists.

Nevis had read a good bit on poltergeists and knew they were always linked to a young person in the household with strong and disturbed emotions. He thought it was very likely Radomir *was* experiencing a strong emotional contact with something. He wondered if it was a beautiful French friend of his who had died of AIDS the year before, and who had first become ill while he was staying in the house. *Maybe it's André come back,* he thought. *It would be just like him to fall in love with Radomir and not make the slightest effort to contact me.*

"He's trying to communicate something to me," Radomir went on. "I feel him around me. He pushed the two little porcelain busts on the dressing table in my room together so they were kissing."

That evening when Nevis was giving Radomir what was becoming an expected and usual massage he slipped his pajama bottoms down to massage the hollows of his buttocks to see if he objected. Radomir said nothing, but the defenselessness and childlike look of his lower back touched Nevis. It made him think of his own nephews when he tended them as babies, and of their sweet, soft cuddliness when he changed their diapers. Radomir's heavily developed upper body and long curving back and his relatively short legs gave a childlike quality to his stance, as his rounded nose and cheeks, forehead, and lips gave to his face. Which didn't keep Nevis from having an aching hard-on while he gave him his massages. And a fairly explosive masturbation session later.

~4~ Radomir's Side

So he's here. What gives with this guy? I'm kind of glad to see him, but I really don't ever want to lay eyes on him again. I owe him a lot, but I hate him. He's been trying to get into my pants since the first day I met him, and he just won't give up.

But to be fair, it wasn't always that way. When I first came to France I hardly noticed him. He was just a friend of Larry's from New York who had a house in the Loire Valley. An old friend. And I mean old. God, he was way into his fifties. He had a big job in advertising. Larry said he could write his own ticket as far as jobs went. He was nice, you know. Very gay. Not so much swishy as tall and thin and very nicely dressed. Too nicely dressed. When you see guys like that you say to yourself, what else could they be? The kind of men who know all the words to all the old songs.

He was kind of funny that way. I mean really funny. He would just sing out wherever he was. Walking down the street, sitting in a restaurant. It embarrassed some people. But not me. It didn't embarrass his niece either. Amanda. She was there that Christmas, too. With her boyfriend. She was a model working in Barcelona and Madrid. I broke it off with Larry while we were in France because she and her boyfriend seemed to be having such a good time together. And I wanted to be like them.

When I first met Larry in Germany I have to admit I was crazy about him. I thought he was so handsome. And he had been the lover of Dan Danforth, the guy I had broken up with when I left California. He really loved Dan, and Dan didn't give a hoot in hell about Larry. So fucking him was like giving him what Dan wouldn't. It's always the same old crap, isn't it? Larry wanted Dan; Dan wanted me. I wanted Larry and got him. Not that he wasn't a really great fuck. The first time I was with him we had four wonderful days and three fantastic nights together.

So when I went back to Germany to live with him it wasn't as though I was using him when that job I had been promised just failed to materialize. I did want to be with him. But I was always thinking about Esther back in California, too. And when I was in France and Amanda and her boyfriend were there I remembered what it was like to have a girlfriend and decided to go back to that. I gave Larry a really good fuck in that little bedroom on the top floor of the house in the country one morning and that was that.

Now I kind of wonder why I thought my time with Esther was so great. She had that other boyfriend she wouldn't give up. We even had a threesome at her request. Maybe so she could make a real on-site comparison. I don't know what she decided, but she got hers that night. We were both probably trying to outfuck the other guy. Clever girl. The only hitch was I wouldn't have minded throwing a fuck into him, too, while I was at it. I could have fucked him while he was fucking her. It occurred to me, but I was pretty sure he wasn't up for it, so I didn't try anything. And that would have really clinched it with Esther. All the attention was supposed to be on her. Not on either of us. But he definitely had a nice ass.

That's how I came to Europe. Esther wouldn't leave that guy, who had a nice ass but was definitely a loser. I got that job in Rome through the company I was working for, and when I got there the job didn't exist. So they sent me to London, and I went by way of Germany and started that little affair with Larry. London didn't have a job for me either, so I went back to Rome and there it was real obvious that I was just being given the runaround. Somehow I just couldn't go back to the United States. I didn't want to see Esther again. I didn't want to see Dan Danforth again. I'd broken it off with him when I was getting serious about Esther, and I didn't want to back over the same ground again. So I wound up with Larry. And because of Larry I ended up in France.

I was never really involved with Nevis. I was involved with his house. The house really got to me. I've always been interested in that woo-woo stuff. And he had that really strange house out there in the Loire Valley. It's all staircases and halls running off this way and that and attics rambling around up above and a couple of caves under the house with strange things in them. I just fell in love with that house. So when I got back to Germany I wrote a letter to Nevis and asked him if I could renovate it for him. He had been talking about how it really needed to have all the old wallpaper pulled off and the plaster repaired and be repainted and there were lots of little things he wanted to have repaired and changed and he just hadn't found the time to do them.

Of course, I knew he was interested in me. I'm not that dumb. And I made sure that he saw my body a couple of times while I was there. Just to make sure, you know. I mean, he had a big job in advertising. You never know when those things will come in handy. And he seemed to be a nice enough guy.

I knew he'd do it. He wrote back and said he wasn't so sure that I'd like living full-time in a little French village but that I could give it a try and if I didn't like it and wanted to call it quits that would be fine with him.

Actually, it was cool. Nevis kept an old car out there and gave me money to buy paint and supplies and I got busy. I'd done a lot of that kind of stuff with my dad when we added a back wing to the house, and I'm pretty disciplined. I can cook for myself, and I kind of got off on that little village with its two grocery stores and the butcher and the baker. It had everything but the candlestick maker.

Of course, it's pretty gray in France in the wintertime. And wet. But the house had central heating, and I loved making a big fire in the kitchen fireplace and staying there most of the time I wasn't stripping wallpaper or plastering or something. And there were some other Americans around.

There was Fritz, who was doing pretty much the same thing I was to an old house down the street. Fritz had been the lover of a French friend of Nevis's who had died of AIDS. This all took place in California. Fritz was pretty upset. He had been to France with his lover and decided to come visit Nevis. Which he did, saw that a house was for sale, and bought it. I think he wanted to be near Nevis. I think he wanted to have an affair with Nevis, who wasn't having any. Which was a real mistake in my opinion. Fritz has a gigantic cock.

Fritz and I hung out together a good bit. I used to fix dinner for him, and when we needed two people to lift or haul something we helped each other. He was a really good guy, but he tended to use drugs a lot when he got lonely. Prescription drugs. He slept a lot. He said it was because of his asthma. He was a real redneck, good 'ol boy from Alabama, Fritz was. Very good-hearted. I think there had been a big insurance policy on his French lover and Fritz collected a lot of money, none of which he gave to his lover's parents, who lived in the next town. That was just a fluke, Nevis told me. Fritz had known the French lover in Paris and only later discovered he was from the same area where Nevis had a house.

I wonder if the French lover had been a lover of Nevis's before Fritz? I never asked. Probably.

Fritz had been in France at least a year before me and didn't speak a word of French. I told him once I thought he should try to learn, and he said, "Hell, ah don't even speak English!" Which was kind of true, although he told me that at one time he had taught in a private girls' school in San Francisco. I wonder what? Those girls must have had some pretty funny accents when they got out of that school.

I started studying French right away with the wife of the assistant to the mayor in town. She was an American married to a young Frenchman she had met in school in the United States. Elsie was her name. I went to Elsie three times a week. She had a crush on me. I could see that. I wasn't about to get involved, though she was pretty nice looking. You could tell where all that would go. She would want to leave her husband and marry me. Then we'd go back to the States. Etcetera. Etcetera. Definitely not in my game plan.

I kind of led her to believe that I was interested in Angelina. Angie. The daughter of some Americans who had a house across the river, about five miles away. They were friends of Nevis's, too. Angie was staying at her parents' house for the winter, so she and Fritz hung out together quite a lot. I don't know quite what Angie's story was. She was older than I was by a few years, younger than Fritz. They went out to bars together. They took me to the one gay bar in Blois. Which wasn't very gay. Kind of a mixed crowd. I guess they thought they might each find somebody there. There wasn't a whole lot to choose from the night I stopped in. I was definitely the hottest guy in the place.

Angie would have liked to get it on with me—that was clear. But that wasn't in the cards either. Well, maybe. I couldn't tell why she was fucked up, but fucked up she certainly was. Fritz told me that they sometimes discussed trying to go to bed together, but that didn't happen either. When I think of it, it was kind of strange that Fritz never came on to me. I guess any attention he could spare from his house and his sleeping pills went to Nevis—who was always very nice to Fritz, but clearly there was nothing doing.

In my own case I wasn't so lucky. Nevis came down to the country every other weekend to see how I was doing and to give me a hand with things. To his credit, he was a good worker and pitched right in with the painting and wallpaper peeling.

On the alternate weekends he had me come up to Paris so I wouldn't get too bored. I could tell he was falling for me, but he was always the perfect gentleman. And he could be very interesting. There were always exhibitions in Paris to see. Weird ones on erotic Greek pottery or photographs of French film stars from the 1930s. We took the trip in the sewers of Paris by boat, definitely weird. We walked through the catacombs carrying those flickering candles, another weird trip. No, you could not say that Nevis was boring, and he always concentrated on the other person.

I think my big mistake was in the country house when I had a stiff neck and Nevis started to massage it. He is very good at massage. I said, "You can give me a massage any time." Partly because I do love a good massage and I think probably I was getting a little tired of his tight-ass "I'm not going to touch you" routine. Fritz walked into the house just as Nevis was massaging my neck, and he got the picture right away, I could tell. The world is just full of people not getting what they want, I guess.

~5~ Nevis Speaks

You don't fall in love with someone all at once. At least I don't. You fall into it, step by step. Like falling down the basement steps. Bumpty-bump-bump-bump.

That's how it was with Radomir. I saw him come out of that airport door and my hackles rose. This was going to be trouble. He flew into the air when he jumped up on that stone gatepost in Amboise like an avenging angel and something inside me flew up with him.

But it was on that second trip in search of *Le Grand Meaulnes* that I think sank the hook in so deeply I couldn't escape. I had always loved the magic of Alain-Fournier's book. It has the kind of magic that Halloween has when you're young. True beauty, but something spooky and inexplicable, too. It's the same thing that John Fowles's *The Magus* has. It seems mysterious, but you're sure that if you try to understand it you'll find another level of reality there.

I gave *Le Grand Meaulnes* to Radomir and he loved the book, too. He was a good sport about venturing forth, and together we went to the Sologne to find the town where it supposedly took place. It was disappointing. The Sologne is only a few kilometers from my little town in the Loire Valley. When driving to it, the rolling storybook countryside of the Loire abruptly ends and your car enters flat pine barrens. Few houses. And an occasional small lake or pool. The hunting is supposedly great and the reason that many aristocratic families have large rambling country homes there. It's a gloomy countryside in which to pursue a gloomy preoccupation: the killing of living things. The French of course love that. Anything the kings did they want to do. As long as it's *comme il faut* they would never ask themselves if they were actually having a good time. There is no such thing as having a good time in France for the French. There is only doing that for which other people will envy you. That's even their expression for "would like to." *Envie*. "I have envy to do this or that."

When we reached the town that was supposedly the site of *Le Grand Meaulnes* I bought a green hanging lamp in an antique shop. We wandered about. There was nothing in the town, the atmosphere, the air, the sky, the trees that suggested that this place inspired a magical book.

Then I read the cover copy of my guidebook more closely and discovered that Alain-Fournier spent summers in this town in the Sologne with relatives, but that he actually had grown up in a small town to the south. Beyond Nohant, where George Sand lived, deep in the region of Berry. So we set out again another weekend, Radomir and I, in my ancient black Peugeot.

Radomir preferred driving and I preferred riding, so he was at the wheel as we headed south. It must have been April because it was chill and clear and precise. The fruit trees were flowering and about every twenty feet there was a Vincent Van Gogh painting. A fragile pear tree, a fluffy apple tree, occasionally a violently pink cherry tree in frilly blossom. Each one a perfect subject for one of Van Gogh's saner days.

There were very few cars on the road. The French don't weekend that early in the season. We stopped for lunch somewhere south of Nohant. One of those small town hotels. The large, empty, sunny room all varnish and white tablecloths. A few large local people in clumps here and there. They look at you with little interest. If you're not French you are never of interest in France.

The menu is always the same. You have the soup and the chicken and a green salad. And red wine. The French virtually never drink white wine. They think it makes your digestive system acidic.

It was so perfect I almost cried. The big room, the sun pouring in, the warmth after the cold car, Radomir across the table looking muscled and American and completely out of place and loving it.

It was a long drive to Epineuil-le-Fleuriel, where Alain-Fournier's father had been a schoolteacher. It was well into the afternoon before we approached it. Across long, green fields with not a sign of a telephone or electric wire along the narrow, winding road. We could have easily been in pre–World War I France. I suppose they must have had macadam roads by then.

The town was tiny. Really just a crossroads in the fields with a small café and a few houses in each direction from where the roads crossed. A sign indicated the schoolhouse a few doors away from the café. A small square stone building. The teacher and his family had lived upstairs over the two school rooms below. Now it was a small closed museum. Probably Mme. Fournier taught the little ones. It was not at all a typical French town. The houses were surrounded by lawns, each in their own little plot of land, rather like an American town. There was no forbidding rank of stone houses edged right up to the street, shutters closed or about to be. No feeling of stony indifference. It must have been a lovely town to grow up in around the turn of the century.

I had a guidebook that said a local chateau may have been Fournier's inspiration for the chateau in his book. We circled around the outskirts of the town and saw a red brick building back in a grove of trees. Two rutted tracks formed the drive. As we turned into it the sun was setting sideways. The chateau looked deserted. Suddenly in front of the car a large bird flew up. I thought it was an owl. "An owl?" I said.

"At this time of day?" Radomir answered.

In front of the chateau there was a battered-looking Land Rover kind of car. But no sign of life. The large windows were uncurtained, but the building seemed to be well maintained. Gentlemen farmers most probably. It was gloomy now in the grove of trees surrounding the chateau. "Let's go," I said to Radomir. We had had our *Le Grand Meaulnes* experience. This could easily have been the chateau that the young Meaulnes finds in the night when he is lost returning from the train station. Inside all those weirdly assorted guests could easily have been getting into their eighteenth-century clothes, preparing for the evening ahead.

The sun was squarely above the horizon as we headed back north for the Loire Valley. It threw Radomir's profile into dark silhouette as I looked at him, the dark, damp brown of fields behind it. The sun passed through his light brown eyes. It is at moments like these that you realize how much we are like large dolls. Eyes like clear glass observing the images about us.

Radomir had said very little during the day.

"This has been a wonderful day for me," I said. "It was an effort coming here, but now I think I have felt what Alain-Fournier felt."

"I loved it," Radomir said.

I was surprised. I never really knew if he was perceiving and enjoying what was going on around him or if he was just dutifully accompanying me.

"When the bird flew up I thought it was an omen. The bird was waiting for us. It *was* an owl. And owls aren't out wandering around on the ground during the day. It was an omen telling us that we had come to the right place. That we were in the heart of the mystery."

He went on. "I love this country. I feel like I really belong here. I felt that the first time I came to your house. It was something like coming home."

"There are two sides to you, Radomir," I said. "There's the American boy side. And there's the magic side. It's the magic side I love."

He turned and looked at me. "You're the only one who sees the magic side," he said. "You're the only one I let see the magic side."

And I fell down another step. Bump. There in the cold spring air of the end of day I really fell in love with Radomir Pulkanovic.

~6~ Lunch in Plakias

After Nevis finished the sparse taverna breakfast he repeated the walk of the night before. Wild and windy then, now it was in blinding sunlight. The disco snoozed behind its skeleton of empty neon, and the few tourists from the one tour bus searched for something to buy they hadn't already seen endlessly repeated in Chania, Rethymnon, Heraklion, Agios Nikolaos, and Sitia. The dusty little town made Nevis think of Mexico. The barren hills, the square stucco buildings, the shops of repetitious factory-made junk. He finally found some espadrilles and bought a black pair and a white pair.

He walked back to the taverna and took a seat on the terrace. Radomir came over and, leaning against the railing, lit a cigarette. He hadn't smoked when he left Paris.

"I'll be out of here at noon."

"Do you want to have lunch here?"

"Absolutely not."

"Well, let me take you to one of those places in town, one that's right on the water."

Which is where they went. Radomir told Nevis where he'd been since he left Paris. The young married couple who had shown up from California and with whom he'd hurriedly departed had gone with him from Paris to Monaco to Florence. Radomir had grown less enchanted with them as it became quite clear that their Europe-on-a-shoestring plans did not include spending money to enter museums or even the least expensive restaurants. He had seen Michelangelo's *David* by himself and then described it in detail to them on the train that bore them away to the port for Corfu. Corfu, it seemed, was pretty but covered in debris.

The trip he described was one Nevis had never taken. A series of youth hostels with seemingly the same mixed bag of wandering European and American kids, none of whom had a very clear idea of where they were or what was to be done there. The point seemed to be to hang out together with a minimum of expenditure and a maximum of free time in which one did as little as possible. From Corfu Radomir and his friends had come to Greece, traveled by train to Athens, seen the Acropolis, and come by boat to Crete. In Crete they had moved slowly from one north-coast town to another and hearing at their youth hostel there was a companion hostel in the town straight south had come across the island. And there they had stopped. *Probably because it's so much like California,* Nevis thought.

A number of young foreigners were working in the local hotels and restaurants. Local management needed their language skills for the tourists and obviously enjoyed paying them less than the locals and avoiding taxes by paying them in cash. The dazed owner of the taverna had taken a liking to all three of the new arrivals and offered them jobs. They had automatically turned him down, but Radomir had thought it over, and when the Californian couple moved on to similar beaches in Turkey, he stayed behind and took a job at the taverna.

Radomir said, "I was sitting on a wall up at the hostel having a beer and looking out over the water at the sunset and I felt so happy. I decided why not stay? And here I am."

"You know I was looking for you everywhere while you were gone," Nevis said, tucking the paper napkin under the edge of his plate so the wind wouldn't blow it away. The sun was high and brilliant over the white-railed terrace. An English couple at the next table, rather close, had stopped talking. The woman, whose back was to them, was obviously asking her male companion what Radomir and Nevis looked like, as he was studying them and talking in a low voice. Nevis didn't give a shit. Radomir didn't seem to notice.

"That's funny. Just this morning one of the English girls who handles the tours told me she had been on the other side of the island and someone told her there was a person calling all the hotels looking for me." Radomir ordered a funny kind of steak. He had hypoglycemia and had to eat full meals three times a day or he became emotionally unstrung. Nevis ordered shrimp.

When Radomir left Paris he had told Nevis he planned to travel to Greece for a week and fly back from Athens to his parents' home in the Midwest. Nevis had not had a real chance to say good-bye, as Radomir had dropped by the apartment the day before he had left when no one was there, leaving the keys and a brief note with about a thousand dollars in francs he felt he owed Nevis.

Two days later Nevis, feeling somewhat badly used and rather relieved that Radomir had left, was walking up the street toward his apartment at the end of the day. Suddenly he realized that Radomir was no longer in Paris, and he felt as though someone had punched him hard in the stomach. He stopped and had to steady himself against a building for a moment. *This is going to be awful* flashed through his mind. And it was.

There was that feeling that he was about to cry right behind his eyes that never went away. There was the compulsion to bring up Radomir in conversation with anyone who knew him, just to talk about him, mention his name. He was sure he'd be able to talk to him in the United States as soon as he arrived there and, having to go to New York to work the following week, he called Radomir's parents. He considered just flying there without advance warning, but a last fragment of control prompted him to call first. When he did they said they had heard nothing. His mother told him Radomir had written before leaving Paris to say he would be home in several months (not in a week!) and they rather thought he would be. Nevis felt the hysteria mounting.

He talked to Fritz, the friend down the street in the country, who gave him the advice that Nevis himself would have given anyone else. "Don't do anything," he was told. "Just sit tight. At least he's in Europe. He'll be back. You know he will." Nevis found himself unable to do anything except the most obviously programmed and desperate stratagems of all deserted lovers. *And we weren't even lovers,* he admitted to himself. But as Radomir's absence lengthened he became increasingly frantic.

He wrote Radomir a long letter every week, neatly addressed to him in care of his parents, and stored them away in a cabinet on his desk.

Fritz received a card from Radomir. He was in Greece. Nothing suggested he was leaving, staying, or going anywhere else. Nevis's niece Amanda called from Madrid to say she'd had a card. From Florence.

Nevis called all of Radomir's friends he could bring to mind. He remembered a woman Radomir had visited in Arizona when he'd gone back to the U.S. for a brother's wedding. He called the woman in Arizona who said she had heard from Radomir. He was in Crete; he thought he was going to get a job in a hotel and stay all summer. No address, though. Nevis asked the woman, who wasn't unfriendly, if she could decipher the name on the card of the town from which it had been sent. She wasn't any too sure, but it looked like M-Y-T-H-I-O-S to her. And, she added, Radomir was going to send her an address to write to soon. Nevis asked if she would call him in Paris with it when she received it, knowing she wouldn't.

In June Nevis went to the Cannes festival for advertising films, always a nightmare. The agency had asked him to go at the last minute and had trouble finding a hotel for him. What they found was like so many third-rate hotels where he'd been his unhappiest. He thought how perfect it was for his present love-bereft condition. The single bed sat awkwardly in a corner of the L-shaped room. The curtains and bedspread hung stiffly as though paper had been used in their synthetic mix. The cheap bureau and chair stood forlornly, nicked and marred with a thousand kicks and tears.

Oh, God, he thought, *what a place to be sad in.* The autoroute cut sharply around the corner of the pension, making getting out the front door hazardous.

He dressed and walked into Cannes. In a flashy lamp shop he saw a beautiful carved wooden male torso. Big. *I'd like that,* he thought. In a restaurant he ran into Nika, the creative director of the Milan office. Short, bleached-white hair and a big grin gave her something of the look of the "Me Worry?" boy. He told her of his sad hotel and she said, "Oh, come over to the Gray d'Albion. I'm there and I'm sure they'll have a room. Lean on them." Nevis, who always had to boost the morale of others, now felt boosted. And at the Gray d'Albion they said he could come over the next day.

That night as the cars roared past the dusty little garden outside his window he turned fitfully on his thin and beaten pillow and felt less sorry for himself, knowing he was escaping in the morning.

He spent the day with the worldwide creative director, who kept him waiting for an hour on the terrace of his hotel. While sitting there the dwarfish creative director of the Paris agency passed the table and said, "You look very angry."

"Only at you," Nevis replied.

That evening as Nevis walked into an expensive restaurant high in the hills behind Cannes with the worldwide CD he saw the tiny monster again at a nearby table. This time it was the tiny monster's turn to look angry.

The next night he opted out from the agency entertainment. Chatting up the clients was exhausting. And missing Radomir as he did, it was particularly hard to be vivacious with the emptiness eating away at the edges of his heart.

He remembered sitting beside a pool at the Majestic at an earlier festival and saying to a friend, "I'd rather just go upstairs for twenty minutes and get it over with." But that would be too unsubtle for a business based on being amusing and fun and attractive with clients who weren't and would never make any attempt at being so themselves. *Agency people and homosexuals,* Nevis thought, *we're just like geisha. Always amusing. Always attractive. And never allowed to show unhappiness or irritation. It is a courtesan's business.* And he decided to not get up and dress and go to the large party in the hills. No one would even notice he wasn't there. And if they did he'd claim he was at another party somewhere else.

He remained lying on the large bed in his luxurious room at the Gray d'Albion after eating dinner from a room service cart. He looked across the terrace to the rooftops setting into the dusk. An hour so mournful in the United States, but never so for him in France where the purple-blue skies of "L'Heure Bleu" had always seemed promising, not nostalgic.

From the terrace it was four stories down to the gardens below. Suddenly he had an urge, as though some exterior force had seized him, to get up from the bed and feel what it would be like to fall face up through the air into the gardens. The terrace doors stood invitingly open. The breeze below softly moved the flowered draperies. It wasn't despair that moved him. More the temptation to stop feeling the sadness that seeped from him down through the mattress and into the carpet beneath.

No, I cannot do this, he thought. And he mechanically stood up on the far side of the bed from the inviting windows. Turned on the night light. Shut the doors partially, pulled the draperies, and got into bed with his book. He didn't feel shaken but only as though the temptation to fall through the air was like a low-grade cold. Always there, lurking, needing to be quashed from time to time.

There was a meeting the next day for all the creative directors from around the world. Nevis showed the work done for his client, one of the world's largest beauty houses. The tiny monster who headed the creative department of the Paris agency raised his voice to say he thought the work could be better. And the even tinier German art director, who wanted Nevis's job, joined in. Nevis stared at them from the head table where he was standing and did not reply. The worldwide creative director, who was supervising the meeting, looked at them with his Dickensian schoolmaster's face, colder than ever, and said, "Be quiet."

At the farewell party that evening many New York acquaintances who were in Cannes for the festival came to the agency party. Chatting and laughing with people he knew well only pointed out for Nevis that he was in a foreign country where no one meant him well and that he was disabled with a broken heart. A malady few people in the room would have allowed themselves to have, and would certainly think laughably inappropriate for someone of his age and rank in their industry. He was glad to return to Paris the next day. The large wooden torso he'd seen in a store window he purchased on the way to the airport. It was under his feet as he buckled himself into his tiny seat aboard the plane. The torso was too poorly packed to be checked, too large for an overhead bin. He had brushed past the stewardess assuring her it would go under his seat, which it wouldn't. With his knees under his chin he thought, *At least something beautiful has been rescued from the awfulness of Cannes.*

Back in Paris he called Radomir's parents again and they had heard from him. Radomir had called. He was in Crete. Their card was from Rethymnon. Nevis checked out the other card that his friend had received. It didn't mention Crete, but it was from Chania. And in the several guidebooks Nevis had bought at Galignani he found Chania among the towns in Crete. One of the guidebooks said the only really good map of Crete was published in Austria—the Freytag and Berndt map.

Working in Vienna a few days later, Nevis sought the map out and began placing the towns in his mind. As he looked at the carefully detailed map he realized it must certainly have been prepared for the German invasion of Crete during the war. A great, unfolding work, it gave the impression that Crete was as large as Europe and one would have to drive hours between cities, which were in fact villages and only a few miles apart.

Nevis went to a travel agency and, posing as a prospective tourist trying to join a friend already in Crete, got a listing of the hotels they represented with addresses and phone numbers. He called the Lissos and the Porto Veneziano in Chania. He called the El Greco, the Ideon, the Orion, and the Rithymna Beach in Rethymnon. Just to leave no stone unturned he called the Horizonte Ikaros village, the Kernos Beach, the Malia Beach, and the Sirens Beach in Malia. (Because it was spelled a bit like Mythios.) And because Radomir's father was sure about the spelling of Rethymnon on his card, he tried Hersonissos also, calling the Creta Maris. At the Creta Maris an obliging desk clerk said there were no Americans employed there but he believed there were three of them at a nearby hotel. Nevis asked him if his hotel was the only one in Hersonissos. "Oh, no," came back the answer, "there are dozens." Nevis realized that perhaps Crete was as big and complicated as the Freytag map suggested, but perhaps he'd had luck. Maybe the three Americans were Radomir and the Californian couple. The obliging desk clerk didn't have the other hotel's number but he promised if Nevis called back in a few hours he would check it out and get names. Nevis gave him Radomir's full name. And when he called back at six o'clock, heart beating as though an Oscar was about to be his, the desk clerk had bad news. There was only one

American at the other hotel, his name was Bill, and he'd been there five years.

Then he called the Hendriz, the Kriti, the Alkazi in Chania. One clerk also mentioned the Olympic, the Panorama, the Santa Marina, and the Irena, but he was sure there were no Americans there. In fact, all of the clerks expressed great surprise, and many great suspicion, that someone would be calling from Paris looking for an American working at their hotel as all the employees were Greek as they were required to be.

Undeterred Nevis attacked Rethymnon. He was beginning to feel like a very compulsive Sam Spade. *Thank God obsession gives you energy,* he thought as he spent the evenings calling, each call taking three or four sorties into the erratic Greek telephone system.

He called the John and the John Apartments in Rethymnon. *Weird name,* he thought. Followed by the Calden Beach, the Leskonica, the Xymia, the Olibyc, the Monos, the Striti Beach. These followed by the Calden Sun. *Who* are *the Caldens,* he wondered. *Probably some awful English people who fill their hotels with pale, plodding guests, treading the sands in large, straw hats and rubber sandals.* He could imagine it all. And then called the Dies, the Sandy Beach, the Rethymnia Bay, and the Mesali.

He called the town of Hersonissos again, adding the Silveama, the Nicol Village, the Hersonissos, the Golden Beach, the Cretan Sun, the Marimate, the Maura, the Nona Beach, the Firena Beach to his list. No Radomir.

And again, many of the people he talked to thought he was some kind of government spy from their suspicious reactions. "Why are you calling?" they kept asking. "There are no Americans working here."

Then Nevis remembered once wandering past the Greek Tourist Bureau near the Place Colette and dropped in on a lunch hour. They had a brochure of Crete, listing hotels. And there Nevis found the village of Mirthios. *Almost* Mythios. *She must have gotten it wrong,* he thought. Only two hotels were listed. The Esperides and the Myrthios.

Both hotels in Mirthios professed to have no Americans. One clerk told him there were only 500 people in Mirthios, so he was sure of what he was talking about. But perhaps it would be worth calling the Petrovilla Apartments, not listed in the guide Nevis had. The Petrovilla wasn't answering, so Nevis called a restaurant on the beach one hotel had given him the number for. Radomir was unknown at the Acti. But the Acti suggested the Flisvos. The Flisvos suggested the Porto Marino. The Porto Marino suggested the Votsolos.

Finally there was someone at the Petrovilla. A rather nice man who spoke rather terrible English. But (Nevis's heart stopped) he did know an American man who visited some people who were living at the Petrovilla. "Very nice," he said. "About twenty-eight. Dark. Nice guy. Quiet. Right?" Nevis agreed he was right. "I'll get him. He be here at six o'clock. You call back." Nevis felt like a gold miner who finally saw a few flakes in his pan. The prisoner who feels the bar he's been picking away at with a nail file for weeks give a little, just a little. The man in the haystack who suddenly feels a little prick of metal that could not be hay.

While waiting for six o'clock to inch its way into being he had vivid fantasies of Radomir in Mirthios. The desolate, sandy dry Greek town on the beach. Radomir walking disconsolately through its streets, hands in pockets. Very much like Maria Schneider had in the dusty square at the end of Antonioni's *The Passenger*. Working in some beaten-out taverna on the beach. He briefly revived some of his fantasies about the English woman with a taverna with whom Radomir was sleeping, but dismissed it. There was something even sadder going on, a running out of energy, a not knowing what to do next. Of that he was sure.

Feeling faintly sick he called the Petrovilla Apartments again at six and got through on the third try. "He's here!" was the announcement when he told the man who he was. And a voice he had never heard before came on the line.

"Hello, who's this?" Nevis said.

"It's Paul. Who's this?" came back on the line.

And Paul, a young American who had been living in Mirthios for a few months, told him he was sure Radomir wasn't there. He might have passed through, but he wasn't there now. Paul told him there were many more restaurants than he had called, and certainly a number without telephones, but he was sure if another American was living there he would know it. "Why are you looking for him? What's his connection to you?" Paul wanted to know. Nevis wondered how Paul would handle being told that the man he was searching for was the man he loved and that he was going to crack up if he didn't find him very soon. Then he decided to say, "I'm a friend of his family and they're worried about him. I'm trying to find him for them." Paul took his name and number and said if he happened to run into Radomir he would ask him to call. He also said Mirthios was a mountain village, not on a beach. Nevis was confused. And then they said good-bye to each other.

The next day Nevis called Radomir's parents again. They still had heard nothing, according to his mother. Earlier when he had told the father that he knew Radomir was in Crete and that he was working in a restaurant his father replied huffily, "Can't he do any better than that?" Nevis explained that it was a lark and that any job at all for a foreigner was a great accomplishment and left him mollified to a degree.

During this call the mother seemed airily unconcerned about her son, from whom she hadn't heard in a month, and ended their conversation by saying, "Oh, I'm sure he just wants to get away and think things over for a while."

When Nevis told this to his neighbor, Fritz said, "She knows where he is. She just isn't telling. I'll call her and see what I can find out."

He did, and the following day reported that Radomir's mother did know where he was, but that Radomir had sent a list of people who could know. Fritz wasn't on the list, nor was Nevis.

Radomir and Nevis left the restaurant and headed for the beach. Although Radomir had made the point that he was always nude on the beach, Nevis noticed that he had put swimming trunks on under his shorts before leaving for lunch. Nevis had, too.

The beach curved away past a row of tamarisk trees and as they walked through assorted families and aging American couples Nevis was finding it a little difficult to imagine stripping to the buff in this holiday camp atmosphere. But as they walked further along the beach breasts began to appear, and then buttocks. *Thank God I've still got the body for this,* thought Nevis as he saw some tanned but sagging buttocks pass by. He thought there was nothing worse than a man's buttocks when the muscle tone was gone and the flesh hung down like a folding Gladstone Bag. Or an elephant's rear end. *Elephantiasis of the ass,* he thought. *Not nice.* It hadn't come to that yet in his own case, so when they stretched their reed mats out he dropped his trunks before Radomir had to lead the way.

~7~ Radomir's Body

As they lay side by side under the Cretan sun, he thought about Radomir's body next to his, and of how well he knew it. There was the little scar on the hairline above his forehead. He inquired about it each time he massaged Radomir's scalp. Radomir didn't remember precisely how he got it. Nevis gave Radomir massage and scalp treatments like his own, which Radomir allowed him to do somewhat grudgingly. What Nevis didn't tell Radomir was that his hair seemed to be thinning already on the top of his skull, and the hairs in the tub and sink didn't look promising either. But he said nothing of this and had gotten an electric hand massage unit to give even more circulation to Radomir's scalp.

On Radomir's left eyebrow at the corner was another small scar. When he was in high school some friends and he were drinking one evening at a playground. They decided to upend some bicycle racks and managed to do so with two smaller ones. They got a larger rack on its way up, but it began to skid on the wet grass. One of the boys just let go, and the entire weight was upon Radomir. As the rack fell his head got between the wheel holders, and ricocheting back and forth, he got cut badly. His friends took him home, but his parents were out so neighbors got him to the hospital. To avoid explaining that the prank began with getting drunk, he told his parents he had fallen on the metal steps of the store where he worked part-time.

His opposite cheek didn't have exactly the same conformation of its partner because of having been smashed in an automobile accident, also in high school. Speeding down a country road at night, the driver tried to make a turn and the car went off the road, smashing into a telephone pole and some trees. Radomir's cheekbone was crushed, but his doctor left it unset. Several years later the unset cheekbone continued to give him trouble and he had to have it rebroken and reset. At the same time he had his nose altered slightly.

When looking very closely at Radomir, you can see two minuscule scars under his nostrils. The shape of the nostril hides each scar unless one looks very closely. At the time that his cheekbone had to be redone, Radomir decided to have the width of his nose reduced. When Nevis asked Radomir what his nose looked like before the operation, he said, "Like my father's. You'll see it someday."

There were other small scars here and there on Radomir's body, some of which may have been due to a second automobile accident he had on an approach ramp to a highway in Chicago. The steering wheel of the car he was driving jammed; his car struck an oncoming car and went through the guardrail, falling on a grassy slope below, and turning over. Neither Radomir nor the friend who was with him were injured. They clambered out of the car and scrambled back up to the ramp to see what had happened to the other car. When a policeman arrived on the scene he didn't believe they had been the occupants of the car below. They finally convinced him they were, and also convinced him they were neither careless nor drunk but had actually had a steering failure.

This accident caused a major confrontation between Radomir and his father when he got home, as his father didn't want to hear any details and was immediately convinced that the accident was Radomir's fault. Radomir remembered the scene particularly clearly, as it was one of the rare times that his mother took his side and the two of them stood up to the old man. Radomir ran out of the house and down the street and stayed overnight with friends without telling his parents where he was.

Radomir's lips were rather thin, and his teeth were small in size, the incisor on the right side a little bit shorter than the other teeth. Radomir never showed his teeth very much when he talked or smiled. Neither did the Empress Josephine, Napoleon's consort, or the Empress Elisabeth of the Austro-Hungarian Empire. Both were self-conscious about their teeth, and the Empress Elisabeth practiced an almost inaudible murmur to avoid opening her lips too far.

Radomir's rather narrow jaw gave him a very different appearance from the front and in profile. When Nevis first met him he continually changed his opinion as to whether Radomir was good-looking or not. From the front his features tended to close in upon one another. The forelock that fell over his forehead made his brows and eyes seem even more beetlelike and deep set than they were. And there did not seem to be enough space between his nose and upper lip. The absence of a sharp jawline also seemed to focus the lips and eyes too closely to the nose. But in profile, another face altogether was suggested. The line of brow, nose, lips, and jaw was sharply drawn and boldly masculine. It was always a surprise when that strong profile turned and the too-tightly grouped features appeared. Nevis encouraged Radomir to push his hair back off his forehead. He frequently mentioned how handsome Radomir would be with long hair, knowing the long hair would fill in the jawline. Radomir experimented with pushing his hair back from time to time, but not until he was in Crete did he start using a gel so that it was always swept back.

As for letting his hair grow, he had only once let it grow out a bit but found it uncomfortable or unmasculine and had it trimmed short again.

Radomir's shoulders were those of a swimmer, heavily muscled and forming a strong, unbroken curve with his back down to the base of his spine, with one shoulder, the left, sloping more than the other. From lifting weights, the neck muscles, too, were thickened, and he tended to carry his head forward and his chest depressed. *Some day,* Nevis thought, *he'll have trouble with second chins, dewlaps, from not holding his head erect.* Nevis from time to time would put his hand on Radomir's back as they walked together, spreading his shoulders and making his pectoral muscles lift up into place, pushing his head up. It gave Radomir an extra inch in height, but he wasn't comfortable with his body held in this position. His slouchy athlete's walk was natural to him, and he felt better posture was a body attitude that suggested he was aware of the beauty of his body, which although he certainly was, he made a great point of pretending he was not.

Radomir's chest was actually rather well developed from his weight lifting, but because of his body stance it seemed flat. Radomir's arms were his second-best feature. They were very powerfully muscled as a result of his years of weight training in California.

He had told Nevis that at one time he had weighed considerably more than he did when they met. Had run regularly and was evidently quite a bruiser. When he was lying on his back with his arms raised over his head, the form of the muscles rising out of his back and spreading into the fine, white skin of the underside of the large muscles on his upper arms were complex, sculptured, and beautiful. Radomir did not have much underarm hair, and the sharp, clean lines of the muscles framing his head were in somewhat surprising contrast with his features, which were round, curving, and much less finely molded. His facial skin, too, was coarser and more porous than the fine skin on the inside of his arms. Although very male looking, Radomir didn't have to shave very often, perhaps every two days. When they first met Nevis noticed that he had no hair on his chest but some months later noticed a handful of fine hairs sprinkled across his pectorals. They were too pronounced to have newly arrived, so Nevis concluded that Radomir had been in the habit of shaving them.

Radomir's best feature was his abdomen: very flat and very hard. As a child and a young teenager he claimed to have been very thin. What remained was his very flat and tough rib cage, descending directly toward his crotch without a hint of bulge. He had a very small waist, out of all proportion to the width of his shoulders. Sitting on the edge of a bed, with one knee up pulling on a sweat sock, the curve of his long, powerful back ending in the small waist, held tightly in the elastic band of his jockey shorts, seemed almost improbable. The silhouette had the sharp line of the Petty and Vargas girls of the old *Esquire* magazine. The rarity of these idealized proportions in actual existence makes the eye wonder if it is seeing correctly. The proportions were much like the subtly smiling kouros of the early Greek period in sculpture. Radomir had done much to create the body he walked around in, and Nevis felt there was much to be known about him by studying that body.

As Nevis turned to look at Radomir in the sun, he saw that he was lying on his back, resting his elbows. The powerful arms and shoulders braced the flat torso that moved down to the groin without a pause. One knee was up. The tan was uninterrupted, and Nevis could see that the skin of his cock where it fell between his legs was even darker than the tan of his skin. A large vein showed under the dark skin, skewing somewhat to the left side.

The curious thing about Radomir's cock was that, although they had shared an apartment for the better part of a year, Nevis had never had a really good look at it. His only real impression was from the gymnasium where they both went, Nevis taking aerobics classes, Radomir doing his weights. Nevis was in the shower one day when the curtain flared out as another body flashed by into the next stall. In that moment he saw a jaunty, uncircumcised penis bob by at the base of a flat stomach between a pair of sturdy thighs. *That's Radomir,* he thought, but didn't speak out or rap on the wall. But from that time on he was convinced that he had seen Radomir's cock, as jaunty and bouncy as Radomir himself often was.

Now on the beach he realized that the passing cock had not been Radomir's at all. In fact, when Radomir rose to get into the water he saw that he was quite extremely circumcised, a quite long expanse of exposed skin reaching from where the foreskin had been cut away to a fairly sizable head. A really good-looking, rather threatening adult cock hung between Radomir's legs, not the bouncing bit Nevis had seen on someone else. Nevis felt relieved, because he had recently read that the incidence of AIDS was much higher among uncircumcised men than circumcised.

As Radomir walked down the slope toward the water he showed his brown buttocks. He had said in a phone conversation from Crete, "Even my little tushy is brown." Radomir had a babylike quality and was aware of it himself. His buttocks were, in Nevis's opinion, his least-good point, as when they were massaged they did not have the taut tone of the rest of his body. But Nevis had been a dancer at one time and perhaps expected more of buttocks than is normal in the average athletic body.

On Radomir's right leg was a small recent scar from a fall he had had in the bathtub at the country house. It was the day they were leaving to return to Paris for the winter. The country house had been repainted, replastered, reputtied, repaired in every way imaginable, and Radomir was changing residence to start serious study of French. Shortly before friends with a car were to come, Nevis entered the bathroom, saw a towel rack ripped from the wall, a wet towel on the floor, and thought, *What in the hell is going on here?* He went downstairs and in the kitchen found Radomir wearing blue trunks lying on the floor and the young woman from New York, who was spending the weekend with them, applying an ice pack to his leg. "I fell getting out of the tub," Radomir said, looking at him upside down from the floor. Nevis looked down judiciously. "I know, I know, nothing is by chance," Radomir added immediately.

Nevis processed a number of ideas immediately. Since it was Sunday, what local doctor would be on duty? How had Radomir fallen out of the tub, bruised his leg badly, then gotten into blue shorts and down to the kitchen without his hearing anything? It was all very curious. He examined Radomir's leg where a large lump had formed on the front of his shin. It was very painful, maybe a fracture. He called the local doctor where a recording told him the name and number of a doctor in a nearby town who had the Sunday duty. Another call got that doctor to the house in under fifteen minutes. With the help of the young woman from New York, Nevis got some towels under Radomir and left him lying on the floor until the doctor examined him. The doctor quickly said that no bones were broken, wrote out a prescription, and left with his 500 francs. When the car came, Radomir hopped out to the car on one leg and left. Nevis and the girl from New York followed by train.

In the water, Nevis saw Radomir pulling something from below the surface. A fishing line. Radomir started pulling it in. There were large hooks on it at intervals. As he pulled the line stretched off far out to sea. Nevis shook off the sand and went in the water to join him. He wound part of the fishing line around his hand, pulling hard. *So this is the Sea of Libya,* he thought. Many small rocks and larger ones were underfoot. Radomir waded out further and the two of them pulled and wound yard after yard of the hook-hung line. Radomir's cock stood straight out in front of his body in the clear water and looked much diminished from its more impressive appearance ashore. Nevis thought of swimming under the water and putting it in his mouth but realized that such a plan was out of the question on this nude and prudish beach in Crete. It had to remain something that had occurred on another beach with another person several oceans away many years before.

When they had successfully wound up what seemed a good mile of line and hooks they took it up to the beach and buried it.

~8~ Radomir Speaks Again

I want to be fair to Nevis. He taught me a lot. We went on lots of drives around the country and saw things that added up for me. I don't know if maybe I lived a previous life there. I like the idea that I did. I've always liked the presence of things you can't see and can't explain. When I was a kid in that house on the Indian burial mound in Sandusky there were lots of unexplained incidents. Bureau drawers would be turned upside down. Papers would get torn up. Pictures would fall off the wall. All that kind of stuff. And the funny thing was that it didn't faze my parents, who are really very white-bread kind of people. No fooling around. No reading horoscopes. Not at all religious. But when they got phantoms in their house, their solution was just to live with it.

So when I felt that old house in the French countryside calling to me, I just went with it. And I guess I knew that that wasn't going to be all there was to it. So I wasn't so terribly surprised when the ghost started to try to communicate with me. A funny thing about spirits is that when you sense them they seem to defuse your fear mechanisms. You aren't particularly frightened when you hear footsteps overhead and you know no one is there.

I woke up one night and heard footsteps coming up the stairs. I always slept in the bedroom beyond the bathroom on the front of the house, and the staircase is pretty much below the head of the bed. I was sure someone was coming in. I knew that the guy who drove me here from Germany had said he might come back this way, and I thought maybe Fritz had given him a key. I called out "Bob?" and the footsteps stopped. I got up and went out in the hall. No lights were on. I put them on and nothing was there. I went down and checked the front door. It was locked. I didn't feel frightened. I just understood that something was there that wanted to get in touch with me. I went back to bed and fell right asleep.

Not long after that I noticed that someone had been fooling around with the things on the dressing table in my room. Nevis has a dressing table in every bedroom, not that I would ever use one. But he thinks they are necessary for women guests. And he uses the one in his bedroom. It is always covered with stuff he uses on his face. He doesn't have many wrinkles. I'll give that to him.

On the dressing table in my room were two little porcelain busts, heads, whatever you want to call them—a kind of devil or faun and a pretty young woman. They were sort of on opposite corners, but one morning I noticed that they were kissing. I thought that maybe trucks rolling by had sort of shook them together. But there are very few trucks passing in this town and none in front of the house directly.

Did I tell you that the National Truck Drivers School is in the old abbey across the street? It's just another weird thing about this whole town. I kept my eye out to see if there were any cute ones but never spotted any, although you see a lot of great-looking ones out on the road.

No, those figurines were kissing because somebody had put them there like that. But nobody had been in the house. Fritz had keys, but if I was out of the house I was usually with him, and besides that I was sure they hadn't been in that position yesterday. I moved them back to where they usually stood. Now I was kind of waiting to see what would happen next.

I began to resent it when Nevis came down on the weekends. He was getting in the way of my spirits, spirit, you name it. Something was there and I knew that he, she, it wasn't going to come out when Nevis was around. He always says that he has never heard or sensed anything in the house, although he thinks presences are possible. He's just such a practical person that a spirit wouldn't waste its time around him trying to get noticed. Actually, I think I could say of Nevis that under all those Pierre Cardin clothes and Bulgari jewelry there is a rather plain person posing as an interesting one. He's lucky that he's gay or he would really be boring.

And I got so I really didn't want to go to Paris on the weekends either. I didn't want to be away from my ghost. More and more I got the idea that it was a man. A young man.

He touched me once, in the night, and I jumped and yelled. Not because I was frightened, but because I was surprised. What a jerk. I had just gotten into bed; it was eleven. I turned over, pulled the covers up over my shoulders, and then I felt this touch on my back. I yelled and it was all over. I sat up in the dark, well, not so dark because the street lamps in front of the abbey were on and the room was quite light. I never closed the shutters at night. But there was nothing. I sat very still for quite a long time, but he never reappeared. I didn't sleep very well that night. I was really angry with myself.

Then I saw him. All the time I was working around the house or cooking meals or just sitting reading I thought about him. Who could this young man be? Why was he trying to get into contact with me? Was the two figures kissing a sign that he was falling in love with me? I know I was falling in love with him. How much more of a mysterious stranger could you get than a ghost? And then I saw him.

It was in the afternoon and for once I wasn't thinking about him. Maybe I'd been in the toilet and was just coming in to wash my hands. There's a sink in my room. And as I came through the door he was there. Shortish, long dark hair, dark eyes, in a kind of baggy-sleeved white shirt. I was kind of aware of some kind of dark pants. And then he faded. His eyes went last. They looked at me like someone who was in love. I threw myself down on the bed, paint-covered jeans and all, and hugged the pillows and wanted to cry but I couldn't. It was awful. I knew he was there and would always be there, but I would never be able to hold him in my arms and he would never be able to crawl into my bed, his hot body pushing itself down on top of me, his tongue in my mouth, maybe turning me over to fuck me from behind. It was never going to happen and it was all that I wanted to happen. No wonder I hated Nevis.

Nevis was falling more and more in love with me. I guess I egged him on when I said he could give me a massage any time. It had become a ritual. But it was funny. I hated him but I liked the massage. He massaged my head a lot so I wouldn't lose my hair. I used to wonder if he was seeing something up there I couldn't see.

And he'd push my T-shirt up and pull my boxers down, but never too much. Once when I was giving him a massage he tried to get me to lie down on top of him but I wouldn't. It really made me mad and I told him so, but he only laughed and left the room. I was really stuck. I didn't want to leave France, I didn't really have anywhere to go, and I particularly didn't want to leave Hervé. I was calling my ghost Hervé now.

And one more reason I didn't like the massage sessions was that I imagined that Hervé was right there watching. I was certainly not going to do anything with Nevis that I would have liked to do with Hervé. That would have been awful for Hervé. Is this all too crazy?

Finally it all came to an end when the house was finished and the summer was over and everyone was going back to Paris. It had been suggested by Nevis that I move up to Paris, live in his guest room, go to the Alliance Francaise to improve my French and then do some work for him at the advertising agency. I draw pretty well and he thought I could do storyboards. Was I supposed to say no? There was no way for me to stay with Hervé even if he was dominating my masturbation fantasies. I had gotten to know Hervé's body very well. He must have been a horseman, because he had very strong thighs and he was a little bowlegged. He didn't have very long legs, but they were nice legs. He had a very strong upper body and that white pearly skin that some Frenchmen have. His pubic hair and the hair under his arms was that bushy straight kind. Sticks straight up and there's lots of it. Other than that there wasn't a lot of hair on his body. And he wasn't circumcised. I never looked at his cock very much but I know he had a foreskin. I hoped that imagining him in my masturbation fantasies might work for him and he could be there, too. I wondered a lot about when Hervé had lived. There was something about his hair that made me think of Victor Hugo, or Balzac. Or somebody like that. And his breath also. It wasn't bad breath but it didn't smell like people do today. It sort of smelled of grain and wine. You know, I think Hervé had to be a real ghost because I could really imagine him so well even though I had only glimpsed him that once. I couldn't make up those things about him. They weren't like somebody else I have known, and I haven't read all that much about French history. He wasn't at all like something from *Le Grand Meaulnes*. There was nothing like the Victorian period about him and he didn't seem like someone from the eighteenth century. No wig or anything. That was why I came to think that he had lived in the early nineteenth century. Maybe he had lived in this house. Maybe he had taught at the abbey. Maybe he had taught riding and had fallen in love with one of the students and had killed himself. In my room. Is that romantic enough for you? I didn't believe all of that, but I thought it. So it all came to an end on a sunny Sunday afternoon. Famke, a friend of Nevis's from New York, was there. She and I were going back to Paris on the train and Nevis was riding back with his cat with friends. The parents of Angie, in fact, who were now living permanently in France. I was taking a shower standing up in the tub and was reaching for a towel when suddenly I fell. Lots of people had fallen on the steps in the house, to the point where Nevis had a railing and ropes on the wall, and rubber guards on the edges of the steps. He warned everyone to be careful and I think thought that perhaps there was a ghost who was pushing people. Not people, women. It was always women who fell on the steps. Perhaps it was Hervé. I kind of liked the idea that he didn't like women. And then he pushed me out of the bathtub. I went over like a ton of bricks. I grabbed at the towel rack and pulled it right out of the wall. My legs hit the edge of the tub when I went over and I thought one might be broken. There were some shorts there on the floor that I had been wearing and I got them on and crawled over and opened the door. Famke was in the hall. She said, "I heard the crash." I said, "It was me. Maybe my leg is broken." She got me up and helped me hop downstairs to the kitchen. Just then Nevis appeared. He'd been out. He looked down at me. For someone who loved me so much he didn't look very sympathic. Scorn, is that the word? He looked scornful.

I said, "I know, I know, nothing is by chance. I think I broke my leg falling out of the bathtub." Evidently he had gone upstairs before he came into the kitchen and had seen the towel rack torn loose and water all over the bathroom and all of us about to depart for Paris. He was pissed off. But he said nothing. He went into the living room and started calling doctors until he found one that was on Sunday duty. Then he called Angie's parents and asked if they could leave a little later. Then he figured out what trains there were later in the day. Even when he's pissed off Nevis is good in an emergency.

The doctor showed up, a tall skinny guy from the next large town. My leg wasn't broken. Nevis paid him, brought down some clothes for me, and packed my bag. When Angie's parents showed up he sent me to Paris with them. They weren't very pleased but agreed that they would help me into the building and up the stairs when we got to Paris and take the cat up, too. Nevis took my suitcase with him. Famke and he took the train.

The next day my leg was fine and I started going to my French classes and Nevis went to his office. My new life in Paris had begun and I wasn't going to like it half as much as my life with Hervé in the country.

~9~ The Terrible Christmas

While they were on the beach Radomir asked about Nevis's niece Amanda.

Nevis remembered the previous Christmas which Amanda had spent with them: a very cold December for France, and a wretched time. Someone had said to Nevis long ago, "We always have to do what you want to do." And he had replied, "If we do what I want to do we'll all have fun. And if we don't do what I want to do, I promise you nobody will have fun." Which was pretty much what happened.

It was Radomir's second Christmas in France, and he was thinking that he might go home to see his parents. "Go home?" asked Nevis. "You don't even like those people." Nevis didn't want Radomir to leave, and by chance a request for storyboards for the Caribbean-African market came in. They had to be done by the first of the year, and Radomir needed the extra money he got for drawing these storyboards. Nevis was relieved that he had a legitimate reason for asking Radomir to stay.

It was in this emotional climate that Nevis asked Radomir if he wouldn't like to take a weekend driving trip before Christmas down into the Berry to see a series of chateaux he'd read about but never seen. Radomir was sulky but not uninterested. On an extremely cold December morning they set out in the old Peugeot from the country house. Nevis brought a blanket to cover their knees. The old car no longer had heat.

The car stalled as they passed through a nearby town, fortunately not far from a garage. The garage owner wired a piece of cardboard in the front grille. "It's too cold for your engine," he said.

They stopped for lunch in a town on the edge of the Berry region where a wealthy department store family had completely renovated a late-eighteenth-century chateau. The chateau was Nevis's dream house. Each room was prettily painted in pastels, and the curvy eighteenth-century period furniture was upholstered in flowered or solid pastel fabrics. Everything was cozy, pretty, safe, and charming. Radomir said, "There are very good vibrations in this place. It feels good."

Later they stopped at George Sand's family home, Nohant. Nevis had been there before in summer weather. Now Nohant seemed bleak and a long time not lived in, unlike the pretty chateau they'd just visited. There the family seemed to have just stepped out. At Nohant whatever energy George and Chopin and Liszt and their cohorts might have generated was dissipated. George's bed was pushed up against the wall and hardly seemed large enough for the two people her biographers suggested so often shared it. And her drop-leaf desk where she sat up all night writing, so that the house parties might go on and on, also seemed small and inadequate for the miles of writing that had poured from it.

Nevis had reserved a hotel, which turned out to be a slapped together modern little place at a highway intersection, only slightly different from an American motel. They were both cold and tired and laid down for naps. Nevis got up and slipped under the covers of Radomir's bed and wrapped his arms around the warm body lying there. Radomir was reading. He neither stiffened under Nevis's touch nor relaxed. He was just there. But Nevis didn't care. He had been so chilled that holding Radomir's body close to his own finally stopped his shivering.

They ate a nondescript dinner in the nondescript dining room. Radomir was a little chattier. He had an interesting day, and then to bed they went in their joyless room.

The next morning they started their chateau visiting early. Through the chilly fog they went. It was colder to the south here in Berry than it had been in the Loire Valley, closer to Paris. Every blade of grass was coated in ice, and the tree branches were coated in crystal. The only landscape colors were the shades of white, silver, and gray of the iced-over plants, backed by the darker silver of the sky waiting to snow.

In a little village they ventured down a muddy lane to find the entrance to the chateau. They rang and knocked on the doors. No one was about. Finally the chatelaine emerged, a portly lady looking more

English than French in her cardigan sweater and glasses. She conducted the tour of the ground floor and was particularly eager to sell her canned chicken and preserves in the gift display. Nevis bought a large jar of canned chicken because he had never seen chicken in a glass jar before.

The rest of the tour was turned over to the guide, a very small young woman in a red coat who had just emerged from the early morning fog. Under five feet tall, her skin was pale, her features slightly disjointed, and her dark eyes and hair made her seem even unhealthier. Nevis could imagine the ugly room she must have arisen in. So cold it was difficult to button her clothes. A bath or a bathroom unthought of. Maybe a comb straggled through her hair, and rushing breathlessly down the muddy hill knowing the chatelaine, three times her size, would berate her for her lateness, tourists or no tourists. At least it would be warm at the chateau.

And then two American men to haul around the ramparts, pointing off into the distance where a famous battle may or may not have taken place.

The little guide carefully showed the defenses, the portcullis, the machicoulis. On a large terrace she explained that below were the dungeons where all the prisoners from an ancient nearby battle had been kept. An entrance stood in the middle of the terrace: a dormered doorway she had difficulty swinging open. She stood to one side and pointed downward into the gloom. "*Vous pouvez le visitez,*" she said. Nevis demurred. He felt he was in the opening sequence of a film where dopey Americans wander into dungeons. He could imagine the door swinging shut with a clang behind him and the pale little face peering through the bars before scuttling away. Radomir, too, was not eager to go downward into the gloom. Did the little guide sneer? Or smile knowingly at their perceptiveness? It was hard to say.

They attempted visiting several other chateaux going back northward. They were all closed. Somehow, despite the disappointment, they felt closer to each other after their escape from the strange little woman in the red coat in the fog.

When Christmas came Amanda arrived from Madrid with the same boyfriend as the year before, Randy, but there was no fun and frolic. The strain between Nevis and Radomir made it impossible to capture any feeling of gaiety. At gift time on Christmas Eve Nevis was given a large, heavy box by Radomir that contained six framed 1920s prints for children with small songs printed under each charming art deco drawing. They were prints Nevis had seen in an antique shop that was never open, and when he had finally found it open the prints were gone. He had come home and cursed the shop roundly to Radomir, but it had been Radomir who had found the shop open and bought them for Nevis.

Nevis was both thrilled to have what he had thought were lost forever and very unhappy with himself that he couldn't be careless and jolly. He tried, but it was no go.

Amanda came into his room one evening and asked, "Is everything all right?" Everything was so not all right that Nevis flew into a rage and muttered things about "people always bothering me" and "I just want to be alone."

Amanda looked at him judiciously and said, "You know, Garbo never said, 'I want to be alone.' She said, 'I want to be left alone.'"

"Well, she had it about right," Nevis said sulkily and threw himself down in the chair at the dressing table. *I look like shit,* he thought. Amanda left thinking he was acting exactly like Miriam Hopkins in a particularly bad 1930s movie.

~10~ Amanda's Take on Things

I had no idea. I mean, really. My uncle is so discreet that when I found out he was in love with that kid Radomir I was stunned. I mean, he's a very cute guy but, you know, nothing that extra special. Nice arms but short legs. There are tons of guys like that in California. I guess having him isolated in the Loire Valley made the difference. I'd sleep with him in a flash, but I don't think I'd fall in love with him. He's really too young for me, not to mention Uncle Nevis.

And all the time we were there that Christmas Radomir thought Randy and I were so in love. He wrote me all about that during the period that he decided he was going straight. Said how much he envied Randy and me, our romance. Randy and I had a lot of fun together, but we were on the verge of splitting up that Christmas. We weren't even sleeping together. He wanted to marry me, but I wasn't having any. I didn't really love him, and considering how hard it is to live with someone, you should at least be able to tell yourself that this is the person you love. Or, make that past tense, loved.

Uncle Nevis and I often discuss all the marriages we see that seem to have occurred without either party having been in love. They were graduating from school. They were getting older. His career required a wife. Her self-image required a husband. It must be horrible to be saddled with someone and you weren't ever crazy about them. At least if you were once nuts about them you know how you got into the pickle you're in.

I confronted Uncle Nevis when he called me in Madrid after that Christmas in the country. I said, "This isn't at all like you. You've never had lovers who were much younger than you were."

He said, "Oh, you know I like to lay myself out like a doormat to see how they plan to walk all over me. This one appeared while I wasn't looking."

"I thought you were interested in that guy from Dallas you brought to Spain with you. He was crazy about you," I said.

Uncle Nevis said, "He had the look of somebody's chauffeur. You know. Black suit. White shirt. Very pale colorless skin and hair. When he took out his change purse and dug through it to give some money to a beggar I knew I could never love him. You know that line, 'I fucked him but I *never* dated him.' You do have to check people out and he *was* very large."

"Randy stood next to him in the loo when we went to Las Chinitas together. He said it was enormous," I told him.

"In his case it was an encumbrance." He went on, "What can I tell you? I like living with a man. You can leave the toilet seat up all the time. I guess I just stopped having an age requirement. I feel neglected. I guess I'm looking for someone to look after me. I've never had anyone look after me."

I said, "Oh, honestly. That's like hearing Genghis Khan complain that no one ever looked after him. Or Hurricane Andrew. How could anyone look after you? They'd have to catch up with you first. And you might kill them when they did."

"Oh, don't say that," Uncle Nevis said.

"It sounds like self-pity to me," I said. "Do you think Pamela Harriman was given to self-pity and bemoaned that she needed someone to look after her?"

"After her jewelry, maybe."

"Perfectly right. As you've told me many a time, please don't complain, it makes you so unattractive."

"I know, I know. Perhaps you and I should co-author a television series called *All My Boyfriends,*" Uncle Nevis said. "But it *is* awful being so old you have to face the fact that you can't take anyone away from his wife anymore."

"It's sobering," I had to admit.

"More than sobering. It's disgusting."

"I'm sure it makes you feel powerless."

"Exactly. And with all I know about fucking."

"Well, there you have it, Uncle Nevis. The next time you're in Madrid I promise we'll go out somewhere and have fun."

"Spoken like a true friend and a good niece and a real trouper. What do you think? Shopping or the movies?"

"Do you have any objection to both?"

~11~ The Second Day at the Beach

The first day that they went to the beach together they saw no one Radomir knew, although he talked about a crowd of friends who worked in the tourist hotels, in the youth hostel, ran tours for British tourists, even one American who worked in the olive oil factory up on the hill behind the town.

There was a mysterious romantic couple who lived at the hostel. Nevis wondered why this love-struck couple would be in the most obscure resort on Crete living in a youth hostel where privacy, romance, and lovemaking would be extremely minimal, if possible at all. Radomir had no explanation.

On the second day two friends did appear. There was the blonde, Natasha, a little Australian waif who strongly resembled one of the current crop of top models with whom Nevis worked. He told her this. It triggered her confession that she was very interested in the world of fashion photographers, top models, hairdressers, and makeup artists that was a daily routine for Nevis. Natasha had a kind of elegance to her manner that Nevis found attractive. She said she had been in Plakias a year. She had run the youth hostel at the foot of the hill all that time, staying there alone much of the time in the winter when the youth-tourist traffic ran low. Soon she was returning to Australia, she said. She wandered away to remove her clothes and walk into the water gingerly in the distance. Nevis was beginning to see that there was a certain code to nude sunning and swimming that he wasn't likely to get the drift of in the few days he was to be there.

Tony, a young blond Canadian, was working as a cook in a hotel beyond the beach, some distance from the village; he was a pleasant, chatty pal of Radomir's. All three of the young people seemed to agree that they didn't like what they were doing, had lots of problems with their Greek employers, whom they thought were taking advantage of them, and gossiped a great deal about the other young people they knew in Plakias. Nevis got the impression they weren't so much in Plakias because they wanted to be, but rather by chance. Life on hold. He tried to remember if he had a similar period in his life. He couldn't remember one. He didn't point out to Radomir, who denounced California and swore he would never return, that Plakias, with all its English-speaking young people, was probably as close in style and climate to Southern California as one was likely to find in Europe.

After Natasha and Tony left the beach Radomir and Nevis lay side by side on their mats under the sun. Nevis thought, *We never lay this close naked in our lives, yet here we are.* And he remembered the modest level of sexual encounters they had in the year they had spent together.

One evening they had eaten at a candlelit restaurant at the top of Montmartre. It was called Le Pierrot. Pierrot dolls, paintings, and sculptures were everywhere in the black and white costume and mask. The owner, although thoroughly French, looked as though she had wandered in from Greenwich Village: all blonde hair, portly body, toreador pants, and lipstick. The standard out-of-work New York actress, somehow French and somehow aground on the top of Montmartre. It was a silly, romantic restaurant and they had not been planning anything so elaborate as candlelight and champagne, but it got to them all the same.

They wandered down the hill to Pigalle later, and during the now almost-nightly massage, Radomir turned over to have his chest and shoulders rubbed with no demurring. He also liked to have his stomach lightly rubbed in a circular fashion; he said his mother had often done that when he was small. As Nevis rubbed his stomach he pushed his pajama trousers down and touched the root of Radomir's penis. It was very flaccid. Radomir said in a slightly drunken voice, "No, don't do that. I don't want our relationship to be like that." So Nevis pulled up the pajama trousers and returned to the circular stroking of the stomach, feeling less frustration than he thought he might.

As the massages continued, they became more physical. Radomir allowed his pajamas to be pulled down enough to have his buttocks thoroughly massaged, but there was no more full frontal nudity than before. Nevis always had a terrific erection while he was giving the massages, so he felt he was getting something out of it.

Radomir also massaged Nevis, with lesser and greater degrees of enthusiasm. He frequently liked to straddle Nevis's buttocks, sitting squarely astride him to massage his neck and shoulders square on. One evening when they were in Radomir's bedroom in the country house Nevis took Radomir's forearms and pulled him down on top of him. Radomir didn't object, but bracing himself on his elbows and knees, he kept his crotch slightly elevated above Nevis's buttocks. They lay that way for some time. Theirs was an unspoken negotiation: one testing cautiously to see if the bond could take any more pressure, the other offering no real resistance, but also never acquiescing.

It was in this same bedroom perhaps a month later when Nevis sensed that something erotic was hovering over the massage. He lowered Radomir's pajamas. He was using a body lotion for the rubbing. Kneeling over Radomir, he lifted his body by the hips and massaged under his hip bones, reaching deeply into his stomach muscles. He felt Radomir's erection, reaching downward between his slightly spread thighs. He reached for the body lotion, intending to dribble some on Radomir's penis to masturbate him. A hard, dry voice came from the inert body beneath him. "Please stop," it said.

He did, pulling Radomir's pajamas back into place. He laid down beside Radomir, who was propped up on one elbow and looking furious. "Why do you keep doing that?" he demanded. "I'd think you'd be trying to help me not do things like that, rather than pushing me toward them."

Nevis considered the possible responses and decided to laugh. "Well, (A) I don't think that homosexual acts are as dreadful as you do. And obviously, being in love with you, I'm always interested in some of those kind of acts. And (B) I'm never sure that people haven't changed their minds about what they'd like to do. My first major lover cried for his mother after the first time he made love to me. And before we separated he was giving me blow jobs. And not at my suggestion. People can change, and you can't blame me for testing the waters from time to time."

Radomir seemed surprised that Nevis found it funny and not dramatic, and after a few more words Nevis left the room and went to his own bedroom. He was glad that he hadn't run out in a huff at Radomir's crackdown, which had been his first reaction. But they never ever came this close again to a real sexual encounter, although Radomir didn't seem to mind if Nevis laid across him with one leg between his legs, as long as they were fully clothed.

There had been a kind of intimacy to their massage sessions, that although not sexually expressed, was when Radomir gave the most of himself. There, lying with his head twisted into a pillow, was when he would talk about himself and answer Nevis's questions.

There, having his shoulders massaged, he had said that his niece, a little girl of two, didn't like him. She would never let him hold her and always ran from him. One time she spat at him when he was trying to be nice to her. He admitted that for much the same reasons, he did not like one of Nevis's cats who avoided him. The cat, Hester, avoided everyone, but Radomir took it personally.

It was also there that he spoke of the poltergeists that had invaded the family home when he was young. His mother refused to discuss their presence except to refer to the presence as "them." One of his brothers had experienced having someone enter his bedroom, go to his bureau, and then stand over his bed before leaving. He had assumed it was Radomir or another brother, but then realized neither were at home. The next day, when opening his bureau drawers to take something out, he found them thoroughly disarranged. The phantom presence had searched through them all, turning their contents topsy-turvy. There were other noises, fallings, crashings, and inexplicable events. No one seemed to have felt that Radomir's presence had conjured them up, nor did he himself until Nevis told him that although the poltergeist phenomenon is accepted and it is unknown how it operates, it is always related to the presence of a child in the home, one who is usually unhappy and hostile in their circumstance.

Radomir also talked a lot about his family, a topic much drawn out by Nevis. They were Yugoslavian on both sides, emigrants to the Midwest in the generation preceding his parents, who had grown up in the same neighborhood. On the maternal side there was a good bit of talk of descent from minor aristocracy or major landholders. The great-grandmother had supposedly climbed out a window and emigrated to the United States under her own steam, joining family members who had gone to the United States ahead of her. It was her daughter, his grandmother, who lived with them when he was small and to whom he was very attached. It was also she who told him something in the hospital where she lay just before her death which she told no one else. He said of this, "I know I will remember what it was she told me one day, and when I do I know it will be very important."

It was this same grandmother who accumulated several small apartment buildings and a store in Chicago. Radomir's mother was brought up above the store and with a variety of relatives in the adjoining apartments.

There was an uncle whose death revealed that he had bought large amounts of electronic equipment, clothing, and much else which he never unwrapped. His home was full of the overflow of an abundant America. Perhaps stunned by the fact that the goods were so available and that he had the money to purchase them, he had continued to buy. Radomir returned from one of his trips home with a large supply of socks from the hoarding uncle. The flashier ones he gave to Nevis.

There was an unhappy alcoholic girl cousin near his own age, married to a handsome policeman, who certainly betrayed her. She had surprised Radomir by writing to him when he lived in California and telling him if he ever needed anyone he could count on her.

There was also the disappointing cousin who had promised intellectual achievement and instead opted for an interracial marriage, largely to discomfit her mother.

There was an aunt who wore muumuus in her winter flat in Acapulco and drank a lot of tequila. There was another aunt married into the dreariest depths of dull normalcy in a small town in Indiana. The very antithesis of her sister, Radomir's mother, who in her sixties enjoyed wearing short shorts and high heels, and dueling with sticks with her husband in the forest when they took walks.

There was the father, always a stern martinet, who on one of Radomir's returns home from Europe, had told him that during the war he had worked with the CIA and now felt deeply unhappy about the dishonesty and disloyalty he had seen there. There was the older brother who had been almost completely unmanned by drugs, and who had been held back from the brink by Radomir's parents. Nevis thought,

We have all been through horrible things. But horrible things are very different when you're single and in the fast lane from horrible things when you're married and in the farmlands. But they are all horrible.

There was another brother who had devoted himself to being the "good son." He had the college degree, the pretty wife, the nearby home with the neat lawn. And the brother closest to Radomir in age. Radomir had returned to the U.S. to serve as best man for his wedding. The brother had insisted several times that Radomir return for the wedding to be the best man. When Radomir returned to Paris he said that the brother had waited until the wedding rehearsal to tell him that someone else was to be the best man. Nevis was angrier about this than Radomir seemed to be. It was at that wedding, also, that Radomir's father distinguished himself by refusing to wear one of the silly chorus-boy outfits favored for American weddings and insisted upon wearing a simple tuxedo. Nevis thought perhaps he had fallen in love with the wrong member of Radomir's family.

It was during a massage while Nevis was rubbing his swimmer's body that Radomir told about being missing from the family swimming pool as a very little boy. After much diving, searching, calling, and general hysteria, his mother had found him in his own little bed, where he had crawled, tiny wet trunks and all, because he was exhausted from his infatuation with swimming. Nevis thought about this. He had not been very young in this same time period. At that time he had been very much in love with a rising Broadway actor who looked like Tyrone Power and who was now a fairly unattractive antique store owner. It made him feel very old.

Radomir also told Nevis that when he was small he was fascinated by the miniature paper umbrellas stuck in summer drinks and ice cream treats, and used to unroll the paper forming the knob of the umbrella. Made of bits of oriental newspapers, they were covered with oriental characters, which he used to study and wonder about the foreign land from which they came.

They also discussed fears during one of those muscle-probing sessions, and Radomir admitted that he had a deep fear of spiders, which Nevis already knew about. But he added that he had a horror of needles, and also chickens. Nevis wished he had paid more attention when studying psychology. Certainly these pointy, prickly, crawly things added up to something meaningful. He also remembered having seen Radomir burning flies with a cigarette as they crawled across a windowpane stunned with heat. When he mentioned this as needless cruelty, Radomir had told him that he also pulled the wings from flies and put them in spiders' nests. Nevis hoarded all these stories to think about later.

The sun over the sea was still high, but Radomir had to return to the hotel to shower and prepare for work at the taverna at six o'clock. Nevis stood up and brushed the sand from his buttocks and pulled on his black bikini. Radomir pulled on his faded blue Speedo swimming trunks. They trudged through the sand toward the tamarind trees in the distance. A woman with somewhat pendulous breasts who had carefully watched them getting up continued to watch them walk away. Nevis noticed quite a few nude and nonnude voyeurs on the fringe of the nude beach. At the tamarind trees they stopped and Nevis put down his beach mat to brush the sand off his feet and put on his espadrilles. Radomir was wearing sweat socks and high Reeboks that he'd put on with his shorts and an oversized tank top.

The long, sandy road that ran along the beach back toward the hotel passed a sweep of grain fields on the landward side, running back to the descending hills. Nevis could imagine the Minoans, long before the glory that was Greece and the grandeur that was Rome, trudging this same sandy strip beside their little clutch of grain fields. *No wonder they are dark red in the frescoes,* he thought. *They probably had great tans.*

Halfway back to the hotel Nevis realized he had left his beach mat wedged into the cleft of a tamarind. "You go ahead," he said. "I'll go back and get it."

"Are you sure?" Radomir asked.

"No, no, you go ahead. You've got to get ready for work. I'll be right along," Nevis told him and turned around.

He started walking back quickly. After a few hundred yards he turned to watch Radomir walking away. In his shorts and loose top and lace-up shoes he had the air of a very small boy, walking alone down an empty road. Nevis felt that awful hand grabbing at his heart. It felt like he was watching his child walking away alone on the first day of school. He put his hand on his heart to clutch it and forced himself to run down the road toward the tree that held the mat.

When he got to Radomir's room at the hotel, Radomir was coming out of the shower. There was something in the manner in which he wrapped his towel around his hips sarong style that always made Nevis think he had just been admiring himself in the mirror. With his all-over tan he was something to admire. Nevis wondered if sometimes he took the towel away and admired himself in the mirror, and if sometimes he masturbated in front of the mirror, excited by the physical beauty that confronted him.

Nevis had known a dancer who told him that his reflection in the classroom mirror had often given him an erection. *Well, beauty is beauty, I guess,* thought Nevis, *even if it's your own.*

"Before you get dressed show me what you look like in that green bikini I bought you," demanded Nevis. Passing through Galeries Lafayette one day he had seen a Brazilian bikini in turquoise on a mannequin in the men's department. He had bought it for Radomir, who tried it on in the privacy of his bedroom and said he would never wear it. "It does cover my pubic hair, but that's about all," he had said. Nevis had noticed that it was among his effects in his room, even so.

Radomir disappeared into the bathroom and returned in the bikini. Cut high on the leg, it gave him the length of leg he needed, and his narrow waist rising to the broad shoulders and built-up biceps was relatively dizzying for Nevis. "It looks wonderful on you, but I do understand why you don't want to wear it," he said. "It's too provocative."

"That's right," Radomir said and went back into the bathroom to take it off.

When Radomir went on duty, Nevis went back to his room. He lay down on his bed for an hour, then showered and dressed carefully. Knowing he would be in Crete only three days, he had packed lightly but preplanned so he would not have to appear at dinner in the same thing twice. Years of moving from Helsinki to Paris to Guadeloupe to Los Angles to New York made it possible for him to program what he would wear days in advance. He had often explained to people who wondered that he could leave for such jaunts with one suitcase: "If the same people aren't going to see you, you can keep wearing the same thing. It's just your underwear that's a problem." The day when he dressed to amuse himself was lost back in a time he barely remembered.

This evening he wore the white T-shirt he'd bought in Madrid with white pants and put on the extremely tight black espadrilles he'd bought in the village. He tied a black sweater with Matisse color blobs he had bought at the store Corolla in London over his shoulders. He looked quite tan when he passed a mirror. He had not been liking the way he looked for several years now, but he was still thin enough and blond enough to meet his own standards.

He took a walk through the village again before returning to the taverna terrace. Radomir came out and brought him a kir. The Greek wine with which it was made got him a little woozy immediately, but he thought, *What the hell. If I'm going to get out of control, it might as well be here.* He smoked several cigarettes, too, while he drank his kir. An infrequent smoker, he found he was smoking fairly incessantly on this trip. It was smoke or scream, he decided.

He could see Radomir moving around inside the taverna. Every time Radomir disappeared from sight he felt panic rising inside himself. Having found him and followed him this far, he was living with a dreamlike feeling that none of it was happening at all. For some reason he had come to this obscure resort and fantasized that Radomir was here. Every time Radomir reappeared from behind a pillar he felt a surge of relief. *This is really crazy,* he thought. *He's here. He's not going to disappear. Now calm down.* But he couldn't.

At 10:30, having long finished his dinner and having smoked many cigarettes, he saw Radomir emerge from the inner dining room. He came to the table and said, "Let's get out of here. He'll find something more for me to do if I don't split." "He" was the taverna owner, the dazed man who had given a room key to Nevis the night of his arrival.

They walked back into the village and found a table on a terrace by the water. They ordered drinks. "I was surprised that you had dinner with Minerva," Radomir said.

"She called me and she sounded so lonely I thought I should," Nevis answered.

"I guess you figured out that she and I were seeing each other," Radomir told him.

"Minerva told me you were her best friend in Paris. And that when you never wrote her she decided to just forget all about you."

"She probably told you that to keep you from thinking anything was going on," Radomir said.

"I remember when you first met her," Nevis went on. "When she forced her way into that weekend in the country. You came back and talked about her. You didn't even like her."

"Yeah," Radomir said, "but then I got to know her better." Nevis wondered what really had gone on. Nevis dropped it. At least he had made it to Plakias, and Minerva hadn't.

They left soon, as Radomir was tired. At Radomir's door in the alley behind the hotel they hugged briefly and Nevis climbed the stairs to his room. He was tired, too.

~12~ Radomir's Perversions

"I'm perverted," I told Nevis one evening in Paris. He said he'd never heard anyone say that before. "I've known hundreds of perverts in my lifetime, but I never heard anyone actually say it. They all thought they were perfectly normal," he told me.

Then I told him about the threesome I had with Esther and her boyfriend in California. I didn't tell him the truth, actually. I told him that I went out with my boss and boss's girlfriend and that we all went home together. Somehow I didn't want him to know that it was my girlfriend and her boyfriend. And in fact I did work for her boyfriend. Kind of fucked up situation, that.

When I think of it, Nevis and I had a sexual relationship. A kind of one. I enjoyed talking about sex: the things I've done sexually. And he enjoyed hearing about them. I guess he realized that that was all the sex life he was going to have with me.

"As far as perversion is concerned, I think that depends on what you do in bed when you get there," Nevis said.

"She got hers that night, that's for sure," I said. I didn't say anything about thinking about screwing the other guy, too, but I told Nevis he was a health nut and a marathon runner and had a great body.

"He was probably hoping that in the heat of the night he'd cop a little action with you, too. I've known a lot of those physical fitness freaks. Finally they all want some guy to sock it to them."

Damn, I thought. And I blew it. Actually I don't think Esther would have been very happy seeing one of her boyfriends shoving it up the ass of the other one, no matter how it would have turned out. Or maybe that was exactly what she wanted to see. What a weird, weird world.

"I don't think that really comes under the heading of perversions. Two guys sleeping with one girl. More under the heading of experimentation," Nevis said. "You should read *Portnoy's Complaint* by Philip

Roth. There's a threesome in there. His girlfriend eggs him on to have a go with a whore they pick up in Rome. He claims that when he was slipping it into things, he didn't even know what they were or whom they belonged to. I think most men see sleeping with two women as an exciting achievement. Of course, he blames his girlfriend the next day and she gets mad because she thinks he's suggesting she is a lesbian."

I told him that it sounded interesting and he said he'd get it for me. He was always getting me things to read. He got me *Lolita* twice and I never read it just to spite him. I'm sure it was to sort of explain his huge old crush on me.

"How about when I used to take phone calls for that call girl in Denver?" I said. I had already told Nevis about when I lived with Beverly in Denver. He knew that I had wanted to go to school in Colorado and that my father refused to pay for an out-of-state college, so I had just set off by myself. I finally moved in with this call girl I met in a bar. Beverly always wanted to make it with me, but we never did. Well, once if you can call it that. She wanted to demonstrate her blow-job technique and I let her—in the kitchen, me sitting in a straight-back chair and her kneeling on the linoleum. I really am perverted in ways I'd never tell Nevis about or he'd think he had a chance. I'm not all that interested in women, but if it's doing something kinky I can get excited and it doesn't matter if it's a woman or a man. That was so strange with my blue jeans down and old Beverly's blonde head bobbing up and down that I really got into it. It was exciting kind of waiting for a neighbor to knock on the back door at any second.

Beverly wasn't really good-looking at all, overweight, not a pretty face. She had nothing going for her, but I always admired her just going out there and making money and getting all these guys on the telephone all the time.

"I saw my first porn video at Beverly's," I told Nevis. "It was about some young woman who doesn't want to sleep with this older guy. And so he shows her what he plans to do with her with an older woman first so she can watch."

"That kind of sounds like a scenario from the Marquis de Sade," Nevis said. "An older man wants to deflower a young girl. Lets her watch while he boffs an older woman who expresses a great deal of pleasure, making the young girl jealous."

"That was sort of it," I said. "Beverly was playing the video for some guy, probably to get him excited. I just wandered in by chance and they asked me to stay and watch it." I always acted a little naïve with Nevis. Of course, I got the picture right away. Beverly thought that the guy might like a threesome and she might get to score with me. I kind of get a kick out of letting people think I don't know what they're up to.

"Beverly sounds like an okay kind of dame," Nevis said. "You showed me those pictures when she took you up into the mountains for your birthday." It had been fun playing in the snow. How old was Beverly then? Thirty? Maybe not even. With me she was kind of acting like the girl with a cute boyfriend having fun. Something she really never had, I suppose. "Of course, Beverly fucked a number of guys to pay for the trip," Nevis said.

"That was her business," I told him.

"Of course, that *was* her business," he said and laughed.

"Didn't you ever feel bad about Beverly working as a hooker?" Nevis asked me.

"No, that really was her business. It wasn't mine. I worked as a hooker once myself," I said, just to sort of shock him thoroughly. "Yeah, Beverly had this male friend who was a prostitute. He was the first guy I had sex with, to tell you the truth. Herbert was his name. Funny name for such a handsome, sexy guy. I think Beverly sort of set it up when I told her I had never really gotten it on with another man. Herbert set me up with one of his clients."

I didn't tell Nevis that I had fallen in love with Herbert. He had a gorgeous body, not too muscular but with great stomach muscles. And a really perfect cock. He was tan all over. He went to the tanning parlor every week. And he was very professional. When we slept together he fucked me, but very carefully so it hardly hurt at all—plenty of K-Y and he used a rubber. He was a great kisser, too. I fell in love with him, but Herbert wasn't having any. We slept together a couple more times, but I guess he felt he was giving away what he could be making money from.

"I thought I'd give it a try. Everybody I knew was doing it. It was awful. The guy sent a limousine for me. His limousine. He was fat and really disgusting. All I could do was let him give me a blow job. I didn't even take my clothes off. Afterward his driver took me home and on the way stopped and bought me a cup of coffee. He told me I wasn't cut out for that kind of work and I shouldn't do it anymore. He was so right." I told all this to Nevis, who didn't seem particularly surprised.

"All of us have sold it in one way or another," Nevis said. "Think of all those women who marry for money who have to lie down under some disgusting guy just because that's part of the deal.

"I never slept with anyone because there was something in it for me, but I have slept with men from time to time when I didn't feel like it just because they wanted to so much. Always a mistake, it's always a mistake. For me that's the worst thing in the world, sleeping with someone when you don't feel like it. They are having a wonderful time and you feel like it's a bad day at the gym. Talk about inhabiting two different worlds. I guess I'm lucky that I have had very few experiences like that. For some people it's a way of life.

"When I pass whores on the street I always think they are going to go straight to heaven when they die. Imagine sleeping with four or five different guys a day. A lifetime of unattractive men banging your box all day long every day. You've already been in hell."

Nevis had a point there.

"I almost had a threesome a couple of times in California with my best pal," I said.

"The one that looked like you?" Nevis asked. "Is that the one that you told me that if you didn't get lucky in the bars picking up girls you went home and screwed each other?"

"That's the one," I said. "We did a lot of crazy stuff. We'd go to gay bars and pick up some guys and really get them hot to trot and then run out on them. We called it 'wrecking 'em.'

"We both used to help out this woman who handed out the winner's cup in Indianapolis when they had the races there. We used to wash her car and hang out with her. She always said she loved having cute guys in their bathing suits around the place. She would have loved making it with both of us at the same time I'm sure, but we never did. We were sort of into letting people eat their hearts out over us."

"Like me," Nevis said.

"Like you," I said. "Once we went to a party where a girl was getting engaged and we got the bride-to-be out in a car and got her real hot and tried to get her to go away with us and get it on. She almost did. I was doing a lot of drugs in those days, and I think that maybe made me do all those wild things."

"What happened?" Nevis wanted to know. "Why'd you stop?"

"I almost died," I said. I told him about my having a mouth infection, which was gonorrhea of course, although I didn't want to admit it. When I went to the doctor they gave me a shot of penicillin and I went into shock. I didn't know I was allergic to it. I went right down on the floor and my heart almost stopped. I remember lying there almost completely out and praying to God and promising I'd straighten myself out if I didn't die. When I got home I looked at myself in the mirror as I was getting ready to take a shower and I was thin and terrible looking and from that day on I quit drugs and got myself in shape.

This little story did stop Nevis a bit. "That's kind of impressive," he said. "I've had lots of friends go all to hell with themselves with drugs but I don't think any of them pulled themselves together without help. And some of them didn't pull themselves together at all. They're dead. I never did drugs because I was afraid they'd ruin my looks. You know that awful gray look addicts have. As if you just push their skin a little they'll just crumble and collapse." Then he added, "What happened to your cute friend?"

"I don't know exactly. He was from Arizona and he went back there to live with his sister. He was sick," I said.

"Did he have AIDS?" Nevis asked.

I didn't answer him. I said, "Do you know what that shithead Larry wrote me the other day from Germany? Today actually. He wrote me that Dan Danforth tested positive for AIDS. Just sort of casually in the middle of the letter. Like it was nothing. As though both he and I haven't both slept with Dan a lot. He really is a prime bitch."

"Is Dan Danforth the man you left behind in California who had been a lover of Larry's?" Nevis asked. I explained that Dan had ditched Larry just before I met him, then I ditched him. Larry told me that one reason he was so hot for me was that I had given Dan the gate. Dan wasn't all that great.

"I didn't quite get it myself when you showed me his picture," Nevis said.

"Oh, he was a very good fuck. So was Larry. But I never really cared about either of them," I said.

"You told me that you were in love with Larry," Nevis said.

"Who said anything about love?" I said. "He could tuck those ankles right up beside his ears and he really loved having it stoked to him."

"Of course that is a very attractive quality," Nevis said. I looked at him to see if he was kidding. Or making fun of me. You never could tell with Nevis.

He immediately became his reassuring Nevisian self. "You can go get a test tomorrow. If you were always a top, AIDS isn't all that easy to catch. It isn't communicated by kissing very often. It seems highly unlikely that you can get it by giving or getting a blow job. Since it has to get into your bloodstream, only those people who take it up the bum and have some kind of cut or opening are going to catch it. Which means people who take it up the bum a lot."

"Whew." I said no more. Nevis went on.

"You ought to get in touch with that girlfriend you left behind in California, too. She should get a test."

"I will," I said, but didn't tell Nevis that I had no plans to tell Esther that she had been at risk for AIDS. He didn't put it together that the girlfriend in California was the same girl that was in the threesome and I wasn't about to tell him.

"Why did you break off with that girl?" Nevis asked.

I told him, "I don't know exactly." But of course I did know. Once we did the threesome I knew I could never trust her again. "It wasn't love; it was lust," I said. "I just thought seriously about Esther one day and decided that I could do better." I realized I had said too much from the look that Nevis gave me.

I said no more. I didn't tell him that I not only had no intention of telling Esther that she should have an AIDS test, but I wasn't so sure that I was going to go get one myself.

~13~ Minerva Minot

Dozing in his room on the way to sleep, Nevis's brain snagged on Minerva Minot. Would he have the courage to ask Radomir more about her? Was it even a good idea to ask? Did he even care to find out what had been going on with Minerva Minot?

Shortly before leaving for Crete he had had a call from Minerva. She was a friend of Radomir's from the Alliance Francaise and Nevis thought it was very possible Radomir was sleeping with her before he left Paris.

Nevis remembered well the first time Minerva's name had come up. Radomir had invited some friends from the language school to go out to the country. Nevis had decided not to go because he thought the friends would see Radomir and him together, draw their conclusions and—zut—there went Radomir's image at the school. He told Radsomir why he wasn't going and the reply was, "Oh, I don't care about that."

When the weekend was over Radomir complained because the young girl from Guatemala he'd invited hadn't been able to get away from her au pair job, and she had asked if the American girl, Minerva, could come in her place. Radomir thought Minerva had pushed her way in, and had kept on being pushy all weekend.

Later Nevis had come home to find Minerva visiting and had listened to her long story of pursuing a career in singing in Europe. Her air of an earnest rabbit from Texas wasn't going to serve her very well on the cabaret circuit, he thought, but he'd seen stranger careers come into being.

Now Minerva wanted to know when she called if he'd heard from Radomir.

He told her Radomir was in Crete and if he heard more he'd let her know. Minerva had received a postcard, but without an address. She added, "Radomir said I could come join them if I came back from the

United States early enough, and now I'm here and I don't know where they are!" Nevis wondered which of Radomir's lists she was on. Since he knew she called his parents from time to time, evidently she was on the "Address Unknown" one.

Nevis suggested, to cheer her up, that they were probably in some dreary youth hostel somewhere with sand in their sleeping bags. "I hear there's a lot of wild sex at those beaches in Greece," Minerva said, a note of jealousy flickering in her voice. Nevis immediately registered that she most certainly must have been sleeping with Radomir. He decided to hate her but then relented. *Just another member of the Radomir Pulkanovic Walking Wounded Club,* he thought, and felt a bit sorry for the Texas rabbit.

"I'm alone here now that he's gone," Minerva went on, "but I'm going to try to keep reaching out to people all the same." Now Nevis did feel sorry for her, and he said they should have dinner together sometime.

Poor Minerva hung over his head during the week. He also wondered what she knew about Radomir that he would like to know and could worm out of her. He called her and they made a date for dinner.

The evening of their dinner Minerva came by to pick him up as the restaurant was near his flat. When he came down the stairs she was wedged between the mailboxes and the door in the entranceway. He thought, *You have been granted a stay of execution, Minerva. I'm not going to strangle you for having slept with the man I love. Not tonight at least. Although I may feel like it before this dinner is over.*

Nevis remembered Radomir telling him he felt sorry for Minerva because her parents sent her the money she needed for her studies and to live on, but they didn't want her around. Nevis thought Minerva had a pretty good deal. Sleeping around Europe, all expenses paid.

At dinner he found Minerva rather restful as she enjoyed doing most of the talking. The previous year she had spent in the Italian countryside with some man who was now history. She conceded that he was Italian and that he was not her vocal coach.

When Nevis brought up Radomir and said as cheerfully as he could, "I'm sure he'll be back," Minerva took her paw-like hands out of her salad and said firmly, "I don't think so. He felt he was too dependent upon you." After this Minerva felt she had said too much perhaps and Nevis sensed her guard was up. Nevis felt quite inadequate at leading her into revelatory admissions and changed the subject.

He asked her if she still saw the girl from Guatemala whose place she had taken on the fatal weekend in the country. "No, she's really not so interesting, you know. I call her and she never wants to do any of the things I'm planning to do. She's really too young." Nevis guessed that both girls had been interested in Radomir. Certainly he had spoken far oftener of the Guatemalan girl. And Minerva, being older, stronger, and more aggressive, had won out. Nevis stopped feeling any pity for her. He hoped the Guatemalan would revenge herself well on Miss Quiver-Nose.

He did learn that at the present time Minerva was having an affair with a French musician whose apartment she had gone to look at. She hadn't liked the apartment, but she had liked the musician. As for Radomir, "He was my best friend in Paris. And he left town on the spur of the moment without writing. Just a postcard. I'm going to forget him. Just forget he ever existed."

You can say those kinds of things when you're young, Nevis thought. You can revenge yourself on those who desert your love by forgetting their existence. Or you can try. Later you know it's not so easy. They keep turning up. And much later you know your love's all used up. They got the last of it and made off, leaving you with just the hole where the transfusion used to be. And the love for them that's left just keeps leaking out, dripping on the sidewalk behind you when you walk, useful to no one. Nevis felt as though he was several pints short on his love level and that it was very unlikely he was ever going to get them back from anyone else. He wanted to go home.

Nevis allowed Minerva to drop him off at his apartment. Not very gentlemanly, but he wasn't feeling very gentlemanly. As they crossed on the rue La Bruyère she walked uphill slightly ahead of him. He saw her less-than-slender buttocks bobbling in her slacks. *I know exactly what her body's like,* he thought. *Already flaccid. Poor muscle tone. Not very large breasts, already drooping. And this is who Radomir prefers to clamber upon. My ass is much nicer, much firmer. Pound for pound I'm more beautiful now than she ever was or ever will be. And I'm sure I'm a ten-times better fuck.*

This little burst of hatred out of the way, and it really wasn't directed so much at Minerva as at the whole way that most people got their sex lives together, Nevis said good night pleasantly and wished her well.

When he got inside the message button was blinking on his answering machine. When he played it back it was the voice of Radomir's female friend from Arizona. "Nevis," the voice said, "I've got an address for Radomir. It's Number Twenty-Four, Hydranthos Beach Hotel, Plakias, Crete, Greece." She spelled "Hydranthos" and "Plakias" and then said, "Mirthios is where they mail letters. It's nearby. But he's in Plakias. Good luck."

Nevis stared at the address in his hand. "This is it" ran over and over again in his brain, as though the tape machine had transferred itself to his head. He turned to his desk and started a letter.

~14~ The Last Night on Crete

The few days left on Crete followed the same routine. Nevis appeared in the dining room for Radomir to bring him some breakfast and then strolled the town. He found the *Herald Tribune* in the general store, only one day late. He returned to the taverna terrace and read the paper until Radomir could leave. They lunched in the town and then went to the beach in the afternoons. The friends drifted on and off the beach. They talked about a more isolated nude beach where the Greek boys walked up and down along the water's edge with erections. "Nothing beats advertising," Nevis said.

The night before Nevis was to leave he had two kirs before dinner and smoked even more than usual. The preceding evenings both Radomir and he had retired relatively early to their separate rooms. Radomir talked about how much rowdy partying they did and Nevis was determined to not leave Radomir and his friends to party on by themselves if the evening were to develop in that direction.

He also had a small bottle of Greek wine with his meal and they ordered more in the village. It was chilly and no one was on the terrace except three or four of Radomir's gang, who joined their table. As the restaurant closed there was talk of going to the disco but the girls in the party, Sacha and Carla, begged off and left for the youth hostel where they lived. Radomir, Nevis, and the blond Canadian boy, Tony, went to the same disco where Nevis had searched for Radomir the night he had arrived. Nevis was feeling dazed by this point but took a seat at the bar between the two younger men and ordered an ouzo along with them. A young Greek who played the records at the disco joined them. The Greek man rubbed his hands over Nevis at frequent intervals as they talked. *He fancies me,* thought Nevis. *This is bizarre.*

As they left the disco an hour later a small open truck was passing. "Let's go to the other disco," shouted Radomir and what was apparently every pedestrian in the street piled into the back of the truck.

Nevis scrambled over the back board with the rest of them, and they bobbled off into the night. The other disco turned out to be a barnlike structure along the beach road that they had passed every afternoon walking back and forth to lie in the sun on the nude beach.

The large black room was empty except for three or four couples lurking in the shadows. Their party advanced to the bar and ordered more ouzo. The disco music blared and Nevis flung himself onto the dance floor with the others. He wasn't sure how much longer he would be standing. When the music stopped they went back to the bar for more ouzo. Nevis was so drunk he knew he wouldn't get any drunker. Radomir was sitting on his left. Nevis crossed his arms and grabbed the under side of Radomir's nearby arm to steady himself. Radomir was talking to a small, pretty German girl all in red. Then he was kissing her. Very long. With a lot of tongue, Nevis guessed. He felt he was not only drunk but that something was collapsing within himself. Then Radomir was kissing the German girl again. "That was nice," he said as he pulled away. The German girl frolicked off onto the dance floor. "You stay right here," Radomir said to Nevis. "Stay right here and don't go anywhere."

Nevis would have liked to run out one of the side doors that stood open on the black Cretan night, but he thought it just as well to not finish the evening passing out in the nearby grain fields. He wasn't sure that anyone would bother to look for him. Radomir floated into view just as the disco music changed. "We have to dance this one," he said. "This is the one we requested." Nevis could see him on the dance floor. He had a kind of floaty, ice-skating style that covered a lot of ground.

Then they were leaving. There was no one left in the disco except Radomir and Nevis and the Canadian boy, who struck off in the opposite direction toward the hillside hotel. Nevis took Radomir's hand in his and pushed them both into his pocket to give him support as he walked. He had that stiff-kneed gait that told him he was very, very drunk. At this point he wasn't at all sure he was going to make it all the way back to the hotel.

They passed the taverna, which had the same ghostly off-season look it had the night Nevis arrived. They turned into the alley behind the hotel and paused in front of Radomir's door. Nevis was not at all sure he could negotiate the stairs to his room all by himself. Then he flung his arms about Radomir, sobbing into his neck. "Let me just come into your room. Just to lie beside you, that's all. I just can't make it without you." He sobbed harder and harder. The falling away that had begun in the disco collapsed and the pain and sadness of being alone during the past months roared through him. "I just can't make it without you." He continued to sob and then realized that he had to sit down or he wouldn't be conscious. He groped his way to the step in front of Radomir's door and continued sobbing. Radomir stood beside him with one arm over his shoulder. Nevis clung to Radomir's legs. "I'm sorry, I'm sorry," he said. A man passed in the darkness of the alley and looked at them curiously. But not too curiously. The sky was beginning to lighten over the ocean.

"You're going to have to help me up to my room," Nevis muttered. Radomir had not said a word. As they dragged through the alley toward the stairway to Nevis's room he said repeatedly, "I can't. I just can't. I just can't." Out of the depths roaring and rushing through him Nevis felt admiration for him.

In his room Nevis clawed his clothes off and fell on the bed. "I hate myself for what I'm doing to your life. I'm shit. I'm just shit. This is awful what's happening. Oh, God. Oh, God." While he sobbed and mumbled and pounded on the mattress with his fists, Radomir stood in the doorway and looked at him. Nevis was aware of the look of disdain on his face. Radomir said, "I'll see you in the morning. I'll make sure you're up in time to get your taxi for the airport." As he left, Nevis fell asleep. It was six o'clock.

At eight Nevis woke up. He did not feel too terrible, although a little floaty. He shaved, dressed, packed, and carried his suitcase down the stairs and through the alley toward the taverna. As he passed Radomir's room Radomir was in the hall locking his door. He looked surprised to see Nevis up and presentable. "Did you sleep?" Nevis asked him.

"No, I went for a walk on the beach and read."

Nevis took a table by a window in the sunlight and Radomir brought him some breakfast. The cab came. Nevis shook the dazed taverna owner's hand, and Radomir walked him to the cab. All he said to Nevis was, "You shouldn't be so hard on yourself." They shook hands. As the taxi rushed Nevis away up the hill past the hostel he looked back. Radomir was walking back into the taverna. It was early in the morning in Plakias and Nevis was leaving.

~15~ Lo De Coy

I don't think I would have gotten through that awful winter in Paris with Nevis if it hadn't been for Lo De Coy. I met her in my French class at the Alliance Francaise. She was from Guatemala. Spanish really. She said that her family was descended from the conquistadors. Then she laughed and said that everyone in Guatemala said that.

Minerva Minot and she and I became pals because we were the only ones from the Americas in the class. We always sat together. Lo was a lot better than we were because her first language was Spanish, but her English was excellent, too. We were probably an interesting-looking trio. Kind of like the cast from of a B movie about young Americans in Europe. Minerva was blondish and blue-eyed and kind of pudgy, and Lo was very dark and had a muscular sort of body, and then there was me. Cute American me, I suppose.

Both the girls had families who didn't really want them. Minerva had parents in Texas who sent her money to live in France and pursue a singing career, but they obviously didn't want her around. And I always wondered about that career. She never seemed to have a singing teacher and I never heard her sing. Well, once. She was at the apartment one day when Nevis was singing, "Look me over once, look me over twice, examine the line of my spine." From *Die Fledermaus*. You always learned a lot of obscure things from Nevis. Minerva got the music and sang it for me frequently when we were in the country together. I never had the heart to tell her that Nevis sang better than she did. But then he had had a real career singing and kicking his legs higher than his head when he was a chorus boy. As he always said, "Right after the Civil War."

Lo was something else altogether. She had the strangest story. Her parents had separated, each to marry someone else, when she was about five with sisters ages three and one. Neither of the parents wanted the children, so they were sent to live with her mother's parents, where they stayed until Lo was about fifteen. Then both grandparents died and two aunts inherited the house. They didn't want to inherit the girls too, but everything looked up when both the spouses of their father and mother died, and their parents remarried. But they still didn't want the children with them. They said they didn't have room for their children and so they put them in a rooming house, where Lo, real name Loretta ("I hate that name"), lived, keeping an eye on her sisters. Now the sisters are eighteen and sixteen and Lo saw fit to depart for Paris. In comparison to Lo I have never had any problems at all, yet she rises above it all with no hard feelings.

I said, "If I had parents like that I'd never want to see them again in my whole life!"

"Oh, no, it is not at all like that," Lo said. "They are quite demanding that we are all present for their birthdays and the holidays and especially Christmas. They look forward very much to our presents."

"Presents! I'd give them a bomb," I said.

Lo looked at me pityingly. "You must remember that they are always willing to pay. They just don't want to see much of us. But later when they are very old they will want to see a lot of us."

"And revenge is a dish best eaten cold. That's a Spanish saying," I said. I had learned that from Nevis.

"Well, not too cold," Lo said. "You don't want them to be dead. Or so old they don't even realize that it is revenge."

"That must be the Spanish way," I said.

"Of course, I don't know any other," Lo said.

Lo became my confidante and Minerva became my girlfriend. I'm not sure quite why or how. Of course, I concealed that Minerva and I were sleeping together from Nevis, although there wasn't much to conceal. She didn't ever really move. I think we slept together because there really wasn't anyone else around. I say that, but I could have slept with Lo, I'm sure. But Lo didn't care one way or another. Minerva needed desperately to be doing something with someone. And I needed desperately to be doing something with someone other than Nevis. So Minerva was it.

I talked a lot about Nevis with Lo, and sometimes Lo and Minerva together. Minerva took my side. Lo not always. When I said he was controlling she said, "But look, Radomir"—she never called me Rad as a lot of my new friends in Paris did—"what's the problem? You have a nice place to live. You have warm clothes. Even better than that, nice clothes. You have very nice clothes and that is very important in France. You never are without food. There's always something in the refrigerator at Nevis's apartment, isn't there? You do those little freelance projects for him for which you get paid. It is not as though you are being kept. And, and this is a big *and,* there are no strings attached. Is that what you say, there are no strings attached? You don't have to sleep with him. So how is it that he is so controlling?"

"He always has to know where I am all the time. And he always wants me to do things with him all the time. I don't feel free."

Lo said, "Well, he's in love with you. Maybe you don't know how that feels. It is like a dream that you are always afraid is going to end. He is afraid that suddenly you will meet someone and fall in love with them and go away. I understand that; don't you?"

I said I didn't understand it and that I didn't plan to.

"You will some day, you little boy," Lo said. Lo is four years younger than I am, but I think she has seen a lot more or felt a lot more than I have. Maybe it's another one of those Spanish things.

She went on. "And as for doing things with him, if you don't want to go I'd be delighted. I would be delighted to run down to Milan for a few days. I'd be delighted to go to Casa Olympe for a really good dinner. And he even bought you a house in the Loire Valley. I'd be delighted to go there."

"That you can do, Lo," I said. I invited Lo and Minerva and some other friends to come down and help me work on the little house Nevis and I owned together in a big town not far from his country house. We were there taking people to see the local chateau one day and saw this little house up a side street. I have my magical side, and this little place hit that streak. It was kind of perched on a hillside and when we got inside with a real estate agent it was like something out of a fairy story, all little steps up here and down there and a big walled garden behind it. From the top floor you looked into the tops of the cherry trees, and they were full of cherries. You could reach right out the windows and pick them. It was a great little house. So when Nevis suggested he buy it in both our names I said that would be fine. Which he did. I started going down on weekends to work on it. Scraping beams and painting walls and all the same kind of stuff I did on his house.

The first time Minerva came down it was because Lo couldn't get away from her au pair job. I kind of hated her. She was very pushy and always knew the best way to do everything. But she really worked. She got out and cleaned up the garden and made bonfires and I came to like the fact that she was really helping me. Lo wouldn't have done that. In fact, she looked at the house with a very skeptical eye.

"Is there something you're not telling me, Radomir?" she asked. "You don't like this man. You are using this man. And then you let him buy this house for you. It doesn't look right. Are you sleeping with him and not telling us? You know, it's all right if you are. It would actually make more sense with all that he does for you. If you're not you are going to regret this. I don't really want to help you with this house. I think it is unhealthy."

I knew what she meant. We had just learned *malsain* in French class. It means "dirty" in the way we use it in the United States, like a dirty book. But it translates as "unhealthy." I knew what Lo meant. But Minerva didn't. She thought everything I did was fine.

That whole winter was awful. We had a rotten Christmas down in the country. Amanda was there again and tried to keep things going, but Nevis was in a real snit. Everything everyone did was wrong. He hated everything. We went for a long walk to talk things out and that only made it worse. I kept telling him he was trying to control me too much and he said he didn't know what I was talking about. He wanted to fuck and I didn't. That's what it boiled down to.

In February we went down to the country and I decided to go out with Fritz and Angie on Saturday night. Nevis wasn't invited. He called a taxi and took the next train back to Paris that evening, leaving me there. I apologized when I got back to Paris, and I could tell he was feeling shitty for having made a scene and run away. Things weren't good, and I was looking forward to making my getaway in the spring. I wrote some friends in California, Lauren and Bixby, and we made plans to take a tour of Europe together. What I was going to do at the end of it I wasn't sure.

I always liked Lauren and Bixby a lot in California, and I was looking forward to our trip. Nevis was very cool about it. He took all of us out to dinner the night before we were leaving, gave me a generous last payment so I had plenty of money to travel, and seemed perfectly happy to see me go. On our way out of the office in the Montparnasse Tower on the last day . . . I had been over there delivering some storyboards . . . he said, "Just remember, Radomir, to read the small type before you get into another situation like the one you've been in with me. Not everyone is willing to give you something for nothing." That really pissed me off. At the beginning of our relationship I thought it was really a friendship and of course it always boils down to the same thing. They want a piece of your tail.

Every day on the trip I came to like Lauren and Bixby less. Nevis had said, "She has too many gums." And I began to find it true—that irritating smile with all that pink flesh showing along with that big mouth full of Chiclet teeth.

In Florence they didn't want to spend the money to see Michelangelo's *David*. They just wanted to have me tell them about it later on the train. Stuff like that. Totally uncultured, and Bixby is supposed to be an art director. Lauren got looser and looser as the days went by. We had a picnic on the beach in Greece at a youth hostel, and she wandered off into the night with some guy. I told Bixby he should go look for her. He wasn't planning to. He did and they both looked like they'd been made to do something they didn't want to do when they came back to the campfire.

When we got to Crete we finally wandered down to the south shore and decided to stay there. I asked for a job at the hotel in the café and they hired me. There were lots of English and Australians and some French working around the village and it looked like it would be a lot of fun. Lauren and Bixby decided to go on to Turkey and then back to the States, so we said good-bye there and I haven't heard from them since. I had no plans, so there I stayed.

The only person I wrote to was Lo. She didn't answer. I think she thought I was crazy.

~16~ Fanette

Nevis returned to Paris. Through the hassle of the wild taxi trip to Heraklion; the discovery that his ticket had been written incorrectly and he had only five minutes at the Heraklion airport before his flight departed; the mob scene at the Athens airport where he had to wait in a giant queue to change terminals; the strangely somnambulistic quality of the international airport where the waiting passengers moved as though they were underwater or perhaps only seemed so. Through all this Nevis moved numbly. He kept waiting for the drunkenness and the brief hours of sleep to hit him, but they never did. He felt as someone must who has been narrowly missed by an avalanche. The relief provided all the energy he needed not to fall apart.

Once back in France he was gripped by an enormous compulsion to complete the renovation of the country house he had bought in both Radomir's and his name. A strange fairy-tale house he had seen with Radomir on a curious winding lane leading into the nearby town of Amboise. Out driving one day they had noticed the unusual cliff-perching site with the *À VENDRE* sign and had routed out a local real estate agent. The house made Nevis think of a drawing from *The Toys of Nuremberg,* a childhood book he had loved. A gate in crumbling green paint opened directly from the street into a small courtyard. In front and to the left green-painted doors opened into caves, cut directly into the cliff the house sat upon. A barred window beside one door gave the whole ensemble the look of a small prison in a Mozart opera.

On the right an iron-railed stone staircase wound round upon itself to a balcony where the green-shuttered front door opened into the house itself. They entered this door after the agent struggled with a clutch of keys. Once inside they found themselves in a small room painted navy blue with acid yellow trim. In an alcove a photo view in color of a Pacific lagoon had been pasted like wallpaper from floor to ceiling.

The agent opened another door, and up a short flight of steps they found a stone-walled garden with cherry trees full of fruit filling the sky overhead. From the edge of the garden one looked down on the lane below and across the valley to not-distant hills.

Behind this garden through a gate, they found another larger and wilder garden reaching to another wall of cliffs. This garden had many terraced levels, fragments of old walls, shreds of old stone staircases, and entrances to caves even more ancient than the ones below the house. Each cave had stone fireplaces and indications of having once been inhabited.

Back in the house they wandered up through different levels. The red-and-white kitchen's casement windows opened flat with the lawn of the garden outside and matched the color of the fruit filling the trees.

Up a tiny winding staircase was a black and candy-pink bedroom. The bedroom window looked directly into the cherry-heavy branches of the trees outside. From the attic room above it one could reach into the treetops and pick the cherries.

As they leaned side by side out of this window looking through the tops of the trees and to the valley beyond, Nevis had thought, *If I could spend one happy night here with him I could stand the rest of my life, however it might be.* He didn't tell Radomir this.

Radomir, too, seemed caught up in the fantasy quality of the house. He said, "It would be wonderful to live here, wouldn't it?"

They left the real estate agent, and as they walked to the car Nevis noticed a small plaque on the front of the house. It read FANETTE.

He had no reason to buy Fanette, didn't really have the money to buy the house in fact. But Radomir was increasingly ill at ease with him and the house was a subject they both enjoyed discussing. One night at dinner in a tiny Japanese restaurant in the Montmartre foothills he suggested that he buy Fanette in both their names. Radomir looked down at his plate in the flat-faced, choked-up, noncommittal manner Nevis had come to know meant something important was going on inside. "Would you like that?" he asked. Radomir suddenly moved from a mood of sulky recalcitrance to one of open enthusiasm. They discussed what could be done with the house through the rest of the meal and as they walked down the narrow cobbled streets past the tough transvestite hookers. Nevis had found something Radomir loved, even if it wasn't Nevis himself.

In one of the few times they had been at Fanette together before Radomir left Paris, Nevis had discovered that the hillock rising in the back of the grounds was actually earth covering the foundations of an old house. At the entrances to the caves there were remnants of old windows and doorways in the hillside that suggested this, but while working on the hill with a hoe he discovered a hole. Poking his head and a flashlight inside, he saw that the walls still stood inside the hill, though the room was largely filled with dirt.

He told this to Radomir, who wanted to look, too. Radomir put his head and the flashlight in the hole and then suddenly thrust himself backward out of the hole, sliding down the hill. "Spiders!" he gasped.

When Nevis first went to look at the house alone on a wet spring day shortly after Radomir had gone, he found Radomir had been working on it the weekends he had gone to the country by himself. In the bedroom the alcove beam had been scraped to the bare wood, as had several of the cupboard doors that framed the fireplace. One coat of white paint dimmed the vividness of the bright pink walls. A large can of paint remover, a scraper, and a pair of paint-begummed gloves lay together on the floor. Nevis ached when he looked at them and realized Radomir had cared enough about Fanette to make a start. Before he left for Crete Nevis had finished the paint removal in the bedroom and had put another coat of paint on the ceiling and walls, so the room looked fairly finished.

Now on his return from Crete he felt swept up in a tide of needing to do as much as he could to finish the work on Fanette. Radomir had written soon after Nevis returned that he was coming to France in July, coming to rendezvous with a California friend, a woman he had worked with at one time. He had written repeatedly from Crete, "You know I'm not coming to see you. I'm coming to see Savannah." His friend's name was Savannah Dickens. A very Californian name, Nevis thought.

First Nevis attacked the woodwork of the lower sitting room at Fanette. It seemed modest at first: a beam separating the alcove containing the view of Tahitian beaches, a closet door, a door to the kitchen stair, and an old wooden fireplace front. But soon he found the ancient wood was very resistant to paint remover. He borrowed a sander from Fritz, his American neighbor. Couldn't find the right size of rolling sandpaper strips to fit it and finally bought a new sander to fit the rolling strips he'd already bought. His local friends who dropped by obviously thought this was all remarkably unlike him, and the local workmen who had come to take measurements and make plans for installing a septic tank and converting the attic on the stair landing to a bathroom regarded him with amazement in his shrunken sweater, decade-old jeans, and paint-flake-speckled hair, glasses, and face.

Nevis didn't enjoy it. It was more as though there was an unwritten commitment somewhere that he was compelled to fulfill. Finally the paint was stripped from the sitting room doors and the large beam overhead. The fireplace emerged from its layers of black paint. The kitchen door and bedroom door, too, revealed their aged wood surfaces. The last fragments of old gray paint released their tenacious grip on the lower edges of the doors.

Then Tahiti had to go. Slopping a sponge over the huge photograph loosened it, only to reveal large holes in the wallboard, covering even more ancient stone walls, Nevis supposed. The board would have to come off one day, but for the time being much plastering of cracks and crevices would have to do, with three coats of white paint on all the walls and ceiling.

The kitchen in its turn was repaired and painted.

Broken windows were repaired in the bedroom. A broken window latch was replaced. All loose windows were reputtied, and then all the woodwork that hadn't been scraped was lacquered white. Nevis sighed with relief to see the peculiar jaundiced yellow of the living room woodwork disappear, the accompanying navy blue walls having already fled beneath flat white.

The kitchen floor was enameled brick red with deck paint, and the old refrigerator enameled the same blue as the closet interiors above stairs. Next he stripped the little painted table left in the kitchen and put linseed oil on the chairs left in the house.

He bought a settee and some tables from an antique dealer in a nearby town, and a sleigh bed Radomir had said he liked from another dealer. The woman from whom he bought the bed, a sturdy, volatile lady who delivered the bed herself and manhandled it into the house, noticed all the different levels in Fanette and said she believed the house had been built in two different periods. The older house was the back part, she pointed out, indicating a bricked-up window in the top attic Nevis had not noticed. She also noted that the steps descending from the kitchen to the sitting room were stone, and probably exterior at one time.

Nevis had two pieces of old mirror framed and put over the fireplaces in the bedroom and sitting room. He scraped rusty paint off the front door shutters, the descending stair rail, and the front gate, but didn't have strength or time or the desire to repaint them.

When Radomir was last in the country house he had packed up some possessions in a cardboard box and left them with Fritz. While Fritz was in the United States Nevis took the key he had left with him, went into his house, and brought the box back to his own home.

He immediately opened it and laid the contents carefully out on a bed so he would be able to replace them exactly as they had been. There were portraits of Radomir done by Nevis's nephew, the photographer. In them his hair was swept back and he looked slightly upward into the camera in a mixture of sullenness and defiance. Radomir had looked at the pictures and said, "I'd like to look like that someday."

There were a few books, several sweaters, and Radomir's diaries. Nevis had suspected the diaries would be left behind. Radomir wrote in them often.

Nevis had been brought up to think that reading someone's mail or anything not directed to oneself was an unthinkable breach of good manners. Only the lowest person would so much as read over another person's shoulder. He felt deep shame as he opened Radomir's diaries, but he was far beyond controlling himself. *Honor is for the unobsessed,* he thought as he began to read.

He propped himself up in bed and read Radomir unburdening himself in his loneliness when he first came to Europe. Abandoned by his employers in Rome and then in London, chasing back and forth between the cities in pursuit of a job that was never there, he had turned to his writing to strengthen himself. The lover he had left behind in California had suggested he visit a former boyfriend in Germany. He had and there had fallen in love. In his diary he wrote poetically of their first days together. Nevis seethed and at the same time felt as though he had been taken over by a poltergeist himself. Reluctantly, he read on.

The picture of himself that emerged in Radomir's diaries he scarcely recognized. While he had been thrilled to have Radomir share his apartment in Paris, Radomir had been railing about being given no freedom and being checked up on all the time. There were no mentions of affection or even interest in him. Radomir mentioned one conversation on a train where he wrote, "Nevis, as usual, tried to make me feel good about myself." In the diaries were letters from friends, and the woman in Santa Fe in one of her replies wrote, "And as you say, though difficult it is a convenience." Shaken, unhappy, but not regretful, he carefully packed the diaries back in the box with the other things and stored them in a closet.

As he labored alone on the house renovations during that long, cold summer he took the box out a second time and read the contents of the letters and diaries again. Even though it was painful, it was contact with Radomir.

The renovations went on weekend after weekend. Nevis, usually closemouthed, found himself in so distressed a state he couldn't conceal it from friends. Fritz met Nevis at the train from time to time, so he deserved an explanation for Nevis's forlorn looks. When he heard that it was a case of old-fashioned lovesickness he said, "I'm jealous." Nevis wasn't sure if he was jealous because he wanted Nevis to be lovelorn over him, or if he was jealous because he had no one to be lovelorn over himself. Nevis hoped it was the latter but didn't want to ask.

A longtime Swiss painter friend, André, came down for a weekend and spent both days at Fanette doing sketches while Nevis painted walls and woodwork. André found the curious nooks and crannies of Fanette optically fascinating. He loved the curving staircases ascending and descending into irregular spaces. André also spent a lot of time in a straight-back chair in the garden, sketching the strange shapes where Fanette's eaves and roofs and doorways came together.

In the evening André and Nevis sat by the fire and talked. Nevis found it bracing to reveal his foolishness and forlorness to a friend of over twenty years. André and his French actress wife had been the closest to Nevis of his friends in France and had often been to the country house to visit.

In his dry Swiss manner André didn't allow Nevis a shred of romantic hope, and Nevis knew him to be right. On the other hand, the painter did allow him the pleasure of his feelings and saw them as valuable, if doomed. The only concern he expressed, which was shared by his wife, was a fear that Nevis would be caught in an emotional undertow from which he wouldn't be able to extricate himself. Suicide was obviously at the back of his mind. Nevis wondered if it could possibly go that far, and remembered the episode on the balcony at Cannes. *Not out of the question,* he thought, and dismissed it from his mind.

His lawyer and great friend, Anthony Stuart, came down for a long weekend also. He spent time catching sun in briefs while Nevis worked. Anthony, usually brusque and cool and charming and witty all at the same time, could be very human to a friend caught in the pheasant nets of love. "I must say," he said in the evening by the fire, "that I find you being sick and obsessed with love a refreshing change from my other friends, who haven't thought of anything but stock options or real estate in years."

When Nevis took him to catch an early Sunday afternoon train he saw the concern and real affection in Anthony's eyes when he boarded the train. As Nevis crossed the dusty street in front of the station in the hot Loire sun he suddenly burst into tears. *Either I'm crying because I'm exhausted, or I'm exhausted because of so much crying,* he thought. *Either way,* he thought, *it sits badly on a fifty-six-year-old man.* But he saw very little he could do about it.

~17~ This Is a Fantasy

Why do people think that describing sex acts is obscene? Animals lick their genitals in front of humans all the time and most pet owners see it as normal behavior for their pets. But they recoil in horror at the image or description of one human placing another human's sexual organs in their mouth, or even in those orifices which were made for that purpose. Or nearly.

Why this fear? I think Puritanism is based on a great fear of losing control. And that if you lose control you will sink down through layer upon layer of sexual and sensual excess until you are rejected by society, to die alone and uncared for and in filth and agony. Which seems to be where God looks for people to save for the most part. So why all the panic?

No, this fear reveals to me that in fact very few people are able to conceptualize anything except this life on earth. And their eventual end here is of paramount importance, hence the search for fame, power, wealth. To find a permanent place in the worldly firmament of stars, so as to never sink to scorn and rejection. And physical pleasure weakens mental discipline. Of course, we now have film stars and politicians who feel they can combine licentiousness and a pure public image and they seem to get caught at it repeatedly. For most people, letting yourself go sexually means you risk letting yourself sink out of sight socially, the worst possible end to a life. My sense of it is, they want to do it so much that the very hint of it frightens them. They feel the thread unraveling. The candle beginning to flicker in the high wind of passion, starting to burn out quickly leaving only the black night.

Actually, you don't have to fuck very much before you get tired of it. Two or three fucks in a row and you begin to think about getting a good night's sleep so as to not ruin your looks. But people who have never had two or three good fucks in a row don't know this. They think they will then want those good fucks every night and more. So, reader, do not be afraid of the ensuing scene. It won't ruin your life. It really is scarcely more than your cat cleaning under its tail. I was giving Radomir a massage. Could you call it homosocial contact instead of homosexual contact? It was not quite playing tennis together, but somewhere in that area. He had on his jockey shorts. I just had on my undershorts and a cotton bathrobe from Turnbull and Asser. I want you to understand one thing, also. I may be thirty years older than Radomir, but my body is not disgusting. I was a gymnast in high school and college (no contact sports, please) and have always continued to exercise. My thighs are full and the skin is smooth. I don't have much of a waistline, but I never did. I have pectorals and my upper arms aren't thin. I'm not very hairy, and my overall proportions are tall and slender. I was never a Steve Reeves or a Tab Hunter, but men who slept with me enjoyed my smooth skin and slender body. I also kiss with enthusiasm and can get passionate for an appreciative partner. So Radomir's allowing himself to be massaged was not exactly turning himself over to some repulsive and sagging monster, at least as I see it. Am I kidding myself? I think not. I'm still very critical of other people's beauty and compare myself to them.

While I was massaging deeply into the muscles of Radomir's lower back I flashed on something. You know those ideas that just burst in your brain. I believe they have to be some kind of transmission from someone else. Certainly Einstein and Freud didn't dream up their theories logically, A following B. Those ideas sprang forth full grown. Not that my flash was of an Einsteinian level.

I just knew that Radomir would like me to lick his ass. He always resisted strongly any kind of contact that would lead to sexual arousal on his part. No spreading of the legs when I massaged his thighs. When he massaged my back and I pulled him down on top of me, his hips were always lifted so his penis in fact never made contact with my buttocks. Like all men of wide sexual experience, they know what arouses them and keep themselves off the edge of getting truly sexually interested—particularly when they're manipulating the other person's sexual interest in them.

But I flashed and followed the flash by bending down and placing my hot, wet mouth on the crack of Radomir's ass through his white cotton underpants. I soaked them thoroughly. He didn't move. Or say, "Please, stop," which he had done before.

I chewed those underpants good. I pushed my tongue against them and into the cleft between his cheeks. The wet cotton stretched. I pulled his buttocks apart with my hands as my mouth pushed farther down between his parting flesh. He didn't resist. Then he stirred and lifted his buttocks so I could gain better access. Finally I had won. This was the Achilles' heel. This was what Radomir had reserved as his own sexual territory, allowing all kinds of contact with his nipples and penis without getting aroused.

I pulled his soggy jockey shorts down below his buttocks and pushed my face deeper between his lifted cheeks. My tongue was reaching his anus now. I could push the end of my tongue into the center of it like a small penis. Incapable of entering, but hinting and threatening even so. The threat that was no threat built in his blood. I lifted him onto his knees, his chest and head still buried in a pillow. His arms were flung up along each side of his head. His back and upper arms made a massive "V" sweeping down from his narrow waist. His rounded buttocks were now standing high. I pulled his underpants down to his knees. "Let's get these off," I said. He lifted one knee and then the other as I slipped the shorts under them and then pulled them down and off his feet. I threw them across the room. I didn't try for the ceiling fixture, which I like to do when it's within reach and reason.

I bent to my work. I pulled his buttocks apart as far as I could and ran my tongue lavishly up and down the valley between, stopping as I passed over the puckered anus to probe and suck. He groaned. The muscles there were beginning to relax. On one of my down runs I swept lower and licked his hanging testicles. I pulled them up in one hand. I glanced at his penis and could see that it was very erect and pointing strongly down toward the bed. But I wasn't going to jump to that yet. I lifted his testicles in one hand and inserted them into my mouth. He mumbled into the pillow, "It feels like I have two cocks." This was much further into sexual intimacy than Radomir had ever ventured with me before. That was much more exciting to me than the touching of his flesh. The flesh could have been anyone's, but the words from deep inside him were his alone. I felt under the edge of the mattress. I always keep a tube of Vaseline there, in the event it is needed. I sucked strongly on his hanging testicles as I undid the tube and squeezed Vaseline on my fingers. While I continued sucking I rubbed Vaseline over his anus and slowly inserted one finger. He didn't fight it. I pushed the finger in as far as it would go. It felt warm in there. I moved it in and out slowly with the rhythm of the sucking of my mouth.

I lay down on my side between his legs and moved my mouth to the top of his penis. My finger was still moving slowly in his body. He pushed into my mouth. He wanted the warmth. His penis was larger than I expected it to be. From having seen him naked I knew it was good sized, but erect it was stout and of important length. *Is this Yugoslavian?* I wondered. He was now past the point of no return and wanted orgasm. But he had his own sexual skills with himself; he was not frantic to come. He moved slowly in and out of my mouth, pushing in as far as he could, then slowly moving out until just the tip of it rested on my lips, then pushing through again. I pulled off and slipped sideways on it so as to get to the base. I'm no good at getting someone down my throat. It always makes me want to throw up. In fact sucking someone's penis is really for their pleasure. I want them to have the pleasure. As for me, I certainly wouldn't miss it if I never did it again. When his rhythm began to accelerate, I moved my finger in him with the same rhythm. Without asking him, I pushed his body over on its side, still keeping my mouth on his penis and my finger in his buttocks. He was ready. He flung himself on his back on the pillows. His arms were still up, light hair clinging in the powerful crevices of his heavily muscled underarms. His arms pulled his pectorals and rib cage up into a "V" that repeated the form of his back, descending into his small waist and flat little stomach. I couldn't see his penis. It was in my mouth. His pubic hair was light and gathered in small curls around the base of his penis, almost like a wreath. I wondered if this was another Yugoslavian characteristic. Maybe it even traced back to the Greeks and the Romans. It was all part of that ancient world. The sculptors always arranged pubic hair in open curls. Perhaps they were only sculpting what they had seen.

I took my mouth off him but kept my finger in his anus. I moved to straddle him, still in my robe and underpants. I straddled his stomach, one arm reaching back between his legs to keep my finger firmly implanted. With the other hand I found the open tube of Vaseline. I reached behind me and squeezed it on his penis. I was backed up against it. He was waiting patiently, making no move to help me or hinder me. Keeping the tube in hand, I slid the waistband of my underwear down until it was clear of my buttocks and I was sitting on it. I squeezed some Vaseline into my own crevice then slowly lifted and let the head of his penis ride down between my cheeks until it found its entry point. I pressed down gently. I dropped the Vaseline on the bed and used my hand to guide him into me. I pressed into him with the other hand at the same time. I was able to insert my index finger along with the second finger now. He was getting very opened and ready for his orgasm.

Once he was fully within me I sat quietly. He remained quiet, too. I couldn't get out of my robe completely, but I shrugged out of it except for the one arm that was around the wrist that reached back toward his anus.

We were having a little battle of domination here. He pushed up into me in an exploratory manner. I pushed down at the same time. Then I lifted off so that he was almost completely out of me and then slithered down to press firmly into his pubic hair so his entire penis was planted deeply within me. His head, turned to the side, had no expression. He was far away in a world of sensory experience. We repeated this. He retracted his penis, pulling his hips down into the bed, then pushing back. The muscles in his abdomen, pulling and pushing, were exciting. He had nothing but a layer of skin over these muscles, so they were clearly seen, as they pulled his large penis out, then assisted in pushing it back in.

The rhythm built and we moved faster and faster. At one point his penis slipped out and then he reached quickly to reinsert it. Isn't that called "The Fastest Four-Handed Game in the World"?

He didn't put his hands back up over his head but grasped my thighs as I surged up and down on him. He pressed them down as I sank to put more pressure on his penis. He was beginning to move involuntarily in me, pushing in and out with increasing rapidity. I couldn't really move my fingers in him with the same rhythm. I just kept them locked deeply in place as his buttocks plunged up and down. He kept his legs spread so as to allow me full access.

He was sweating profusely, and under his lowered eyelids I could see him looking at me. There was a small smile on his narrow, curved lips. Something like the Attic smile. Maybe that smile you see on the early Greek kouros statues is of sexual origin. His expression was of the most genuine affection I had ever seen on his face. Then it contorted. Agony began to spread over his features. His hands were grasping my thighs as though he were drowning. I moved with great rapidity as he searched frantically inside me with his penis. He was looking for something, it was almost there, and then it was there.

He held his pelvis arced against me. His grimace was frozen in place; his hands clutched me. I leaned forward and kissed him, easing my hand out of his prostate ring, pressing my buttocks against his lifted body. He put his arms around me and held me tightly against his body, then slowly lowered his hips to the bed. His penis eased itself out of my body inch after inch. It felt very, very long. I lay down beside him, pressing one leg between his legs, feeling his still-swollen penis against my thigh. My cheek was against his cheek. He slowly relaxed the pressure of his arms about me, but still kept them in place. Here is a basically affectionate person who has learned to withhold affection, either to avoid complications or control situations, I thought. Perhaps this is true of everyone who seems to not be affectionate.

"You haven't come," he said in my ear. He reached down. My underpants were still twisted about my lower body, clutching my penis to me almost painfully. I lifted my legs and buttocks, and he pulled them off and started manipulating me. I was already soggy; there was no need to look for the Vaseline, now lost somewhere in the twisted bed sheets. "Hold me very tightly," I said, and kissed him. He kept kissing me as he masturbated me. It didn't take long. I was already hyperaroused. I came, as I can, twisting and shaking and shuddering all over the bed. He held me firmly, realizing I needed to be stabilized in my fall through space.

He pulled his mouth off mine. "That was fun," he said. "I'm sorry you came. I'm almost ready to go again." I realized that I had been hanging on tightly to his penis while he was masturbating me and it was engorging again in my hand.

I got up and went to the bathroom where I sat down on the toilet. Strings and clumps of his semen came out of my body and filled the bowl below me. I stared. It was quite a lot. Quite a lot.

Radomir was what I thought he would be sexually. I felt that I had really had sex and it would last me quite awhile. "I always told you that you would really enjoy fucking me," I said when I went back into the bedroom. He had pulled the sheet up to his waist and was lying turned into the room on the far side of the bed.

"I always knew that," he said. "Come here."

~18~ Radomir's First Return

Nevis knew that Radomir was returning to Paris for a short visit in July to fulfill a plan made with his friend Savannah from California. They had long ago planned to meet in front of Notre Dame at noon on the Fourth of July.

Nevis guessed Radomir would arrive on a Monday, as he knew the rendezvous with Savannah was Tuesday the fourth. He told this to Minerva when she called on Saturday, asking when Radomir was expected.

On Sunday, in the middle of preparing brunch for Anthony Stuart and his wife, the phone rang. It was Radomir. He was in Paris. Had in fact arrived the previous day and was staying with Minerva. He sounded particularly sulky but was coming over and, yes, would have some brunch.

While Nevis was waiting for Radomir, several things happened. He let the scrambled eggs stay over the flame too long and they become too hard. As he served the eggs an acrid odor filled the apartment. Immediately his large gray Persian cat, Nada, jumped onto a dining room chair and exhibited little curlicue white-singed whiskers. Nevis snatched Nada up and found singed hair all over his body and concluded Nada had jumped onto the stove to investigate the smell of bacon and had found a gas ring still flaming that Nevis had forgotten to turn off. Anthony and his French wife, Alexandra, chatted amiably through the nervousness of the hard eggs and the singed cat. As they were finishing brunch Radomir arrived.

He was pleasant as he talked with the Stuarts, eating the second round of eggs and bacon that Nevis prepared for him. He explained he was late because after he'd called Nevis he'd called another friend, Lo De Coy, and had coffee with her. Anthony and Alexandra excused themselves when the chitchat had dwindled to nothing.

In the living room Nevis said, "You sounded very angry when I called you last to see when you were coming."

"I was and I still am," Radomir answered. "Because of your letters."

"But you said you'd written," Nevis answered back, "and nothing has ever arrived. Tell me what's bothering you."

"No, I've written you a letter. You'll get it tomorrow." Radomir smiled unpleasantly. He looked hulky, humpy, and handsome, but almost a cliché of the unattainable boyfriend, the guy who instinctively knows his hold on you is that he is unattainable and doesn't care.

Across the room Nevis sat on the settee and said, "The awful thing about this is that when you're about thirty-five you're going to realize what was happening here, and by that time it will all be too late." He felt the tears running down his face as he added, "By then I'll be old, old. Really old." But he wasn't sobbing, just sort of leaking out the overflow of his sadness at the inevitability of his situation.

Radomir didn't seem particularly uncomfortable but said, "I've got to be going. I promised Lo I'd meet her again to go to the movies." Nevis didn't protest. He saw his love disappearing down the circular staircase and thought, *This is a real tragedy. A hard, dry, inescapable tragedy. Because in earlier days I could feel terrible but under it all was the hope for someone else. But now it's far too late. That is your last love you see going out of sight, round that bend.*

During the week Nevis thought of Radomir meeting Savannah precisely at twelve in front of Notre Dame on Tuesday. He thought of going there. Whether just to watch them from a distance or to speak to them, he wasn't sure. But he managed to contain himself and not go to Notre Dame when Tuesday noon came. Radomir was planning to bring her to the country. He would meet her there.

Savannah had written him a polite note from the south of France where she was touring with friends, and he rather imagined her as a large, tending-to-be-plump brunette in her mid-thirties with glasses, originally from somewhere in the South. Hungering for Radomir but unconsummated as she was too nice a Southern librarian type to really go after him. He would meet her when she came down to the country with Radomir for the weekend.

There was finishing-up work to be done on Fanette before Radomir and Savannah were to come down on Friday evening, so early in the morning Nevis was off to the country. He opened his house and put flowers in the separate bedrooms for Radomir and Savannah. He placed a large silver-framed photograph of Radomir on his dressing table, for Radomir and Savannah to see when they arrived at the house. Leaving a note on the front door saying he was at Fanette and suggesting they come over, he drove away.

All day he expected them to drive up, but nonetheless went on cleaning the garden and Windexing the windows. After scraping the last bits of paint off the sitting room tile floor he gave up and drove back home.

The note was gone. They had obviously been in the house, but there was no luggage. They were to have picked up keys from neighbors, so Nevis went to ask if they'd seen Radomir and Savannah. The neighbors said, yes, Radomir and his friend had been there and gotten the key and had come back later for the key to Fritz's house, as Radomir wanted to show it to Savannah. Fritz was out of town.

Nevis left them and walked down the street to Fritz's house. He heard voices in the kitchen, so he wrapped on the window. Radomir opened it. His eyes were very clear and he looked very handsome. Nevis stared. Radomir said, "Yes, it's me. Come on in."

"You must be Savannah," Nevis said to a woman with a dried-up little face and a mop of permanented Chore Girl blonde hair who was certainly his own age or more. A wave of relief passed over him as he concluded this certainly couldn't be a sleeping partner. Radomir was distant but smoothly pleasant. No one mentioned that they were not going to stay with him and that they were taking up residence in a house they had not been given permission to stay in.

Then Nevis realized with a thump there was only one three-quarter bed in Fritz's house that they were obviously planning to share.

He asked Savannah where she was staying in Paris. She looked surprised and said, "With Radomir at his hotel, of course."

He then asked Radomir where the hotel was. He said, "I think it's in the Eleventh Arrondissement."

"You don't remember the street?"

Radomir answered, "No, we just wandered around and found it. I know where it's at."

"Well, how do you tell a taxi driver where to go when he takes you there?" Nevis demanded.

"We don't take taxis," the answer came back. "We always go on the Metro."

With that Nevis realized he was being lied to, and they were undoubtedly staying right down the street at the Hotel des Croisé near his apartment, where he put his visiting overflow, and had been within yards of him all week.

Nevis then started telling about all the work that had been done at Fanette. Savannah interrupted bitterly, "You poor woman. How you work!" Nevis realized her attack was pre-programmed by Radomir, sitting smugly across the table smiling mysteriously. He then forced them to accept a dinner invitation at a small restaurant in a nearby town and left.

The thought of Radomir clambering over Savannah's slack flesh made him feel creepy. *But then,* he thought, *probably no more than my own and she* is *a woman.*

That evening, despite Savannah's continuing hostility, their dinner at the bistro in nearby Montfaucon wasn't too awful. As soon as they seated themselves Savannah had shaken her mop of Bedlington terrier curls and protested that she ate only vegetables, so a large salad and a plate of vegetables had been obtained for her. Like most Americans, she obviously found it hard to imagine that every restaurant in France would not have a health-food platter. Her air of a patronizing sheep became more pronounced as dinner progressed and she drank more wine. She spoke at length about "sharing," "projecting," and "being involved," and also admitted that she had become an analyst because no matter how old she got her patients wouldn't leave her. Radomir sat across the table and said little. He seemed satisfied to let Savannah display enough insulting behavior for the two of them. When Nevis tried to involve him in the conversation he was cool and noncommittal.

After the meal they returned home and Nevis suggested they stroll in the night in the grounds of the abbey. They did so but were determined not to express any pleasure or admiration for the great eighteenth-century facade glistening in the moonlight over its stone terrace and the formal gardens that descended to the river, gurgling darkly below.

Before the evening ended Nevis wanted to surprise Radomir with a gift. He had bought a large Puss-in-Boots marionette, dressed as a cavalier, with sweeping-feathered hat and sword for Radomir. Radomir had a passion for marionettes and had often admired the large cat figure standing in a toy shop window near the Pigalle apartment. He invited Radomir and Savannah in before they went to the other house and gave Radomir the large box. As he handed it to him he wondered if he was making a mistake, but he plunged ahead anyway. Radomir hadn't divined what was in the box and was taken aback when he extricated the large gray cat in its hat. He moved it about and stammered, "I, I just don't know what to say." Nevis was sure if Savannah hadn't been present he would have let down his guard. She had undoubtedly counseled Radomir all week on how to deal with Nevis and was staying within reach so he wouldn't slip off the track she had neatly laid out with her phoney-baloney, jargon-chattering pseudo-psychology. Nevis could easily have punched her.

Radomir placed Puss back in his box on the lavender plaid settee and said he wished to leave him there. Then they departed, saying they would come to Fanette the next day.

Saturday morning Nevis got up, dressed, and left for Fanette to finish his work. There was no sign of life at Fritz's house as he passed it in his old black Peugeot.

During the day, expecting Radomir and Savannah at any time, Nevis finished odds and ends. The small table he had scraped of its red enamel he placed in the middle of the blue-and-white kitchen. The oiled chairs were placed at the table, and others were put in the bedroom above and the sitting room below. A set of pitchers with brick-red edges he put in the kitchen on a shelf. A small wire dish with wooden fruit and a pair of brass candlesticks festooned with metal grapes and wire tendrils he placed on the living room fireplace. He had at first decided against putting the ornaments in place, but there was little else to do waiting for them to arrive.

They still weren't there at lunchtime, so he walked down into the town and bought a small quiche and some orange juice, which made his lunch at the wicker table in the garden.

After lunch he finished cleaning windows, which took appreciably longer than he had anticipated. By the time he had hung a Marie Laurencin print in the bedroom (another expensive gift, the print being one Radomir had often admired in a shop on the Rue de Rivoli), and placed a painting of cherries in a twist of blue paper in the sitting room over the Provincial settee, the day had almost ended. He was tired and decided to smoke a cigarette sitting in the doorway and then would go home, defeated by the deliberate aloofness and hostility.

Just as he pushed the cigarette butt into the geranium plant on the stoop, their car pulled up in the street below. They entered the gate and came up the turning curve of the steps, past the geranium pots Nevis had placed on each step. Radomir's gray eyes were clear in his brown face and he looked particularly handsome. Nevis said to them, "I'll stay here and let you look over the house." He had imagined how the visit would go and had decided it best to let them see things by themselves. He wanted to imagine Radomir gasping with surprise and pleasure, although he knew now this was not going to be the case.

He lit another cigarette and sat down on the stoop again. He heard nothing from within the house. When they returned to the sitting room he went with them into the garden. He wondered if the house didn't seem transformed to Radomir, or if he was frustrated at the work being already so advanced, or if he was impressed but determined not to say so.

Savannah wandered away with her camera and he saw her in the street below photographing the house. He stepped away from the wall so as not to be in her picture. Finally he said to Radomir, who was looking uncomfortably at the eaves, "Would you like to express an opinion?"

Radomir turned and said, "Well, it's really *your* house, isn't it?"

Nevis said, "I thought you'd be very excited to have *your* house so far along."

"I hate all the little touches. Nobody asked you to get the pictures, or the ornaments, or the stuff in the kitchen. I want you to take them out of here," Radomir flared.

"That's easily done. There's just a couple of baskets of things. But why so angry?" Nevis said, trying to keep his voice calm.

"Because I wanted to do this," Radomir replied.

The thought passed through Nevis's mind that spending the summer lying on a beach wasn't the most convincing demonstration of interest, but he answered, "I was so worried about you I had to let my energy out somewhere. I didn't know where you were, I didn't know what was happening, and I thought perhaps you were sick and alone."

"Sick and alone?" Radomir demanded.

"You know, with your friend in California being positive for AIDS, I thought you could be sick somewhere, with no one to help you," Nevis said.

"You would bring that up," Radomir said sulkily from the doorway and turned and went down the stairs. Nevis found he was clinging to the corner of the sideboard, semi-barricaded behind one end of it. He wasn't sure how he had gotten there from the garden where the conversation had started. He walked to the door and looked down as Radomir got into the driver's seat. The Bedlington terrier in the beige raincoat was already inside. After they had pulled away Nevis went about the house. He packed the wooden fruit and the wire dish, the gilded three-prong candlesticks, the matching pitchers, and the blue flowered sugar bowl into a large basket. He put the painting of the cherries in a large plastic bag and prepared to leave. The Marie Laurencin he left on the bedroom wall. He didn't particularly like it and was damned if he was going to take it away.

He stowed the things in the old Peugeot, locked up the house and drove away, winding back across the countryside through the late sun. He sang as he drove, "You go along, never knowing I care, loving somebody somewhere." He sang and found when the spire of his village came into view he could hardly see it he was crying so hard.

That evening he didn't even look to see if Radomir and Savannah were at home. He closed his blinds, steamed his vegetables, ate, and went to bed. The Musketeer cat puppet still sprawled in its nest of cerise tissue paper on the lavender settee in the sitting room as he slept.

~19~ Radomir's Second Return

He saw Radomir off at Orly airport when he went back to Crete. He took the Orly bus from the Gare Montparnasse. The airport was mobbed. The flight to Athens was hard to find. It departed at some weird gate like 27Q. On and on through packs of Pakistanis, tides of Italians, mobs of Moroccans he went. The third world was on the move. At the far end of the airport he found Radomir.

As usual he looked shorter and plainer than Nevis remembered him. *Why am I in love with this guy?* he thought as he saw the shortish figure smothered in a long, black raincoat waiting in line.

"Will you hold my place? I've got to go to the bathroom."

"It's over there. Down the escalator."

As he walked away he handed Nevis his black raincoat. His shoulders were broad in his check sports coat.

Nevis often bought clothes for Radomir, sometimes as a form of bonus for work done on the house and sometimes as gifts. Radomir didn't seem to have any clear picture as to what kind of clothes he liked, but coming from California he wore the kinds of clothes that come off easily and could be frequently washed and left unironed.

Nevis bought him turtleneck cashmere sweaters at Lanvin. And in one splurge got him to agree to the purchase of a black-and-tan plaid sports coat and gray flannel slacks. With a black raincoat and turtleneck Radomir cut quite a dashing figure and seemed very at ease. He also liked a dark blue sweater with cable knit in dark green on its shoulders and sleeves. He wore that frequently.

Because of his broad shoulders he could wear some of Nevis's clothes. A tan linen jacket had its sleeves shortened for him, and he also frequently wore a Saint Laurent sweater in an oatmeal knit with vivid red trim. And he wore an Armani windbreaker with broad shoulders and a belt very often.

Other clothes were sometimes abruptly rejected. A knit shirt in dark green and navy blue panels that looked very handsome on him was disdained, even though it came from one of the best men's stores in Milan.

He was very undiscriminating about shoes, preferring sneakers. Nevis did get him into loafers, which he seemed to think were faintly effete. He liked a pair of brown leather shoes that looked like molasses cookies.

When he returned to Paris from the country Radomir said that Savannah had gone back to the United States. He said she cried when she left the Loire Valley.

Nevis thought that was probably because it was the last time someone under fifty was going to boff her. He said, "That's ridiculous. You never came out of the house before five in the afternoon. She never even saw the Loire Valley."

Radomir's silence either indicated that he accepted Nevis's statement as being essentially correct or was confirming that he, too, thought that it wasn't the Loire Valley that Savannah would be missing.

After his departure no more was heard from Radomir from Crete. Nevis wrote him once: a rich description of the Loire Valley in full flood of sunflowers and purple roadside flowers. Nothing about love. It had been a cold and inclement July when Radomir had come to the country with Savannah. Now its lush, ripe, rich nature was hurrying to catch up after a slow start to the summer. The grapevines flourished, the grain blew golden in the wind, the sunflowers blackened as they turned slowly to face the sun in unison. Shadows from the corners of buildings were hard and square and black on the ground as winds blew steadily through the narrow village streets from the surrounding fields.

Nevis stayed in Paris most of the time. The country was hard to handle. He was traveling a lot for his job, and that helped. On a Saturday in late August he had to go down to the country to pay bills and consult with workmen, but decided to make it a day trip and not stay overnight. He arrived about noon, did what had to be done, and departed again on the 9:40. When he arrived back in Paris he had a message on his answering machine from Fritz: "Radomir is here. He arrived this evening."

Nevis remembered his train rocking with the force of the passing of a down-country train heading in the opposite direction. Radomir had been on that train. Their bodies had passed within a few feet of each other for a moment only, separated by the racing metal.

He then called Fritz and spoke a few moments to Radomir, who said he'd left Crete unexpectedly and would see him later.

Nevis was almost too busy to care. He was in Milan all week, returning on Saturday. He had to work in London on Monday but decided to go to the country on Sunday for the day. He called Radomir at Fritz's and they arranged that Radomir would meet him in Blois at the railroad station with the old Peugeot on Sunday. They would go directly to the best chateau restaurant near Montfaucon, have lunch, and Nevis would depart again in the afternoon from Amboise.

At the restaurant Radomir had no trouble talking. Problems had started as soon as he was back in Crete, he explained over the *frisée aux lardons*. The Australian girl, Na- tasha, and he had gotten drunk together one night and she had spent the night with him. By now he had moved into an isolated farmhouse in the middle of an olive grove, up the hill from the hotel where he worked.

Natasha had been a lesbian in Sydney but now paraded him in front of some visiting Australian lesbians as her boyfriend, saying things like "Isn't he cute?" and "Aren't I lucky?" Radomir's story was that he then explained to her that he thought it was all a mistake, and that he wanted to return to their just being good friends. This evidently was not what the girl from Sydney had in mind, and a great cabal by all the foreigners who worked in the resort ensued. Waitresses from nearby hotels refused to speak to him in the street. Clerks in gift shops wouldn't speak. When he walked up to the bar at the disco everyone turned their backs on him. Only his new roommate, the Canadian boy Tony, remained loyal.

It was hard for Nevis to imagine that in the extremely laissez-faire atmosphere of the Cretan resort sleeping with someone once and not wishing to again could have caused such universal revulsion.

Perhaps Nastasha, too, had fallen under Radomir's spell and, like Nevis, was stumbling about crying and acting shattered. The Millionaire of Love had struck again. Could she have been so disturbed that even her summertime acquaintances decided the situation had gone too far? Nevis could only guess.

Evidently the catalytic event that prompted Radomir's departure occurred on a hot afternoon when he was sunning on the roof of his little farmhouse. Tony was asleep in a bedroom below. Radomir heard a small noise in the courtyard below and saw two French girls who worked in a gift shop stealthily approaching the house. One would advance, beckoning the other to come out from her hiding place in the olive grove. Radomir, hidden on the roof, saw them tiptoe toward the house, peer into the rooms, look about, and then just as stealthily slip off into the olive grove again. Their visit shook Radomir up. They had been good friends before the ostracization campaign. Had they come to warn him about something? Nevis thought they had most likely come to see if they could catch Radomir and his roommate making bamboola in the heat of the afternoon. His suspected proclivity for other men might have triggered the hostilities, Nevis thought. Radomir had certainly confided in his Australian girlfriend that he, too, had known the embrace of his own sex as she had.

Whatever the cause of his being made the community pariah, Radomir had had enough. Rousing Tony, he suggested that they pack, call a cab, and split after work that night without a word to anyone. On the next day they would be gone. They could catch a boat at the north shore port for Athens and go back to Europe. Radomir to Paris and Tony to Holland.

And that was what had happened, with Radomir arriving in Paris on a Saturday. Instead of calling Nevis he went straight to the country and was now living with Fritz, helping him paint shutters and scrape woodwork.

By now the meal was approaching the sorbets. Radomir told Nevis that on the boat fleeing Crete he had some second thoughts and felt more positively about him now.

On their way to the train Nevis insisted they pass by Fanette, the house he had worked on so wildly earlier in the summer. It was completely finished now. Nevis had taken out the paintings and ornaments that Radomir had strenuously objected to before. Now Radomir said he wished to have them put back again. He said that he would like them in the house, and eventually his plan was to pay Nevis for the house and all its furnishings. They then had to race along the river road so Nevis could catch his train, as his London flight left Paris that evening.

~20~ Radomir Gets a New Life

Radomir came back to Paris, moved back into the little yellow bedroom, and came back to work as a freelance assistant to Nevis at his office.

It was messy. Radomir thought the only reason he was there at the office was because Nevis had insisted. In fact, the agency didn't want to spend the money for an assistant, although Nevis needed one badly. And the account supervisor insisted to higher-ups that Nevis was only making work for a boyfriend. Nevis always treated Radomir in a businesslike way in the office, but Radomir exploded one day and said that everyone in the office commented upon how rude Nevis was to him. And he wanted an apartment of his own.

So Nevis bought him the newspapers and showed him where the apartments for rent were listed. He had to go with Radomir to look at apartments, as an apartment would have to be rented in Nevis's name. Radomir did not have working papers. It was also Nevis who would have to put down the sizable fee for first month, last month, and damages.

Radomir found a little two-room apartment to his liking near the Canal St. Martin. Nevis helped him scrape floors and paint, and furniture was brought up from the country house. Soon after, Nevis heard of the nice little house-warming Radomir had had in his new apartment from a young American couple who were there. Nevis hadn't been invited.

The young American couple had a baby now. They had visited the country house occasionally with the baby when Radomir was there. When he saw the baby spread-eagled face down across Radomir's chest, in the chair by the fireplace, clasping him automatically around the neck he felt uncomfortable and left the room.

On another day Nevis was carrying the baby in the garden and the little boy looked at him squarely with recognition and hugged him with speechless affection. He thought of the baby as a love conduit. Held and loved by Radomir and now held and loved by him. The baby feeling affection in both directions. The same soft, sweet little being, sharing his affectionate hugs between them. For the first time he understood why people have children.

As the months passed Radomir became more sullen and bought cowboy boots. Now when he passed Nevis in the hall at the office they were nearly the same height. With his big weight-lifter arms protruding from his T-shirt Nevis had to admit he was quite a sight. The younger secretaries and he seemed to be Radomir's most appreciative audience.

Once in this period, after Radomir returned from Crete and to work with Nevis, they went to the country house together. In the evening, before they went to bed, Nevis asked Radomir to massage his back, which had been bothering him. He didn't suggest that he massage Radomir first, as he wanted to avoid any prelude to seduction overtones. Radomir straddled his buttocks as he often did when giving a massage and proceeded with a really thorough rubdown, with no indication that he found it distasteful to do so. When he climbed off he quickly turned away from the bed and walked across the room. Nevis immediately thought, *He's concealing a hard-on.* And was at a loss to interpret it.

So the winter passed. They spoke impersonally at the agency. He had lunch with Radomir occasionally. He had tried having dinner once after Radomir moved into his own apartment, but Radomir was so impersonal and made it so obvious that the dinner was an obligation there was no pleasure to be had in it. So Nevis didn't repeat it again. They passed each other at the gymnasium. Radomir hulking toward the weight-lifting room. Nevis gyrating and bouncing in the aerobics classes. Then in the spring Radomir announced he was leaving the advertising agency and his freelance job with Nevis. He had a new job at the Paris branch of a film company. So he was gone. Then Radomir called to arrange sending the furniture that he had in his apartment back to the country. He had taken another apartment and didn't want it any longer.

Shortly thereafter Nevis had a notice from a lawyer that Radomir wanted to sell his interest in the renovated house they owned together in the country. All the ties were breaking. His first reaction was to tell him to fuck off, but then realized that was exactly what Radomir wanted to hear and instead was pleasant over the phone to Radomir about it. The several thousand dollars that the legal transaction would cost, in addition to the purchasing of Radomir's part, rankled him more. When he discussed this with Radomir, the suggestion that they split the legal costs was met with great coldness. Radomir wanted out and he didn't want it to cost him any money.

Nevis told him that he would pay the costs but was writing Radomir into his will so that the house would go to him eventually. "That you can't keep me from doing," he told him.

One evening, as Nevis turned from closing his locker at the gym, Radomir was standing in front of the next bank of lockers. As usual, he looked shorter and not as attractive as Nevis remembered him. He called his name. Radomir came over and was friendly in a "We really don't know each other very well" manner. They left together and took the metro together, talking about Radomir's new job and his family in the United States.

Why is it we think it's so important to tell people we love them? thought Nevis. *Maybe it's because we were brought up by slightly chilly parents. And we've been congratulated by friends and lovers on our ability to speak out, to express our affection. Thought well of because we can handle being in a relationship. So we unburden ourselves knowing it's only driving the loved one further away. We just can't help ourselves, poor things.*

They began to run into each other more frequently at the gymnasium. Usually Radomir was arriving as Nevis was leaving. There was Radomir, his brawny back and narrow waist slipped into running pants, on his way up to the swimming pool, or twisting a towel angrily around the flat stomach that nose-dived from his chest.

Can this be love where the more I see of him without his clothes on the more I care? Nevis asked himself. He decided it was.

Leaving the gym together one day, he accused Radomir of deliberately acting unpleasant so as to kill any interest Nevis might have in him. Radomir slipped out one of those little Middle-European squirrel glances of his and said, "You're quite intelligent, aren't you?" From then on every shrugging nod toward Nevis, every sulky "Hello" as he turned his back didn't discourage Nevis.

Their gym closed and chance encounters ended. So Nevis called Radomir occasionally. Hearing his Franglais-mixed message on his answering machine would cheer him up. That voice, placing itself so carefully so it could never be considered anything but masculine, touched him.

In the autumn Nevis's contract ended with the French advertising agency. He began traveling back and forth to New York looking for work. He was tempted to let Radomir drift off into history, but knowing that was exactly what Radomir was counting on, he didn't.

Mutual friends would report they'd seen him. He seemed to be in high spirits. He'd gained weight. He seemed to like his job. He was seen with friends. He was not seen with a girlfriend.

One evening in the neighborhood of Radomir's new apartment Nevis was on his way to eat with the young American couple. Tex-Mex, a novelty in Paris. He thought he saw Radomir coming up out of the Metro. Without his glasses the figure was blurry. He wasn't sure, but it had the kind of slightly lumbering walk of Radomir in his cowboy boots. He was going to shout his name. He didn't. He grabbed the young husband by the arm and demanded, "Is that Radomir?"

The young blond husband turned to look. "I don't see him," he said. As they were waiting in line to get into the restaurant he said, "Gee, you almost tore my arm off."

At the same couple's house a few months later Nevis stopped to chat on his way to Radomir's. He had spoken to him the previous night and Radomir had been open and friendly. They had agreed that Nevis would come by to see his new apartment and then go out to eat.

He called Radomir from the young couple's home and left a message to call him there when Radomir came in. Radomir didn't call back. The couple asked Nevis to stay for dinner. Halfway though the meal the phone rang. It was Radomir.

The phone was handed to Nevis and he heard, "Why do you keep calling me and writing me? Don't you know that I don't even open most of your letters? I just throw them away." Nevis replied, "Why don't I call you back when I get home?" and hung up. Finishing dinner, he went home and called Radomir back.

"You want to know why I keep writing and calling? I can't do otherwise. It's programming. It's nature. I am strongly attached to you. It's not something I can turn on and off. And all your efforts to make me dislike you have no effect on it. But I do love you enough to not bother you if that's what you want. I'll stay out of your way; you have to admit you wouldn't be here, wouldn't be speaking French, wouldn't have the job you have if I hadn't existed. You realize that, don't you?"

In a very matter of fact voice Radomir said, "Of course." And the conversation dwindled away.

~21~ Radomir Speaks His Piece

Why doesn't anyone ever want to hear my side of things? That's what I want to know. It's all poor Nevis, poor Nevis, poor Nevis. What about me?

When I came to France I thought he was some kind of wonderful person. Like an uncle. Very thoughtful. Very concerned about me.

Yes, of course there was always that smily, smily stuff. Everything the other person did was always wonderful. I was always so smart. So talented. Had a great future. All those kinds of things. He was building the other person's morale. And it was always so easy to see through. But he meant well.

And listen, what options did I have? I certainly wasn't going to go back to the United States with my tail between my legs. How was I to know he was going to get so crazy? So obsessed with me.

Of course, lots of people have wanted to sleep with me. I'm a cute guy. I know that. But usually when you make it clear you're not having any they clear out.

It's not like I've never been hurt. That first guy I slept with in Denver I thought was going to be in love with me. And he dropped me like a hot potato. That taught me a lesson. So after that I was going out with both guys and girls. Nothing serious. So they were shocked once in awhile. So some didn't want to sleep with me anymore. So be it. Who cares?

Esther hurt me. I was really in love with Esther. But then she wanted to sleep with her old boyfriend and me at the same time. To make a comparison, I suppose. Who fucked the best. Well, she got enough fucking that night. But I was the one who felt like they got fucked. I'm sure not going back to the United States to get into all that again.

So then I get old Nevis being so helpful and he falls in love with me. Wants to run my life. Tell me what to do. How to dress. I could tell he figured out that I was shtumping Minerva Minot. She used to just lay there like she was dead. No moving for Minerva. I guess she just wanted to be nice to me. But Nevis was smart. He was very friendly to her always. Pretended he didn't know what was going on. He waited her out and it worked.

Then when I went to Crete he really got crazed. Calling my folks all the time back home. Calling every hotel on Crete. Until he finally found me. Wild. And always trying to convince me that he was really only interested in my welfare. But really always trying to get into my pants.

Even now that I came back to Paris and am really treating him like shit he doped out that I was trying to drive him away. He's smart, real smart. So how in the hell do you get rid of a guy like that? It's like having a stalker on your case. A charming, helpful, pleasant stalker. It's like *Fatal Attraction.*

And all his friends think he's so great and that I'm the bad guy who led him on and then turned him down. He's got everyone on his side. But he's the spider in the web. I'm the fucking fly.

I mean, let's get serious. He's thirty years older than I am. When I was born he was already thirty years old. He's old. Seriously old. Nobody is ever going to sleep with him again unless he pays them. And he's never going to pay anyone. He's too proud. Thinks too well of himself. Thinks he's still attractive.

He has that funny way of straightening his back and lifting his chin all the time. Like he's fighting off age that's pulling him toward the grave. Well, he's not dragging me down there with him.

Love, love, love. True love. The love of a lifetime. The romance of the century. That's what it's got to be like for him. If he really loved me he'd just get the hell out of my hair. But no, he's just crazy about love. Maybe just crazy.

~22~ The Prison Fantasy

Do many homosexual men have prison fantasies? I never thought I did, but I surprised myself this morning. I suppose what I have to draw upon as prison fantasy material is very limited. I remember reading something in the *Paris Review* called, I believe, "Letters from an American Prisoner" by James Blake. I was quite surprised. Not at all what you'd expect the editor, George Plimpton, to publish but then perhaps none of us knew the real George Plimpton.

These "letters" were purportedly from someone "inside" and devoted to the sexual shenanigans that went on. At one point the author and his boyfriend make a break for it and while hidden in the long grass beside a railroad track the boyfriend feels the need to possess him. And does. Which seemed to both dismay and please the author. Certainly it was dramatic.

I read another short story somewhere about a young married man whose black cellmate in prison gets excited and masturbates to stories about what the young man and his wife do in bed. Then without warning he pins the man against the bars of the cell and rapes him savagely. Somewhere I heard quoted "Your shit on my dick or your blood on my knife," which is supposedly prison foreplay.

On the side of reality, I have seen a number of photo coverages and it is pretty clear that prison looks something like a hospital, all fluorescent lights and linoleum floors and the loving couples are always some tough Hispanic guy and some kid. As with anything to do with men it all boils down to power and property, rather than romance.

So here is my prison fantasy, just before arising this morning in the half-stupor that seems to be my most imaginative state. Radomir and I are cellmates. He is in a brutal mood and has me pinned against the bars of our cell; his big arms have me crushed against the metal so all breath is squeezed out of me. He is pumping his crotch against my buttocks. He hasn't figured out how he's going to get our jeans down, but it's clear to me he's going to get his way. What isn't clear to me is why he thought I wouldn't want to. He's a little out of his head with some kind of prison drug, and it's the middle of the afternoon. My goal is to get through the whole act of intercourse without getting my ass all torn up. His goal is probably to tear it up. Anger and hostility are clearly part of the deal.

In a reasonable tone of voice I say, "You can fuck me if you want to. I don't mind." He loosens his grip a little. If there's one thing I know about rape, it's "don't struggle." They just love it. "Let's go get on the bed," I say. "And let's take all our clothes off. So you can really get at it." Suddenly he lets go of me and turns away, starting to lower his pants. I pull the sheet off my bunk, the upper one, and tuck it under the upper mattress so it conceals the lower bunk from view if someone passes in the corridor. They'll know what we're doing, but they won't be able to see it. I lift the sheet and he crawls in. He has a very muscular body and a very large erection. This guy is ready for action. I pull my clothes off and grab the bar of butter that is in our little cell refrigerator. I see where his feet are at the end of the bed and dive in, getting his cock in my mouth before he can start any rough stuff. He starts pushing my head up and down on it and groaning, "Oh, yeah, oh, yeah." The anticipated stuff. I do know how to suck cock, and he starts crumbling, falling back on his pillow, and spreading his legs. His thighs are massive from all that time he spends in the prison gym. This isn't exactly the worst way to be spending a long afternoon in prison.

I butter up my ass with one hand while I'm working him over, and before he really gets what's going on I'm sitting on him. His eyes fly open. I can see he's trying to figure out if this is masculine enough for him. But I start pulling at him with my sphincter and riding up and down. He starts pumping in rhythm with my easing up and down. The muscles of his abdomen and thighs are connecting and being held rigid as he lifts himself off the bed and lowers himself again. He's not going to need as much time in the gym this afternoon. He's getting quite a workout as it is. He doesn't touch me with his hands. He puts his hands behind his head and keeps his eyes closed as we really get the big fuck together there behind the curtain. I can handle this without any pain, and I know I can control how deeply he enters me from above. As he pushes up I can lift up to keep him from plunging too far, and once in a while I push down as he goes in so he gets the full treatment. He puts his hands on my thighs to get more control over me. I let him, knowing he can't hold out much longer. Although he's been good for quite a long run, his muscles are dripping and his face is contorted. He stops. He's coming deep inside me. I keep moving slowly and lean forward and put my lips on his. He holds me very closely and opens his mouth. He's not a good kisser, but I run my tongue over his lips and teeth and push it in to touch his. His mouth is passive, but he is still moving slowly in me and holding me down now so I won't slip off.

We lie there for a moment. I haven't come and he couldn't care less. "I want to do it again," he says, in my ear but in a very matter-of-fact tone. This is not a romantic guy.

"Of course you do," I say. I put my hands on his butt and hold him in me as I fall over sideways. This cot is narrow and it isn't easy, but I pull him on top of me, still in place. I pull the pillow from under my head and say, "Lift up." He's obedient and I push my ass up and get the pillow squeezed under me. There is come everywhere. I certainly don't need any more lubricant.

I lock my legs behind the small of his back and he starts moving. He puts his arms under me and his face down toward the bed next to mine. I don't try to kiss him again. He's too intent on his work. "Let me look at you," I say, just to see if it will work, and push against his chest. He kneels and sits upright, still moving rhythmically in and out of me. He is soaking wet, his hair is matted, and he smiles at me. "Feels good, doesn't it?" he says, moving in and out, in and out, in and out. I'm noncommittal. I might have to pay later if I admit I'm enjoying this too much. Which I'm not actually. I start to pull on myself. It's as though he's just noticed that I have a penis, too. "Here, let me do that," he says and starts masturbating me in the same rhythm as his thrusting pelvis. I lock my ankles together and pull him into me with each thrust. He likes that. His action picks up and he is really pounding in and out very rapidly. This is his second orgasm, so it's taking him longer to get there. But I can tell from his concentration that he's not far off. I pull him back down on top of me so the whole weight of his body isn't behind each push. Like a good boy he is still masturbating me from this position. He's not all bad. There is a grain of consideration for others in there somewhere.

"Are you ready?" he says in my ear. I jump. Who would have thought? "Yes," I say and pull his face on top of mine. This time he's really kissing me when he groans loudly and throws his head back, holding his penis in me. He could tell from the semen all over his hand that I had come at the same time. He stroked me gently as he held himself in me. I reached down and fondled his balls with one hand as his orgasm was draining out. That can feel good. He collapsed on me and we both went to sleep. I wake up before he does and my thighs are killing me from having Mr. Beefcake forcing them apart with his full two hundred some pounds while he slept. Not to mention my bung-hole which does not feel as though it had been on vacation.

Suddenly he wakes up and jumps up, pulling the sheet off the side of the bunk as he does. He throws it at me and says, "Here, cover up. You look terrible." Naked he walks around the cell checking out which jeans are his. "I could *almost* do it again right now," he says.

"Come over here." I grab his thigh and pull him to the side of the bed. His jeans are at half-mast. I slip my mouth over his cock. It remains flaccid. I look up at him. He's grinning down at me. "No you couldn't," I mumble.

"After supper," he says. "Get up. We'll work out some until they let us out of here for chow." He goes over to the toilet and pees. Looking at the wall he says, "My, my. Who'd have guessed that they shut me up with the best little piece of make-believe pussy in the whole place." I thought, *This guy has the makings of a really first-class fuck, and I'll bet he'll be taking it up the butt himself before we get done here.*

~23~ Nevis Discusses Things with His Ex, Who Is Dead

As I crossed the sitting room in my Paris apartment the phone rang. *It would have to be from beyond the grave for this to be anyone I really would like to speak to,* I thought.

And if it was, the conversation with my lover of many years, Morgan, would be like this:

ME: When I was twenty-six you told me my body was prematurely senile.

HE: I did?

ME: You did. And I hadn't even had my ten-year affair with Ronny Damico yet. Who just loved to fuck me.

HE: I never said I didn't like to fuck you.

ME: And when I was fifty-five George Voisins marveled that my body was so youthful. And Gary Feldon hated me because I looked so much younger than he did.

HE: It just goes to show.

ME: And now I'm nearly sixty and my body still looks great. Probably better than it ever did. And you . . .

HE: And me, I'm dead.

Which he is, and I really wish he wasn't. He wasn't the love of my life. That was Ronny Damico. As I always said, "When you got fucked by Ronny Damico you stayed fucked for a while." I had been in love with Morgan before then. We slept together for thirty years, and I never didn't feel like it. You can say that for our relationship. At the end, when he died, I loved him, but it was the kind of love you have for someone you crossed the Kalahari Desert with. On foot. Or survived the Black Hole of Calcutta with. Morgan and I had been to hell and back together, but through it all the sexual side of it never waned.

Strange how sexual affairs advance, mirroring the interior state of the participants. The first time we went to bed together he jauntily flopped onto his stomach and said, "First you pogue me and then I'll pogue you." As though we were thirteen years old at boarding school. I demurred. For one, the last thing I wanted was someone pumping away at my behind after I had already had my orgasm. And second, it was far from romantic. I insisted that he lie on top of me and approximate something like intercourse between my legs, which was in no way satisfactory to either of us.

After several years of desultory cocksucking and masturbating something tapped through to a deeper level during a sex session at another apartment I now had on Sheridan Square. Our first sex encounters had all taken place in a cold-water flat I had in Chelsea while I was a dancer. Sixteen dollars a month, later twenty-five when they put in heat. A great atmosphere for throwaway sex that flat had, but it wasn't good for much else.

In my new apartment, which was a real apartment, one evening after the preliminaries had well begun I dragged him over to a wooden chair which had come from my cold-water flat. (I wonder where that chair is now? Someone's using it surely. It was sturdy.) I had him sit down on the chair and lowered myself onto his very large penis facing him. That penis had to be very deeply inside me when he pulled my body to him and pressed his cheek against my chest, holding me tightly with both arms. This was extremely intimate behavior for him. He was probably surging in me and his body flooding with passion. He picked me up still astride him and carried me to the nearby bed where he finished the act with great abandon. This was true fucking between intimates and led us to a relationship with each other that if it was not more interdependent was certainly more profound.

At that time no one ever entered his body, but our relationship was to endure year after year to the point where I would be beneath him in Paris and he would lower himself onto my penis, legs bent beneath him. He would rest there impaled while I masturbated him onto my chest, at which point he would twist his face and sink backward into a deep backbend until his head was on the bed. He was much more supple than I was.

In much later years I would look up from this same position and see that twisted face in orgasm covered in wrinkles— something like a howling oriental sage. Sex had become a kind of spiritual rite for him by that time. He had little else to concentrate upon.

I can just imagine what he would say to me now. When I fell in love with Ronny Damico he said, "That guy is great-looking, but he is going to be nothing but trouble. Just don't come to me with your troubles." And I never did.

He used to say, "You could fall in love with anyone. You just want to be in love." Which is what he'd say now about Radomir I'm sure. He'd say things like, "This is the kind of person you pay for, not the kind of person you share your life with." Or "You laugh at clowns, Nevis, you don't fall in love with them." If he knew I wasn't even sleeping with Radomir he would just shrug and refuse to discuss the subject further. For him, if you weren't fucking you didn't have a relationship. And he was right, of course.

I did say to him once about Ronny Damico, "He's crazy." Morgan just looked at me and said, "No, you are." I'm sure that he would say that to me now. It sobered me up then, and the time to sober up again is heading my way.

~24~ Radomir Makes a List

The other night, as I was lying in bed, I was making a list of all the people I had had sex with. I got up to twenty-nine just counting on my fingers. I wonder if I can write it down and get that many again.

1. First there was my girlfriend in high school, *Cindy LaBreque.* Really. I hear all these stories from other guys about all the sex they had with their buddies when they were teenagers. That didn't happen for me. Even with all my brothers hanging about. Was I too ugly? I don't think so. Maybe because I started going out with Cindy quite young and we started making out. It was kind of dumb. I kind of liked it because I thought that was what I should be doing. I wonder if Cindy enjoyed it. She seemed to, but I'm not sure she ever had an orgasm. I'm not sure I even knew that was what she was supposed to have.
2. I suppose *Beverly* counts, even though it was a blow job beside the kitchen table. I suppose I should have slept with her to give her a break from all those johns. She was always awfully good to me.
3. *Herbert* the call boy comes in here. That was my first sex with a man, and I have to say it was great. If he had wanted to have an affair with me I'd probably still be there.
4. *That terrible fat man* the one night I worked as a prostitute. The less said about that the better. There's a joke about, "What do you call a bad blow job?" "Fabulous." But in his case it wasn't fabulous; it was a grotesque indignity.
5. *Beth* would be next. She must have been about twenty-eight and I was nineteen. She liked being seen around Denver with her little boy toy. She was kind of like sleeping with a boy any-

way. But when she found out I was sleeping with Tim, too, the shit hit the fan and it was all over.

6. And there was *Tim*. I worked with him. He was a really nice guy and I enjoyed screwing him. He was older. I was sleeping with him and *Marianne* at the same time, too, and I don't think either of them cared, or at least I'm pretty sure they both knew but they never said anything. When I left for California I didn't think about either of them very much.
7. And *Marianne,* of course. Another one of those older women I met in a bar in Denver. I was flattered that they wanted to sleep with me and I thought it was kind of kinky going to their apartment and sleeping overnight in their bed. Maybe not kinky. Maybe I thought it was kind of grown-up.
8. *Ned,* my roommate in California, who looked a lot like me. He was cute, but we always pretended that we were after girls and just were screwing each other because we'd had bad luck in the bars. I can't say that I ever really got into being screwed, but I learned to live with it with Ned. We used to take turns and keep track of who went first last time. I always preferred to go first so I got to screw him last. It's kind of a bummer getting screwed after you've already come.
9. There was *Eliza*. She was really beautiful. Ned and I picked her up on the beach. I slept with her off and on for all that time in California. She couldn't have cared less if Ned and I were getting it on or not. Sometimes I wished she had. I think I could have really cared about her. But, you know California. Nevis says they're like television sets out there. You turn them on in the morning. It plays all day, and then you turn it off at night. The video has played, but nothing really happened, nothing was remembered, nothing mattered, life just passed through. But the last time I saw Eliza we were on a terrace at night overlooking Los Angeles and she went to the edge and looked at the city lights and said, "Whatever is going to happen to us?"
10. I kind of went into my girly period out there. There was *Helen,* a girl I knew in high school who moved out there. I only slept with her once or twice, mostly because she wouldn't have gone

out with me in high school and I didn't want her to think I was homosexual. And then Bryce came out and she and I really got a hot affair going.

11. Funny how that started with *Bryce.* She was visiting Helen, and while Helen, was taking a shower we were both lying on the bed so we started making out. It got real hot and we both realized that we had something going. Poor Helen. We even went home at Christmas as boyfriend and girlfriend. That sort of did it. I looked around at my brothers and realized that it wasn't for me. I guess I imagined what my life would be like with a nice wife and kids and me slipping off to gay bars in Detroit or somewhere to get it on with some guy from time to time. So Bryce stayed home and I went back to the West Coast.
12. I guess I have to include *that guy that Ned brought home one night* and once he got there wanted me to screw him, not Ned. What a bummer. I did but I really hated it. With Ned sitting there in the next room. And the guy was zero. I ask you, why do we do these things? I guess it proved that I was better than Ned, which was a point I didn't really want to make.
13. There was *a girl I picked up with Ned.* We each screwed our girls in different bedrooms, probably thinking of each other. Name unknown. She didn't stay overnight.
14. *Another girl I picked up with Ned.* See above. I think this only happened twice. I think I probably got gonorrhea of the mouth from Ned. Yeah, I was giving him blow jobs; I guess it must have been pretty obvious all around that we were more into each other than girls. Denial. It isn't just a river in Egypt, as Nevis says.
15. *Esther.* The girl I thought I loved.
16. *Dan Danforth,* the boy I thought I loved. No wonder I went to Europe. It even looks screwy to me. They both let me down. Esther wasn't ever going to leave her boyfriend. He was our boss and she thought he was a better deal. And Dan didn't really get it that I loved him. I was just an accessory for his life. He gave me a farewell party when I left for Europe and every-

one there was a friend of his. There were no friends of mine there.

17. Now we move to Europe. *Larry.* I guess I thought I was in love with Larry for about fifteen minutes in Germany. Now I think he's such a sleazebag. Where was my head? Between his legs, probably.
18. *Angie.* Poor Angie. Let's face it. Once. Terrible.
19. *Minerva.* Poor Minerva. Let's face it. Quite a few times. Always terrible. My only excuse is that I was really into being straight at the time and hated living with Nevis.
20. *The Swedish girl on a motorcycle in Crete.* Once. Not bad.
21. *The Australian girl who ran the youth hostel.* Once. Not good. Very bad results.
22. Since I've gotten this new job with the American company here in Paris I've been sleeping with *Jackie.* The Barbie doll come to life. She really is pretty and she really doesn't particularly care about fucking.
23. *Beatrice.* The sexpot who works at the office out in Neuilly. She just walked up and said, "Want to come to a hotel with me?" when I was out there one day. I said, "Bien sur." And off we went. I can always get excited doing something a little weird. Beatrice had to sit on top of me and really work herself off. She kept saying, "Don't touch me. Don't touch me." She got herself a bang-up orgasm, and then she let me do whatever I wanted with her. Which was pretty standard but good. Strange woman. And then Jackie found out about it and told me to go to hell. So there you are.
24. *Frederic.* The model I met at the gym. Never returned calls and then after a couple of weeks started calling me. Very athletic Frederic. Beautiful back. Quite a lot bigger than I am. Really loved getting fucked. But I could tell he was just trying to get me to fall hard for him so he could give me the brush-off. I never did.
25. *Phillipe.* Another model I met at the gym. He was a skier. A very nice body. Also liked being fucked. From the front. Frederic liked it better from the back. A very different kind of

person from Frederic. Distant in that French way. Very polite. Very precise and neat and clean. Almost like a store window dummy until he hit the sack and then he let it rip. And then got up as though nothing had happened.

26. And now *Jean-Luc.* I seem to be definitely out of my hetero period and back into a gay one. It was funny, I was really all-out gay from about eighteen to twenty-one. Then I straddled the line out there in California and when I was first in France. And now I seem to be concentrating on the guys. Jean-Luc was my friend Muriel's boyfriend. Another one of those neat and tidy good-looking Frenchmen. We started hanging out together, and one afternoon he was over at my place and started talking about how he knew nothing about homosexuality but was interested in experimenting. So I let him give me a blow job. It definitely didn't come off as a first-time attempt in my book. So we've gotten into this little affair. Of a sort. He really digs those blow jobs. And since I don't really dig him all that much I'm letting it go at that. Except that now he wants to go with me when I go to the gym all the time, and he's hopeless there. But I think he wants to do it just to keep his eye on me so I don't pick up somebody new.
27. I lie. I forgot *the cousin of my friend Jillian.* Jillian used to work with me and now works for a French law firm. She's from New York. Her cousin Petra came over on a writing assignment and we had a little weekend affair. She was really too nice not to. I saw her again when I was in New York on a quick vacation and I told her that we should just chalk it up to experience since I wasn't about to leave Paris. She really liked me. What gives? Everybody likes me. Romantically I mean. And I'd rather just have friends.
28. And there was *Valerie.* I shouldn't forget Valerie. We worked together. A very nice girl. The kind of girl someone should marry. That's my big problem, I guess. I'd love to be married except that I like to fuck guys. Valerie went to the Caribbean for a new job and that cunt Vivian wrote her that I was dating someone new.

I can only hope she didn't know the someone new was named Jean-Luc.

29. And of course there was *Linton.* The most recent. My ex-priest. Quite a good fuck for an ex-priest. But then again, maybe they all are. I shouldn't be so casual about Linton. We really fell in love with a thud when I was back in Sandusky for a wedding. He officiated and we slept together that night. I know. I know. It was one of those new-wave type of weddings where they poured sand into each other's hands and that kind of stuff. An ex-priest was fine for the vows. He was just out of the priesthood and I got right into his pants. A very hot guy, but I can't move back to the United States. I should probably think about that sometime, too.

~25~ Radomir Returns Again!

What kind of book is this that I'm writing about Radomir anyway? And why am I writing it? This troubles me more and more as I proceed. Why is it so important that I find him and his life so fascinating and in need of being recorded?

Some of it has to do with his sexuality and his interest in experimentation and experience. That, because of his physical appeal, he is pursued and can experience things that were never available to me. Also, his ability to sleep with both women and men with equal interest—women being so taboo and frightening and beyond possibility for me. His sexual self-confidence is a source of envy. For me, the idea of putting part of your body into someone else's body is a major and intimidating act. For him, as with most really masculine men, it's about as important as putting your finger in someone's ear. Except more fun. My nature is much more essentially female. I'm not sure I want to stick something in someone else. For me, intercourse and interaction mean the same thing. What it boils down to, I guess, is that when you love another man much of what you love is what you'd like to have yourself: youth, a beautiful body, sexual self-confidence, sexual adventures. You love it because it's one way to have it. And you try to hang onto it and control it.

So, after my not being in Paris for about six months Radomir called me in New York. I'd been in Los Angeles, Miami, and New York trying to whip some life into what I'm beginning to think is a terminally ill career. There's a little work here, a little work there, but in general the response indicates that I'm an aging has-been. With a little added feeling that many of these people have been waiting for years for my luck to run out. And now that it has they're certainly not going to do anything to reverse it. Radomir's call comes as a very surprising occurrence. Not to say stimulating. He wanted to know if he could go down to my country house in the Loire Valley for a long weekend. He had been getting a bit down with the endless Paris winter and might go to Nice or might go to the Loire. This was such a big turnaround from our contact a half a year earlier. I was strung out somewhere between elation and suspicion. I told him that he could go down anytime and that keys were with our mutual friends, the young American couple.

We called back and forth a few times, establishing when he would go to the Loire. I finally asked him, "The overall tone of these calls would suggest you don't think I'm the biggest shit in the world."

"No, I've thought a lot of things over. No, I've kind of changed my mind about some things. Not everything. But some things." And we left it at that. It wasn't exactly the kind of subject for an international phone call. Once started, it was obviously good for a couple of hours.

Hearing from Radomir again made me want to go back to Paris. I had been a little homesick from time to time for that city where any foreigner will forever be a kind of outsider. As a break from being in New York and made to feel an outsider.

As soon as I returned I threw myself into setting my Paris apartment to rights. A number of friends had stayed there through the winter, and it's well-known that no houseguest doesn't break at least one thing. They had rather outdone themselves, knocking out the heating system, the electricity, replacing locks because of stolen keys, and breaking the toilet paper holder. The little retracting tube that held the paper in place had been ripped out and broken. I tried to imagine the desperate attempt to replace the toilet paper.

I called Radomir at his office and we agreed to have dinner on Sunday evening when I returned from spending a week pulling the country house together, which had also had its share of ravaging visitors during the winter.

Radomir was doing well in Paris. He was working in the Paris branch of a big American company and was evidently making himself invaluable. One of the big differences between Radomir and other men I have been in love with was that he could actually work, and do a very good job while he was about it. He relished taking responsibility and could be counted on to carry through projects to their completion. I had seen it in action when he was renovating the country house. In his office he delivered the same kind of capability and had been rewarded for it with a decent salary and working papers. I was impressed. The time he'd spent at the advertising agency as my assistant he'd never been able to even be considered for working papers as you had to be *cadre* level, which required a salary well beyond what someone of Radomir's age could expect to earn. If he was now earning enough to qualify for papers he'd proved himself well, Paris having preceded New York by several centuries as the "If you can make it there you can make it anywhere" town.

The Loire Valley was just like California when I got there. Cold and wet. The young American couple were at home, and I stopped in to see them shortly after I arrived. They said they'd seen Radomir and his friend when they were down. "What was she like?" I immediately asked.

"She?" the husband replied. "It was a he. Tall. Very good-looking. I think there might be something going on there."

"French?" I asked.

"Yes, but speaks good English. Works in the French diplomatic corps. Very nice guy. Played with the children and they loved him. They spoke French to him, which you know they're always reluctant to do in front of us."

I looked around for the truck that had just run over me. Hmmm. This was pretty revolutionary news. I had always believed that one reason Radomir felt so hostile was that I represented a homosexuality he was determined to be over and done with. Somehow I could handle the idea of his girlfriends. I wasn't so sure I was up to young and handsome boyfriends.

The week in the country house was long and empty and filled poorly with cleaning windows and scrubbing floors. I even scrubbed the attic floor and cleaned the back storage wing. I bought a small electric lawnmower and mowed the lawn.

One night I had a disturbing dream that I was departing from an airport and at check-in couldn't find my ticket. I dug through my shoulder bag and carry-on luggage. I was trying to remain calm, but the withering glare of the check-in clerk was disconcerting me. A woman stepped up and asked if she could help me and I realized I was very old and easily befuddled. But not so befuddled that I couldn't see she was one of those people of mysterious Hispanic origins who are always very correctly groomed so as to allay suspicion. "No, no, no!" I cried, sure she was some kind of con artist who would steal from me. At this point the wig I was wearing slipped askew and my desperation was complete. I woke up with feelings that this might reflect my life situation where everything from finances to emotions was almost beyond my grasp.

It was in this kind of tightly reined-in mood that I returned to Paris and to my dinner rendezvous with Radomir. He was living at the top of a very long seven floors of steps.

When he opened the door I was again reminded how much better his body looked unclothed than clothed. Clothed his waist seemed too tiny for the breadth of his shoulders and his legs seemed to need cowboy boots to finish them off. Unclothed there was a flow of form that always made me feel I'd been hit in the stomach.

The apartment had rather low-set windows overlooking the drop of seven floors or more to a courtyard. I sat in a tall canvas-backed folding chair and thought for a moment of pitching out of its shakiness through the window into the courtyard. It seemed for a moment a perfectly reasonable solution to the confounding situation in which I always found myself in with Radomir. Still being wildly in love with him after five years, no encouragement, even active discouragement, seemed more and more to have less to do with Radomir and more and more to do with my not being able to deal with my role as an aging poof.

But is being in love with youth and beauty such an anomaly for the aging? Could we really be expected to fall in love with age and decrepitude? Should we be sexually excited by sagging male breasts and abdomens? Backs covered in hair? Wavering inner thighs? People seemed to expect older people to have a kind of warm and general affection, the kind you feel for dogs and your Aunt Betty, and call it love. Sorry. I guess if you don't lower your standards you've got to lower your expectations. Something's got to give.

What I really wanted to have was full information on the tall, handsome stranger that had gone to the country with Radomir. But I seemed to be in better control of myself than usual. And I *was* actually interested in finding out what Radomir did at his work and what it was like. Though the company he worked for had been going through every kind of shakeup, resale, and reorganization, he was surviving from one incarnation to the next. It was the remains of the same company who had originally sent him to Europe and then abandoned him there. He had the pleasure of seeing all of these people fired from their jobs while he had survived them. In fact, he was the only one of the original company still employed.

I was surprised to learn that he had not gone from his work as my assistant directly to this job, which I had always assumed. In fact he had quit the agency with no prospects, had considered trying to freelance, had decided to leave Paris and try his luck in Miami when the possibility of working for the American company appeared. He had applied, had interviewed, and *voila,* had been hired. And to add to my surprise, he had interviewed in English so his fluency in French hadn't even been taken into consideration. So much for my salvaging my pride a bit in that I had helped him hang on in France while he learned the language.

Radomir in fact had found a job, done well, got working papers, and was making it. His mother once told me, "He was always forty years old." How amazing that I was in love with not only a handsome and sexy person, but one who could run his own life and be successful at it. A first. And I'm sure a last.

We decided to have dinner on the quay opposite Notre Dame where we had eaten before. The waiter, short and swarthy with his receding hair pulled into a ponytail, was quite taken with me. I said to Radomir, "In France, I've always been popular with the short and dark."

"Which includes everyone," he replied.

Toward the end of the meal he told me he'd been going through a period where everyone was falling in love with him and ruining all his friendships. Men and women, no one wanted to be friends. They all wanted to be lovers. He started talking about the man who had gone to the country with him. At last! Patience had been rewarded. He was the boyfriend of a young Irish woman whom Radomir knew. They had become friends in turn, and Radomir had given him his typed up diaries to read, most of it having to do with me. The man, Jean-Luc, had said, "I'd like to meet him, this man who decides others' destinies for them." And knowing this much about Radomir had evidently felt the ground was solid enough underfoot to suggest his own interest in him. Radomir had tried to have a woman friend join them for the weekend but she had failed to do so and Jean-Luc, of the long-lashed green eyes and tall, lanky frame, soon wanted to go to bed with Radomir, too. Like everyone else.

We left the restaurant and I sat on a bench while Radomir stood in front of me. Was he really so concerned that they all fell in love with him? He remembered that I had called him a "millionaire of love." Or did he enjoy all these hearts toppling before him? How was I going to tell him that sexy, solid citizens were in short supply? Particularly those available to both men and women. And did he really want consolation or consultation? He was letting me know what his life was like. And I was finding out that his charm for me was in no way diminished. In my life I'm always waiting for that moment when someone you like reveals themselves to be after all an asshole. As the years moved forward Radomir was moving further away from assholedom. Unluckily for me.

We said goodnight on the quay and I departed in a cab for Pigalle while he walked back uphill to the Roman Arena neighborhood where he lived. He had agreed he would come to the country for a weekend with me. There was no more I could plan for and there I would find out about all the others who were in love with him. And just how much good it was going to do them.

During the week I saw an old school friend who had taken up residence in the old Les Halles quarter. Witty but self-centered, he was fun to talk to even if you had to shout at the top of your lungs to batter through his deafness. His homosexuality had been woven through a marriage and two children, but even so he displayed a lot of classic gay manners and mores. He had accustomed himself to sitting in cafés and "boy watching." He told me that he also sometimes dropped down to the porno tape center, where instead of buying tapes, he rented them for use in the little booths they had there. Nicely equipped with boxes of Kleenex, he explained. He said it was all "Quite correct." I said, "Oh, please, Gary, bring the tapes home so I can at least imagine you sprawled out on your own couch, legs akimbo, whacking off. There's something so French and grim about sitting bolt upright on a hardback chair with your fly open, taking care of business. It's not very sexual." "Not at all, not at all," he answered me, obviously thinking I was ridiculously emotional. Despite the fact he barely spoke the language he had become more French than I ever could be. He did not think of love as playing any part in his life, and I'm not sure that he ever did. He was of that male world where having an orgasm in or around an attractive body was the goal. Letting that attractive body have any control over you because of your love for them was not part of the game. Too threatening, too debilitating, too out of control.

~26~ Nevis Thinks About AIDS

Nevis thought of all the friends who had died of AIDS. His pursuing Radomir to Crete, fearing he had AIDS and had gone away to die, wasn't really a neurotic fantasy. So many of his friends had died. And each of them before their illness had told him of one special, unusual sexual encounter. And some, who were closeted, he had happened upon with a male lover. He thought they may have, in some prescient way, been telling him of the transference of the poison semen without knowing it. They could not have known. And certainly Nevis could not know. But each had mentioned only one encounter.

A young French friend had told him of the South American he had met in a bar in Los Angeles. They went into the men's room and had sex there, as neither wanted to be bothered to take the time to go to someone's home, getting undressed, all the paraphernalia of romance. It had come to that for poor André, and he never described actual sexual experiences. But this one he did. Within the year he became ill when he was alone at Nevis's country house in the Loire Valley. He had called Nevis from there, panicky, described how sick he was, was sure it was the beginning of AIDS. Nevis had reassured him and reminded him of the proximity of his parents and how frequently he was ill when around them. But André's guess was right, and soon he died.

Harry Lieberwitz told Nevis of going to the baths in Miami and taking home some "foreign guy." Harry said he just couldn't suck enough cock that night. The man told him he should go to the gym and firm up a little. Nevis was astonished Harry had done this with no precautions, as AIDS was already sweeping friends off the table. Harry didn't seem to be able to compute this into his thinking. It was the only sex encounter he ever told Nevis of, but perhaps they weren't too frequent for the not-too-attractive Harry. Soon Harry registered positive, and soon after a series of horrifying illnesses began that carried him away.

A former lover of Nevis's, who died of lung cancer complicated with being seropositive, had told him fleetingly of an evening when a group of friends at his apartment got the clothes off a black pickup. Could this have been the fatal contact?

Nevis remembered the television producer from a company he often worked with, so handsome, who was deeply in the closet. He had seen him rushing through Penn Station with a young male model in tow. He had passed within inches of Nevis and ignored him. Was that the love who gave him the AIDS that killed him a few years later?

There was the New York advertising writer he had seen, surprisingly all in black leather, at an exhibit at the Grand Palais in Paris, with a surly black-leather thug. Was that his nemesis? The cause of his death by AIDS? A death that had so surprised his friends back in New York, who all knew his girlfriend so well?

Nevis wasn't into all "that woo-woo stuff" enough to really believe that he alone knew the time or the partner that had killed each person. Knew the specific infection when the virus had entered the veins. But there was one fact he was sure of. If there is one thing an illness should not do, it shouldn't attack you when you're fully in love or fully in lust.

Because of the brief tales and encounters involving friends who had died of AIDS, Nevis both liked and hated hearing of Radomir's sexual exploits. Each one, he thought, might have been the one that would later return in a punishing form. Condoms or no condoms, those tiny viruses are tricky. Radomir told him on one occasion he had totaled up his bed partners and there were about thirty of them.

Nevis wondered how he could continue to listen to stories of sexual adventures when Radomir continued to recount them to him. He had heard the expression "you're only as sick as your secrets." Perhaps not keeping secrets would hold sickness at bay.

~27~ Passage de Salut

This is a strange and brooding house I have in the Passage de Salut. In a town that has plenty to brood about. This small abbey town, lost in *La France Profonde,* has Roman origins. Ancient Roman tombs were found when they dug the foundations of the Mairie in the latter part of the nineteenth century.

This town sits very directly upon the earth. The rich smell of the earth is always in the air, most acutely when the shutters are opened in the morning and when they are closed upon the night air. It is very silent here. Few cars, few tourists come to the Passage de Salut to visit the ancient abbey. It was founded in 1035 by a knight called Gelduin, who had been saved from a storm at sea when returning from a crusade. He prayed to the Virgin and she appeared in a snowstorm and calmed the seas. You may think appearing in a blizzard over the Mediterranean strange, but that she appeared at all is so strange she surely could be accompanied by anything she chose.

Gelduin swore to found an abbey, which he did when he returned to his village. He was known as Gelduin the Girl because of his beauty. He had no heirs. His sister's children inherited the abbey. It all hangs together.

In 1935 the boys' school that occupied the abbey celebrated its nine hundredth anniversary. When I read the history of the abbey I discovered that the sleeping arrangements in the dormitories alternated a monk and a schoolboy, a monk and a schoolboy, down the long rows of beds. When a child had to go to the bathroom in the night the nearest monk went with him and the child on the other side was also awakened to accompany them. Hanky-panky was hard to come by. The boys went to school all year long; there were no vacations. Cultivating any secret vices required a great deal of imagination.

In the evening from my front door the sun falls heavily upon the facade of the abbey and its chapel, Notre Dame de la Neige. Our Lady of the Snows, in memory of that life-saving snowstorm. The ancient stones are gold and sharply outlined against the often lavender skies beyond. Turning around, the fronts of the houses across the square are already dark and the sky above them is pale blue. The classic René Magritte painting. Already night below. Still daylight above. The two views to left and right seem to have little to do with each other.

All the shutters are closed on the houses across the square. They have been since before the dinner hour. In broad daylight the natives close the shutters and sit down to their evening meal under electric light, usually an unshaded bulb. It is a long-standing French tradition to let no one see into your homes. When I first came to France I found it eerie and forbidding to pass through the streets of provincial towns with no sign of life. Now I am used to it and would find it bizarre to see light streaming from windows and jolly people within. I once visited a friend in Holland and saw exactly that. I felt like crying to see people behaving in such a normal, unsuspicious way. I always leave my shutters open and the lights on until I retire in my house in the Passage de Salut. On summer evenings it is a favorite destination for town folk out for a walk. Coming by to see what the American is doing. It probably beats French television.

The streetlights go out when it gets truly dark and everyone is safely in bed. Sometimes with friends I go out for a walk in the brilliant moonlight. The streets lined with their faceless stone houses are at their most beautiful then. The slate roofs gleam like silver in the white light of the moon, which seems particularly close here in the Loire Valley. The shadows are hard and black. It is exactly the romantic look of old lithographs and Hollywood spy movies. I think that it was exactly this in the Middle Ages; and the same when Louis the Sixteenth and Marie Antoinette were on the throne; and at the turn of the century when big hats and bustles passed through these stone doorways and entered these very same shops; and when German soldiers were here in occupancy during World War II, in their metal-domed helmets on their motorcycles as they patrolled this town. No one seems to have minded that much. It is the one subject that is completely taboo and never comes up. One elderly woman school teacher did say to me once, "They were just boys, you know."

Now they have been replaced with Americans. Or at least one American, living in a largish stone house in the Passage de Salut. I cannot say that it feels like my home. It feels more like a birdhouse built for birds of passage. A nest perhaps, but not a permanent one.

Perhaps all the souls that have inhabited these stone walls since 1600 have filled the space so completely with their spirits that there's little room for me to impose my own personality.

This isn't entirely true. When I'm in residence for a while it begins to feel like *my* house, but when I go away and return I have to start all over again. My personal atmosphere has evaporated. The young American woman who comes by to water my plants and pick up mail when I'm not here says the same thing. "It's not your house when you're not here," she has said.

There are only three houses in Passage de Salut. Mine is in the middle, flanked on either side by the village priest's residence and the hairdresser, or what used to be the hairdresser. He's retired now. Monsieur Albert. There is a Madame Albert about and Monsieur Albert makes quite a point about how he lusts after young girls. I wonder. I hope so.

It would be awful to contemplate a lifetime of living in a little stone house with a rather plain wife, her hair dyed a dark red no hair has ever been (by you, no doubt), and two charmless and stocky daughters, and all your life you are longing after young men and endlessly pretending to be an old lecher. My feeling in talking to Monsieur Albert is that he has been pretending to be an old lecher for so long he has become one.

Monsieur Albert plays the trombone very well. In the evening the only sound leaking through the stone walls is the occasional mooing of Monsieur Albert's trombone. It was some years before I realized that the stone walls standing between Monsieur Albert's house and my own were actually one wall. My house must have preceded his and when his was built, sometime in the seventeenth century, the builders just put it lean-to up against mine. They built the three outer walls. The back wall was already there: mine. The priest on the other side has the same construction. His bedroom and the blue bedroom in my house back on the same common wall. Guests sleeping in that room have told me they have heard lashing and cries. I can only hope the mousy little father has some exciting and self-martyring times in there by himself. I once saw a pair of large pink panties on his laundry line. A guest said, "His housekeeper obviously." Well, perhaps.

My house in the passage was three houses originally. The main structure has a front door inserted in what was originally an open passageway. The oldest houses in the village are of this construction. An opening passes through the house to allow horses to be led to a stable in the inner court. The oak staircase and hallways were part of the outdoors then. Only when you closed a room's door and lit a fire in the fireplace were you truly indoors. Perhaps this dates back to the Roman origins of these towns in central France. In the Italian climate there was little need for warmth to be held in.

I have central heating in this house, the only heating of this type in the village. Turning the furnace full up it still takes two days for the house to warm, the stone walls absorbing all the heat until they are fully dechilled. A weekend in winter requires someone passing by to turn on the heat on Thursday morning if there is to be warmth Friday evening. I tried to stay in the house in winter several times before I installed central heating. The first time I arose in the night and pulled the bedroom carpet over the bed. It was still freezing in the bed. These are the feelings that connect us with the past. A past of candles flickering low, wood fires with a few embers still glowing in a cold, cold dawn. Fingers that scarcely bend; gray, soiled skin under stiff and dark clothing. Frozen feet stuffed into wooden sabots filled with straw. Crudely knitted wool socks if you were very lucky.

I have seen older people in the town, bent from reaching for the ground for many years, hands in permanent claws from holding hoes and pitchforks. They were only part of the process of pulling food from the earth and pushing it back through their bodies. Hoping to have a little surplus to sell for handwoven cloth, wooden shoes, some salt, a kerosene lamp.

These stone walls breathe of these hard lives, hard even for those with some money. Nancy Mitford wrote that it was only in the eighteenth century that the wealthy began to exchange splendor for comfort. Comfort can be very beguiling. Only those who have never known it can live without it. Eventually the entire world will be living in Florida.

I was brought up in a house without central heating. A house with a privy in the garden. So this house is not a far reach for me. I do not care that the bathroom is not luxuriously appointed. I have no desire for a "modern" kitchen. In a way it's quite French not to care. I was once shown around a newly decorated apartment in Paris. Long low purple couches ran around the walls. Tall conical Italian lamps lit the red and black abstract carpets on the floors and the pictures on the walls closely resembled the carpets. It was a home for crazed clowns. I said, "Marie-France, what does the kitchen look like?" She replied, "I don't know. I never go there. Let's look."

We did look. It had grease-stained tile walls, ancient skillets and pans hanging upon them. A black behemoth of a stove that must have burned what? Wood? Coal? It must have all dated to the time the apartment was built shortly before the turn of the century. Marie-France glared about and said, "Cook does very well in here. She does not complain." And we left.

I, too, saw no reason to upgrade the kitchen although I could have lived forever without her purple snake-like couches in the salon.

My kitchen in the house in the Passage de Salut is large, a tiled floor in red, a very large fireplace, a little gas stove, a metal sink, a large armoire for dishes, pots, and pans, a long table and many chairs, some matching.

Over the fireplace is a tile map bearing the title *Carte d'Amour*. It shows a land rather like France with a large channel dividing it from a northern isle. Something like England. There are many little towns on this map, separated by numerous rivers. Some are on hillocks. They have names like *Médisance, Folie,* and *Chagrin.* I always tell guests I live near *Les Falaises d' Amour*. The Cliffs of Love. They never respond or ask me to elaborate.

Why my own bedroom is gray I cannot say. My bedrooms in all my previous homes have always been blue. But this one is gray and has always been a little austere. I have never known any nights of real passion in the bed of that room. I said aloud to myself once when I walked into it, "I don't like a bedroom in which I never had a really good fuck." It's true. Perhaps my attachment to Radomir is based upon my trying to make that bedroom one I really could like.

Only on hot summer afternoons when the closed shutters let shadowy light through and I am snoozing on my fat pillows wearing shorts do I really like that bedroom.

At other times, waking in the night seeing the shutters making chevron patterns on the ceiling from the lights of the old street lanterns in front of the abbey across the street, I feel completely estranged from this bedroom. I would like to rise, pack, call a cab, and depart forever. I don't because I have guests.

When Radomir stayed here alone he was never discomfited and the ghostly presence he felt only comforted him.

Amanda claims she has heard steps climbing the wooden stairs from the entryway while she was seated on the toilet below the stairs. She said, "But when I went upstairs there was no one there."

I have no antennae for spirits. I have never felt a presence. I am not a very spiritual person, landlocked in reality and sensuality. That has always been pleasure enough for me.

But sometimes I think that the house's failure to accept my presence and my atmosphere is the resistance of those who have been here before me. It is *their* house. I am only in residence temporarily. Once gone, it will again be theirs. Or theirs and Radomir's. He will inherit this house because I think he is really far more at home here than I am.

~28~ Why Do I Keep Talking About My Sex Life?

I told Nevis I wanted to go to the country for a weekend, so we met at the Gare d'Austerlitz. When he spoke to me on the telephone that morning he asked if the wonderful Radomir or killer Radomir was going to be his guest that weekend. I told him that at least it was going to be wonderful Radomir who would be departing with him. I couldn't promise who would be coming back.

He was waiting where the information kiosk always used to stand. They had moved it, but that's where we always met; so kiosk or not, that's where he was. He said, "I never can be sure if it's you I see coming from the Metro or if I'm hallucinating. I always want to be with you so much that sometimes I think I'm imagining it."

"Actually, it's me," I said, kissing him on both cheeks. I was early because it was the long weekend of the French Labor Day and there might well be a mob on the train. The French just go all to hell with themselves when it comes to fighting for train seats.

We tried to decide which end of the train to get on. It turns around in Orleans because it doesn't go through the city. So you start out riding frontward and wind up riding backward. It's no big deal except when you have a ton of luggage and you get off at your destination to find the station half a mile away.

Nevis seemed nervous. I really *do* wish he'd get over me. But then again, we probably wouldn't be going to the country together if he was. We talked about the complicated series of things to remember when boarding a train in France. When buying the ticket you have to decide on first or second class. The day before you have to decide if you want to make a special trip to the station to reserve a seat. Before you leave the station you have to slip your ticket into an orange electronic post to be punched. Nevis said that when he first came to France there were mean-looking ladies in uniform who sat in a chair and punched your ticket and you weren't allowed on the platform if you weren't taking the train unless you had bought a special ticket for those who were seeing passengers off. The French always have plenty of time to make life more complicated. Maybe that's why they're always bustling about. Even now, if you forget to punch your ticket you get fined fifty francs by the conductor. That's when you fall back on English. They usually forgive you if you're a stupid foreigner.

Once on the train you have to check on the back of the seat you choose to make sure that it isn't reserved. It's in a little sign on the back of the seat. All that done, you can usually rest assured you'll arrive safely. All that said, we, of course, forgot to check if our seats were reserved, which they were, and we had to move.

Naturally we arrived a long hike from the station, but the only taxi wasn't taken and we arrived at the village in a few minutes and were left off in front of the house. The shutters were all closed and it always looks kind of formidable, but we rushed right in and opened the shutters, put on the heat, put out the window boxes waiting in the garden. The usual drill.

Then we walked over to the Brownings' house to collect the Peugeot. Nevis said he didn't want me to spend the weekend working and that maybe we'd take the Peugeot and make a little trip somewhere. But as it turned out we went over to the little house we used to own together on Saturday morning and collected some furniture the tenants didn't want. The sleigh bed he bought because I wanted it and the settee. Which really is a nice antique. The tenants didn't want them. That's the usual routine for Nevis when he rents a house. The tenants love it because it's so charming and then immediately dismantle it so it looks really ugly. As we tied the furniture on top of the car Nevis said, "Bad taste is international." "Le mauvais goût est international" is what he actually said. It's a favorite saying of his.

Somehow that trip took up most of the day and we finished by having dinner in the kitchen. While we were eating Nevis said, "So, tell me about all those people who are in love with you?"

"Do you really want to hear?" I said.

"It isn't a very good image for me, is it?" Nevis said. "One among the suppliant hordes, and rather far to the back among those who are definitely not in the running."

It's probably kind of sick, my talking about the people I'm fucking to Nevis. I could refuse, but I think that's what he wants to know about me. He's always so worried about my getting an AIDS test so I finally got one and I'm negative. I'm not getting AIDS from anyone and I'm not giving AIDS.

"First of all," I said, "I just got an AIDS test and I'm not giving AIDS to anyone. And I'm not bottoming for anyone. Haven't in years. So you don't have to worry about me."

"Whew," said Nevis, wiping his hands across his forehead. I couldn't tell if he was making fun of me or not. But then you never can tell with him.

"How are things going with Jean-Luc?" he asked.

"I have to think about how I feel about him," I said. "As far as beauty is concerned there's no problem there." I don't want to talk about Jean-Luc. Like so many good-looking French men who are gay, they pretend they aren't gay and when they admit it they are just another French girl who wants to settle down and live in the Sixteenth Arrondissement and fuck only on Sunday morning.

So I told Nevis about Jackie, the girl I work with who looks like a Barbie doll. She had recently gone to Crete with me, with suitcases full of clothes. All my pals who were still there called her "Mademoiselle." She didn't make a big hit. I told him about her *"problèmes au lit."* She let me screw her, but she never moved. It meant nothing to her.

Nevis said, "What does she say when you talk to her about it?"

"I don't talk to her about it," I said.

"Your generation is so strange. You do very intimate things together but you're not intimate enough to discuss them. Mine talked about very intimate things but were too shy or immature or awkward to do anything intimate."

"Jackie and I didn't last very long, anyway. She found out that I screwed Beatrice at the other office and she told me to go to hell," I said.

"Who is Beatrice?" Nevis asked.

So I told him about Beatrice after pouring us both a second glass of wine. The sexy girl who abducted me one day and nailed me good. She mounted me and got herself off proper. Then I fucked her pretty good myself. I always love those bizarre setups. Just can't resist 'em.

Nevis said, "She was probably revenging herself on Jackie because Jackie is prettier."

"It couldn't be because I'm a hot guy?" I said.

"Of course you're a hot guy, but a woman can really hurl herself into it with abandon when she thinks someone else is jealous. Men, too, of course. But women more. I always said that for myself I don't care if people like me as long as they envy me. That applies to a lot of people."

"Jackie just called me yesterday. She wants to get back together. She been seeing this older guy again but she wants to see me again. All is forgiven," I said. "Frederic just called me again, too. He wants to see me again. I probably will."

Nevis said, "Frederic is the guy you met at the swimming pool, right? The model. You surprise me. I thought you were becoming a little redneck homophobe. And now you're telling me that you're planning to shag Frederic again, also. I know you're restricting Jean-Luc to blow jobs. How's he going to feel about Frederic?"

I said, "If I sounded homophobic it was because I was in a bad mood because of Dan Danforth out in California registering positive. I kind of blame it on him—running around getting fucked by God knows who all—and then scaring the hell out of me. Hey, listen. I am who I am."

"That's a new tack," Nevis said. "You were sure that you were just going to stop being gay and that was that. Like you were never going to wear navy blue again."

I explained calmly and carefully that I used condoms always. Without any exceptions. And I told him about Frederic being invited to an orgy and when he told the host that he thought orgies were a really bad idea the host replied, "You don't have to worry about getting sick. *Ils sont les gens très corrects*. These people are very correct."

Nevis said, "I'm never sure what *très correct* means exactly. Does that indicate that you always use condoms or does that mean you only sleep with white men of your own class?"

"It might mean that you only do blow jobs and never get completely undressed," I said.

"There's that, too," Nevis said.

"Don't think I don't know what's going on," I told him. "My friend Phillipe, he's a model, hurt his knee skiing, and when they operated they tested this blood and he found out he was seropositive. He got very depressed and wasn't eating so I went around with a pizza and tried to cheer him up but I didn't feel very good about the situation when we said good night.

"I had to go to California for a couple of weeks and when I got back I called and his telephone was disconnected so I went right over to his building. The concierge told me. '*Il est décédé.*' You should have seen the look she gave me. He must have committed suicide and she probably thought it was over me. Or I had given him AIDS. Those concierges know everything."

"She didn't say he had killed himself?" Nevis said.

"No. And I just couldn't ask. But he couldn't have died of AIDS that rapidly."

I thought I might as well tell Nevis about Linton, too. So I told him about the handsome minister who married my friends in Sandusky when I was there for a wedding. A minister who used to be a priest but decided he was too gay to make a go of it.

"His name was, or rather is, Linton," I said.

"That's quite a distinguished name," Nevis said.

"He is quite distinguished. Really handsome, too. I had him come visit my folks, and my sister-in-law Maxine fell in love with him. She threw her arms around him and said, 'Oh, you're so handsome and you can cook. I think I'll get divorced and marry you.'"

"They still don't know you're gay, do they?" Nevis asked.

"No," I said. "My folks do. They have to be figuring something out with me showing up all the time with good-looking guys."

"So where's Linton?" Nevis wanted to know.

"He's back in Chicago where he has a job as a real estate agent. I just couldn't move back there. He said, 'You love a city more than you do me.' I don't know if it was really that. I know I didn't love him more that my life here in France," I said.

"He could have moved to Paris. If he really loved you he could have given it a try," Nevis said.

"You would have, wouldn't you?" I said.

"You know the answer to that," Nevis said.

~29~ Nevis Finishes the Talk

When Radomir came down for the weekend to the country we had one of those long talks, about him of course, after dinner on Saturday night. He's been through quite a few people since we last discussed his private life. His most recent was a very hot and heavy affair with an ex-priest from Chicago. Very handsome. He had some pictures, and in fact this man was handsome. Sometimes Radomir finds men fetching whose appeal goes over my head. And his taste in women I find very elusive.

I'm never sure but what these conversations don't border on voyeurism, but in addition to my really wanting to know what's going on in his interior world, there is definitely a desire on Radomir's part to tell me all about these adventures. But I don't ask all the questions I could.

What I really wanted to know was how their love affair began. Did they fall into each other's arms in a car? Did the minister invite Radomir to his apartment for dinner? Did they begin to neck on the couch and then tear off their clothes and fall into bed? Did they go to a nearby motel and calmly remove all their clothes and get into bed before they had so much as kissed? Did Radomir enter him only, or did he submit to being entered also? Did they make love face to face, or did one lie face down for the other? These are all the things I wanted to know, things that if I had ever been Radomir's lover I would know. What he liked and how he did it. These are the mysteries that are so much more complex and so much more revelatory when two men are in love than a man and a woman. Men and women are traditionally in the missionary position in bed. So much ground work is already established and for many couples more intriguing possibilities perhaps never come up. I thought of Jackie who lay flat on her back wondering why it wasn't more fun.

It was the failure of his romance with the ex-minister that led Radomir to get in contact with the woman who had broken his heart in California before he left for Europe. He had called her. She was living with another man, but seemed to feel her life was not coming to very much. And she regretted having broken off with Radomir. Radomir said, "I had wanted very much to marry her at that time." Remembering how they had once been in love, they started to correspond again. And there was an opportunity for the woman to come to London to do some advanced studies. She had prepared her application, but when Radomir called her to ask if she had heard anything, she told him that the last day of the deadline she just hadn't been able to get up and submit it. She'd been too tired. Radomir was crushed again. He had been imagining going to London to see her. Their old affinities coming to life again. The woman who had once meant so much to him becoming again his great love. And she hadn't even been able to get out of bed to submit an application.

I could easily imagine her in the doldrums of a boring relationship thinking of dropping everything to go to London. Thinking of seeing again an old lover who had done so much more with his life than the dreary man she had chosen, and deciding she still didn't have the nerve to leave the known for the unknown. She would not have many more chances, and soon boredom, routine, and age would place change beyond her boundaries.

In the dim light of the kitchen beside the fireplaces Radomir finished telling me all this. I found it a little hard to imagine that all these romances had been compressed into the space of the year we'd been separated. And I also wondered why I wanted to hear all this.

When I looked at Radomir he seemed tired and lined. The shadows were harsh on his face and I could see how he would look when he was older: the lines of his cheeks deep; his eyes sunken, his mouth tight. It was only the illusion of light for the moment and perhaps when he got older he wouldn't look harsh in this way. The fear of sickness and death that now hung over me when I thought of him only led me to hope that I would live to see him old, however changed he was. If I lived into my early nineties I could hope to see him something close to my own age now. My greatest hope would be for his face to be the last face I saw. His hand to be the last hand I touched.

The last day that we were in the country we spoke more of ourselves. As I came downstairs in the morning he was standing at the sink. I put my arms about him from behind and kissed his neck. His body felt harder and more ridged and rugged than I remembered it. His swimming was toughening him up more than his weight lifting had done. He stiffened slightly in my arms. He had probably been fearing all weekend that I would be embarrassingly romantic at some point.

We talked about how unhappy he'd been working for me at the advertising agency. About how dictatorial I'd been with him. He had mentioned this before, but I have no memory of this. Cool perhaps. But maybe I was and have suppressed it.

He told me that in the large room he shared with others on the creative staff they would talk about him in French, assuming he didn't understand. One woman talking at length with her husband on the telephone about how unfair it was that they had to have his untalented person around when they really should have a French person in his place.

But he said he had once been corrected by a Dutch girl whom I had helped. She had come to the agency as a receptionist through my help and then I later helped her to get a permanent position in an account group. She was now living with the Frenchman who was the father of her baby, and while Radomir was visiting them and telling her lover about what a terrible person I was she stopped him and said, "You and I both owe our careers to him." And her lover had said, "I used to hang around Le Drugstore myself picking up men to make a little extra money. I got my first real job through one of the men I picked up there." The Dutch girl said, "You never told me that." And Radomir probably felt he'd made a good choice by living in France, where no one is surprised or shocked that a young man had made himself attractive to an older man in order to get a foothold in life.

We talked about the terrible weekend when our life together really began falling apart. How he had dragged heavy luggage through the Metro because a car I had arranged failed to show up. We had missed our train and I had only said, "You're late." We both had done everything wrong. He could be forgiven, but I found it hard to forgive myself since experience had taught me how to handle it and I hadn't. I could have risen to his going out to a farewell dinner with his friends in the village, the farewell being the girl I suspected him of sleeping with. I could have accepted her parents' invitation to dinner, which Radomir told me she had requested they make, knowing I'd be furious at being left alone. I didn't have to flee back to Paris the same evening in a rage. I didn't have to make him creep back into the apartment in Paris alone the next evening, undoubtedly feeling humiliated and hating having nowhere else to go. When he apologized the next day I could have been more understanding and not just dismissed his apology. We were in a situation where we couldn't move forward and we couldn't stay where we were. When you are in love you behave in ways you could never accept or understand in other people. And I really couldn't forgive myself just because I loved him so much. I had put him in hell. It took me a long time to realize it. And when I did, I did nothing to extricate him. So do we punish those we love.

Somehow we had survived it. Sitting next to him on the train the traces of how he would look when he was older were gone. That quick chestnut eye of his, that sometimes looked gray, difficult to see under his brow, shone in the sun setting across the fields. He said, "I want to come down regularly to take care of the lawns and gardens. And if you need money I'll pay some bills for you. I believe you'll work again and can pay me back." I felt that pang where crying starts.

I think both Radomir and I have a taste for living intensely. A three-day weekend of high emotional content was the kind of thing we both enjoyed doing. If we share little else, we share a low threshold for boredom.

When he left me on the Metro he leaned over me and kissed me on both cheeks. I felt his beard. I was so glad to have kissed him good-bye and waved from the train as we passed him walking down the platform. Good-byes in the Metro are the worst.

Now that I am back in New York we have spoken several times. The last time he was in the country. When I asked him who was there with him he said, "Jean-Luc." I don't know whether I wished Jean-Luc wasn't there with him. I do wish that whatever they do, they are very, very careful.

~30~ Nevis and Amanda Have Another Chat

I was in Paris on my way back to the United States and stayed with Uncle Nevis in that flat that looks like a miniature dream of the czars. Uncle Nevis always has said that he isn't interested in jewelry unless the stones looked as though they were torn from the crowns of the czars. His apartment looks like it was torn from Tsarskoe Selo, Catherine the Great's country palace—all moldings and pastel walls and big draperies. It's not really so faggy. He says it is designed to look like the home of one of the *Grandes Horizontales* of the nineteenth century. It *is* the sort of apartment where you feel as though you should be making bamboola with someone. Bamboola. That's an Uncle Nevis word, too.

We went for a walk along the river past the *bouquinistes* and he really got on a roll when I said that the disappointing thing about men was that you always had to handle them.

He said, "You really have no alternative except to handle men. If you let them handle you, they drop you and break you. I've been knocked out of the ring three times and I'm not going in there again. I may look like a whole person but I've been severely damaged. And after you quit looking for that warrior lover who was going to make you a complete person, what do you do?

"You amuse yourself with great clothes and wonderful jewels. Beautiful houses and swell furniture, paintings, all that stuff. You have amusing friends and you go out looking like a million dollars and laughing a lot. It's not the same thing of course, but it's not a bad life: It's the life everyone else wants. Little do they know, poor saps."

I said, "If you don't have any more lovers, at least you have a lot of friends."

He said, "You never knew how many friends you have until you get sick and then all their miserable guilts come to the fore and they send you fruit baskets to make up for all the times they didn't invite you to dinner. They don't want your death to weigh on their conscience along with everything else.

"And those damnable fruit baskets. What do you do with them when the fruit is gone? My home is full of those baskets. For that matter, what do you do with the fruit? It all tastes like . . . not fruit. What? Bed pillows."

"I have an idea," I told him. "If your friends are such poor substitutes for a lover maybe you should get involved with S and M. I've been dabbling with the idea. Sadists and masochists are much less critical when it comes to physical beauty."

He looked at me sideways. It was one of those very evaluating glances. "Don't get involved with S and M," he said. "You're too small for S and M. Tell me about your latest boyfriends."

"You know I've been seeing Roger Brodkey in Madrid. He wants to be an actor. He's always talking about when you went to college with his parents."

"I didn't know Roger spoke Spanish," Uncle Nevis said.

"He doesn't," I said.

"What a curious idea to pursue an acting career in a country where you don't speak the language."

"Perhaps he doesn't really want it and is making sure he can never have it," I said.

"That's a good conclusion," Uncle Nevis said. "Many people are like that. I'm afraid Roger swims poorly in the sea of life. It's all struggle and splashing just to keep afloat at all. His parents can't keep afloat at all. Someone is eventually going to have to provide a raft for them. I was hoping it was going to be Roger. But I guess no dice."

My feet were getting tired. "Let's stop for a hot chocolate," I said. "And then there's David Schise. I could kind of like him even if he is a geologist. Except for that name."

"Corot supposedly loved someone named Parfaite Anastasie Osmond. I always wondered if he wasn't more in love with her name than her. But she must have been a lovely baby to get a name like that. Perfection. When you have a name like that you can always believe you are beautiful. No, you're right. Maybe Amanda Schise would be all right in the Midwest. But you're never going to be there."

"Actually there were lots of reasons to stop seeing him. He was very anti-abortion," I said.

"If you eat steak you should have no objection to abortion. They both involve slaughter. I'm quite against abortion myself. Only because I hate the destruction of beauty. Maybe I'd like your David Schise."

"I don't think so," I told him. "He's homophobic, too."

"But I love that. Also men who are anal retentive. Imagine a man who would actually hang up his pants. Morgan used to tell me that if it isn't messy you're doing it wrong and I always told him I preferred to do it wrong."

I knew Morgan all through the many years Uncle Nevis and he were involved. I think I was three years old the first time I met Morgan. Very handsome. A tough act to follow.

"I probably should have stayed with my Argentinean tennis player but he had such bad taste," I said.

"Bad taste leads to crime," Uncle Nevis said. "That's not original with me. I think Baudelaire said that."

"Well, it was certainly true in Filiberto's case. He was always looking around underground parking garages for a car to steal. I probably have so many troubles with men because I don't love myself enough."

Uncle Nevis said, "That's not such a bad thing. At least when you're not in love with yourself it leaves some room to love somebody else."

I said, "None of them are as nice as you are, Uncle Nevis."

He said, "I *was* a nice person. Now I only act like a nice person. But all the time. I'm consistent. Someone should have taken better care of me. Besides God."

"You never know. You always tell me don't get upset about missing a flight. You never know whom you might meet on the trip back into town," I said.

"I am afraid I will die crying for the man I've been looking for all my life and have only caught glimpses of. But let's not complain. It only makes us unattractive. Another hot chocolate?"

~31~ The Trip to Turin

Was the trip to Turin a turning point? My life had lost direction since my contract with the French agency had expired. I really didn't want to go back to New York and get another job. I knew very well how that worked. As a former star, you become a kind of decoration to a big agency that pays you nothing like what you once earned—usually an agency whom you had worked for before, who could now humble you by having you work on diaper accounts. Or sanitary napkins. And I really didn't want to leave Paris because Radomir was there and ridiculous as it was I found myself still revolving around him emotionally.

I was holding things together financially by doing major freelance jobs for different offices of one of the big international agencies. Sometimes in New York, sometimes in London (they hated me there), and most often in Germany, where they seemed to venerate my former status. Very occasionally I had a call to go to Tokyo. All of which somewhat justified my staying in Paris and letting my life drift along.

Just before I had to go to New York for a project I made a quick run to Turin. Have you ever been there? A very strange town. The worldwide capital of black magic. Very few know this. Its arcaded streets have something sinister about them and, as is true in many of these old cities, the people have an air of planning to do things in the most devious way possible just because it pleases them to do so. On the upside is the ice cream, sold from glass cases under the arcades, which is wonderful. One could almost take an ice cream vacation in Turin.

However, I wanted to go there to see a large art exhibit on *Amore*. The *Herald Tribune* had reviews on it and said it was very hot. It included the secret cabinet material from the Museum of Naples, which is rarely opened to the public. I like pornography when it is handled by the masters. Actually, I like pornography whether it is masterful or not, if it is really sexy and not just repetitious and sordid. I have been encouraged in this by Buckminster Fuller, the famous architecht. In a rather ordinary magazine I stumbled upon an interview with him in which he said that pornography is a must as you grow older because it releases testosterone into the system, which keeps your bones and muscles strong and makes it possible for you to have more erections. So off I went to Turin, inviting Radomir to come along. It was really a kind of health mission. And Radomir is a good companion for sex explorations. It is a subject that fascinates him as much as me. It is one thing we truly have in common.

We slept in twin beds pushed together but we had no physical contact except for a few moments on Sunday morning when I rested my hand against Radomir's bare shoulder. I think it was those brawny shoulders and strong arms that captured my attention in the first place. And the flat stomach. He still was hanging on to all these attributes.

Saturday we found the exhibition site, which was as truly bizarre as everything else about Turin. A former synagogue, built in the form of an enormous cube, decorated with a terrifically tall spire. Something like a gigantic birthday package with a carrot on top of it. Evidently this grandiose structure was so overly ambitious that the congregation could never pay for it and it never truly served as a place of worship. Now it is an exhibition hall.

In the center of the vast empty building, which was essentially one great four-story-high room, was a glass box on a wire, which was the elevator that hauled a few passengers at a time up to the turret above. It looked scarier than any amusement park ride.

The exhibit leaned largely to modern erotic art with shiny breasts and couples grappling in a way that may have made some comment on the inherent brutality of sex but was in no way provocative. The collection from Naples was made up of fragments of Roman frescoes and statuary which contained little that hasn't already been in the art magazines for decades. Fortunately there were a few drawings by Fuseli, whose weirdly imagined hanky-panky in the English Georgian period always has so much elegance and distinction.

There was a Fuseli drawing of a courtesan, hair dressed beautifully, reclining on a divan while a robust young man groans in agonized anticipation as her maid washes his organs. This alone was worth the price of admission.

And there were a series of drawings by an Italian Romantic painter showing his mistress and himself running through a fairly complete repertoire of what is possible between men's and women's bodies. Because the artist himself was the male participant, both Radomir and I wondered how the line could be so precise and the sometimes exaggerated perspective so accurate. They didn't seem to be drawn from memory but from live models. Perhaps he used a stand-in. I have great admiration for an artist who can draw with such sureness and exactitude.

I took Radomir to a rather expensive restaurant Saturday evening where he flirted with a young blonde Italian girl at the next table. I love that kind of northern Italian blondness. A really golden kind of hair, olive skin, and greenish-blue eyes. You can have very ordinary features with that kind of coloring and still come off as a stunner. The great model Isa Stoppi had that coloring with even snowier hair and icier eyes, in a tawny skin. She was pretty sensational looking.

This girl was quite pretty and was having a boring evening out with her father. She probably thought Radomir was in the same boat. Or perhaps she was a schoolgirl whore out with her lover. That happens, too. Her little flirtation was interrupted when I paid the bill and departed with Radomir in tow.

Radomir got admiring whistles from teenage girls the next day while we were strolling the arcades. We had gone to see the country palace of Stupinigi in the morning, with its fantastically painted ceiling. I had just read about it in *World of Interiors* and it lived up to its press. Radomir surprised me a bit by saying it was what he liked best about the weekend.

Suddenly on the way to the airport on Sunday afternoon Radomir began talking to me about his friend Tony, who had come back from Crete with him and who now was living in Amsterdam.

Tony had always seemed to be a stable influence upon Radomir, I thought. Living in Amsterdam with his pretty Dutch girlfriend, cooking in a café, not going much of anywhere but enjoying himself in that typical Dutch way. But now it seems there was trouble in Paradise.

Radomir told me, "I went up to Amsterdam to visit him and he was sharing digs with this kind of drugged-out scruffy guy and he told me they were sleeping together. It was Mardi Gras there so we drank too much and did a little cocaine. Then we got it on ourselves, with his girlfriend asleep in the next room. I felt kind of shitty about it the next morning."

The news surprised me. I had met Tony in Crete, a kind of pleasant, blondish young man. Radomir and he had shared a house there for some time. I would have thought the occasion for this would have come up long before. But it was very much in a pattern with other people in Radomir's life: one more friend who winds up as a sex partner and then exits, as so many had in Radomir's life.

The more I thought about it the more surprised I was. Tony had been in Paris and stayed overnight with me while he was visiting Radomir. At breakfast on Sunday morning he told me that Radomir and he had gone to a sex show the evening before. It had been very disappointing. A naked couple dawdled about and finally he touched her parts, a female couple did much the same thing, a single female displayed her unattractive self. That was the show. And then a very large and bossy woman threw on the lights and ordered the audience out. When the audience objected she got really tough with them.

When Radomir showed up for breakfast Tony brought up Minerva Minot, perhaps in the context of the corpselike performers they had seen the night before. "Radomir told me that she laid there like she was dead," Tony said.

"I don't like people talking about what it's like sleeping with someone else. I always worry about what they're going to say about me," I said. Radomir studied the floor.

In the plane Radomir told me more. Tony had called Radomir once he was back in Paris and wanted to come to Paris so they could continue their sexcapades. Radomir declined. Then Tony called again to say that his girlfriend had suspected something and that he had admitted to her that he had had sex with Radomir because Radomir had been so persistent. That Radomir had been trying to lay him ever since Crete. Outraged, Radomir said, "It was completely the other way around. He was the one who was so hot to have sex. I told him our friendship was over. And then he says, 'Does this mean our Canada trip is off?' We had been planning to go to Canada with his girlfriend. I couldn't believe it. I just slammed down the phone."

Back in Paris Radomir insisted on taking me to dinner. He was very jovial and amusing. Maybe he felt he had bent my ear too much about Tony. And then we doubled-kissed good night on the best of terms and I was not to see him again for many, many months. I was just as glad. I had my own life to get in order and I had to work my way out of this Radomir fix I was in.

~32~ Amanda Reports In

Uncle Nevis and I sometimes send poems to each other. It's our sentimental side. Not about each other of course—just things that come into our minds. He taught me to keep a writing pad by my bed. Not for dreams, but those thoughts that come into your head as you're waking up. I sent him a poem that just came to me in one piece.

The light was diffused
We were confused,
I could have refused,
Our bodies fused.

I was just ending this relatively long-term affair with an Argentinean tennis player. Talk about confused.

As a reply Uncle Nevis sent me his poem. Which also came to him as he was awakening. We're not really poets of course.

WE DON'T NEED GLACIERS

We don't need glaciers,
People will do.
Some day people will tear the pictures
 of your lovers from their silver frames
 and throw them away.
Putting their own pictures of loved ones
 in their place.
Children.
Animals.
Not handsome young men.

Someday someone will laugh at the shirt you wore
the night he fucked you so hard
your brains rattled.
You didn't realize he was capable of passion like that.
Or that you weren't.
At least with him.

Someday someone will say to a friend,
"The ruby ring is nice,
But I don't know about sapphires.
Don't they bring bad luck?"
And they'll separate the rings you always wore
together on your left hand,
That Fred gave you.
That you wore for fifty years or more.

We don't need glaciers to push their way
into the house,
Crush the furniture,
Dampen the photographs,
Bury the jewels.
People will do it.
And every detail of your life will be swept away.
You've done it yourself.
You painted over the lavender wall someone chose
so carefully to go with the bedspread.
Put the plate back down on the table
at the flea market deciding against it,
Gave your aunt's napkins away.
Who uses cloth napkins anyway these days?

All this will be swept away as surely as by glaciers.
All that will be left is your memory of someone
holding you very closely as you shuddered
in the night.
Be grateful and remember

The emeralds and the eighteenth-century desk
and the little Vuillard print.
All will be ground away.
The jewels torn from the crowns of kings
Gone.
Because we don't need glaciers,
People will do.

He called me in Madrid from Paris about a week later. I said, "I think you have to have a break from this torchy little love you've got going for Radomir. It's making you feel old."

He said, "I'm turning brown around the edges."

"You're not really," I said. "It's just that Radomir is so much younger than you are. Aren't there any interesting older guys lurking around town?"

"Older guys are never interested in anyone like me. I could go for them, but they are only interested in blond little twinkies. Honestly."

He went on. "And I don't know how honest I am in saying I prefer an affair with someone my own age. No one looks older than when you're looking up at them having an orgasm. So what did you think of my poem? Is it too gloppy?"

I said, "It would probably be great set to music. Like Samuel Barber's 'Knoxville, 1915' or whatever the date is."

"God, Knoxville," he said.

"I was talking about the music not the town," I told him.

"Do you have tango music playing?" he said.

"It's the score from that new tango troupe that's wandering around Europe."

"Whenever I hear tango music I feel I should throw myself away on someone unworthy of me."

"As if you haven't dozens of times."

"It's true. I do seem pretty indestructible," he said.

"If you got into it with a Sherman tank, God help the tank." I told him I could tell he was getting into better spirits.

"Don't mention Sherman tanks, darling. It dates you," he said.

"You mean like referring to the USO?" I said.

"Exactly. What's your favorite thing, Amanda? Mine is the fine skin on men's bodies that has been covered by underwear all their lives."

"Mine is money," I said.

"Having enough money is like a stiff breeze blowing through the house. It clears the air," he said. "Well, that's enough nonsense, honey. I'll talk to you soon." And he hung up.

~33~ Radomir Visits Miami Beach

In the year that passed before I was to see Radomir again I was very occupied trying to salvage my career. Salvaging my life had to come second.

And then, too, Amanda had to be bailed out. She had conceived and delivered a baby in Madrid with her bodybuilding blond lover from Uruguay. A man too much younger than herself, already burdened with a live-in mother and live-in mistress, both who had come from Uruguay with him. I didn't think it was my part to point out to Amanda how much he resembled her father and her brothers. She's no dope.

I think she thought as soon as irresistible baby Boris appeared that Mr. Bodybuilder would insist on marrying her, but that was not to be. After all the adorable pictures of recovering mother and newborn in Dad's arms had been taken, Dad hit the road. What's that old song? "He may be good fucking but he's no fucking good?" That was him.

I had moved to my apartment in Miami Beach by this time. I needed the rent from the house in New York. I'd been renting it for a couple of years, and that essentially was my income as my advertising star faded. However, it was an excellent income. But now something had to be done about Amanda, so I suggested I buy a house in Miami Beach where we could all live together. Amanda could work there as the makeup artist she had become when her modeling career nosedived. Baby Boris could go to the beach.

And so it came to pass, although I hadn't anticipated that the four-bedroom art deco house would soon fill up with Amanda's friends. "The Ladies on the Loose," I called them. And they weren't all ladies. Not at all. And they weren't even all women. There was quite a string of former models trying their luck in Miami Beach before they gave it up completely. All the European magazines and advertising agencies had started coming to Miami Beach in the winter, and it was rapidly becoming a chic destination. People were beginning to call the neighborhood near us South Beach and it was all happening.

Which probably explains why Radomir included it in his itinerary when he made a tour of the U.S. that summer. We hadn't seen each other since Turin, but he called and found me and said he'd like to come see me with the teenage French boy and the French couple who were all traveling with him.

I was on the curved front porch hosing down the front walk when they pulled in from the airport. Radomir looked hunky at the wheel. The fifteen-year-old was portly and serious as only French kids can be. It turned out that Radomir was a friend of his mother's; she had contracted cancer and begged him to take her son along on the American trip, which he agreed to do.

The couple were a good-looking Laotian woman and her sapphire-eyed boyfriend-slash-husband.

It all went pretty well. The Laotian girl and her beau bought groceries and cooked and made beds and dried dishes. Quite a change from the "Ladies on the Loose" and all the other Bedouin tribes of Amanda's friends who passed through all winter.

I invited Don Amour to come down from Fort Lauderdale one evening. Don was a handsome sailor I was guiding gingerly toward a modeling career. Don was very good-looking, kind of a tall Mel Gibson, and was very at ease in front of the camera. I got some tests of him done and he really looked good. I began to think he might actually make it as a model and actor once he got some wind into his husky sails (which made me feel a little less like a manipulative slut). I wanted to show him off a little as a kind of defensive maneuver. Radomir was friendly with Don and struck hunkier-than-usual poses while they chatted.

Of course, Radomir and Amanda got along wonderfully. They always did. They laughed and snorted food through their noses at the table. Something like high school students. I don't imagine they think of each other for a moment once they're apart.

Baby Boris liked Radomir, too. Tiny but stalwart, blond and blue-eyed like his father and mother, Boris had a very Latino temperament under his crew cut. Living with a household of women had given him some unusual set phrases. One morning when I crossed the room to answer the telephone he looked up from his fire engine and said, "Tell them I'm not here."

When we went to the beach Radomir and Boris romped in the water together. I was floating nearby and Radomir suddenly turned to me and said, "When we were in Santa Fe I went to see a medicine man. He told me to go to one of the souvenir stands and buy one of the animal stone carvings. The one that appealed to me most. I bought a coyote and brought it back to him."

He deposited Boris on the beach, who wanted to annoy his mother, and came plunging back in. He obviously wanted to tell me this story which had begun, as was so often the case, with no preliminary. I bobbed up and down as he said, "The medicine man said, 'Oh, the coyote. The Trickster. I thought you'd choose that.'" When he said that there was a sideways glance from those opaque Central European eyes that never give anything away. It was a strange look I've only seen a few times, as though the real Radomir within was sending me a little semaphore message. Then the eyes were veiled again.

He went on to explain that the medicine man had told him of all the positive aspects of being a coyote. That the coyote was independent, explorative, self-reliant. But I remembered the glance. It was like a stone slowly twirling downward through the sunlit water I was swimming in.

When we got back on the beach we lay down beside each other. Radomir's body looked good in his dark blue Speedo trunks. Not quite as taut as it had been when he was twenty-two and first came to France, but still thick-armed; broad shoulders sliding down to his small, flat waist. At one point when Radomir was kneeling on all fours straightening his towel I imagined lying under him with my mouth at his crotch, looking up at his flat stomach.

We did manage one lunch alone together while he and his friends were there, and Radomir told me about an American he had met in Paris on a assignment. They had fallen into something that felt like love and Radomir had recently been out to Los Angeles to visit the man.

They had gone bicycling, to the beach, to gay bars, and Radomir said, "He wanted me to wear long boxer shorts to the beach. It embarrassed him to have people see him with another man wearing a small bathing suit. But he wanted to show me off in the gay bars he went to. I just hated it. I realized that I don't want to live that kind of life again. It was just like Linton, the priest. I didn't love him more than my life in Paris. One night I just cried and cried and cried. I couldn't stop crying. But I couldn't do it."

I told him that it sounded like the same scenario as the priest affair. There was no question of these men giving up their careers to move to Paris.

"I'm not going to say what I said last time we had this kind of conversation," Radomir said.

"Please don't," I said.

All I could think of was that though I would move to anywhere on the globe to be with Radomir he would never "cry and cry" for me. So on the next Saturday morning he got up and I took him to the airport so he could fly back to Paris. I think we both felt it was a kind of strange role reversal. My days of flying off to Paris were over; now he was taking over for me. But not quite. The Germans called on Monday and I found myself heading for Paris just one week later, on my way to Frankfurt. A new shampoo was being launched and they needed my help.

~34~ The List of Lovers Gets Too Long

In Paris, just one week from the day Radomir left Miami Beach, Nevis was with him again at the house in the country. Radomir seemed pleased to be going to the country, saw no problem in catching a train slightly earlier than usual, and had a more "there" presence with Nevis than he had shown for a long time.

On that evening, Nevis set the table in the garden and lit candles. Radomir had gone out for wine. When Radomir walked into the house he could see from the entryway through to the garden and said, "Candles. I hope this doesn't mean you're going to get all gloppy and sentimental." Nevis felt a little flush of relief at not having to feel embarrassed. "Not tonight. Not tonight," he replied, laughing.

At the table they talked at great length. Radomir went out again to buy cigarettes so they could talk, drink wine, and smoke. Nevis thought, *If you don't smoke or drink or eat or fuck, what* is *the context you're supposed to talk in?*

That night Radomir talked more about Phillipe, the boyfriend from the gym who had been a regular sex partner and who had killed himself when he discovered he had AIDS. Nevis felt a quick knowing of fear. Radomir seemed noncommittal. No voice tremor or eye movement suggested he was concerned about his frequent contact with Phillipe. Nevis wondered if he felt immunized by his unvarying use of condoms or was rigidly concealing his qualms. He was very capable of that.

Radomir told Nevis about going to a bar with Phillipe for a drink and noticing at the far end of the bar one man was fucking another. The fuckee, who had entered shirtless, had lowered his jeans and was bent over a bar stool while his barrel-chested, husky new friend prodded away at him. Apparently without a condom, Radomir said when he glanced their way from time to time, not sure he was seeing what he was seeing, although most of the people in the bar had gathered around to watch. When they were done, the husky man hugged his companion and left. But Mr. Fuckable pulled up his pants, tipped his penis into his fly, and ordered another drink.

Phillipe advised Radomir to go outside to pee; the backroom and the toilets were not to be visited. Radomir said he thought Phillipe had probably gone to that place frequently and had contracted AIDS there.

He had also broken off with his friend/lover Jean-Luc, whom he'd led Nevis to think he'd slept with in the spirit of experimentation. He said Jean-Luc had become possessive and jealous. Had gone to the gym with him really to keep an eye out for good-looking competition.

Nevis said, "He was just taking every chance he could to see you with your clothes off."

Radomir said, "He had plenty of opportunities to do that. All he had to do was invite me to dinner and he got that. For someone who claimed to be a homosexual virgin, he got into the swing real quick. He knew exactly what he liked and how he liked to do things." Nevis supposed Radomir was talking about blow jobs.

It was a different tone of voice Nevis was hearing—a tone he'd heard before from good-looking guys who liked their sex and it didn't have to be dressed up in romance. Preferably not. He felt a little sorry for the good-looking Jean-Luc. He'd wanted to try it. Got it hot and heavy and very regularly from a handsome hunk. And bang, one day handsome hunk doesn't want to do it anymore. And as with all dealings with handsome hunks, was told, "You have only yourself to blame."

Nevis remembered Radomir telling him that at one time in California his twinlike roommate had brought home a man who fancied Radomir instead. He insisted he did not wish to be screwed by the roommate but by Radomir. Who then did, although he "hated every minute of it."

Nevis said how sadomasochism escaped him as a source of sexual pleasure. He received the reply, "I tied somebody's hands together once in California." Another Radomir was taking form, solidifying but distorting the form of the Radomir he knew.

Radomir also talked more about Phillipe, the gym friend who had suddenly reemerged in recent months claiming to be in love. Radomir said that after he'd drifted away from Phillipe there had been only one night during a Metro strike when they'd slept together again. Phillipe had asked if he could stay over because of the strike. Once there, Radomir had given him the choice of the floor or sharing his bed. Phillipe had chosen the bed and once in bed Radomir said, "I realized it wasn't going to work. I said, 'Phillipe, I think you'd better sleep on the floor after all. I don't seem to be able to control myself.' Phillipe said, 'That's all right.' And my body took over. I think that's what he wanted anyway. And you know he has a very beautiful body. Shoulders out to here and a small waist." He made a V-shaped gesture with both hands. Nevis thought there was more than one person in that bed who had colluded on that little scenario.

Upon Phillipe's return to his life they had agreed to meet for dinner and talk things out. Radomir had told the jealous Jean-Luc where they were planning to eat and suddenly Jean-Luc had appeared beside their table, saying he'd just dropped in by chance for a drink. Phillipe soon left, not offering to pay any share of the dinner in typical French style, although he had requested they meet. Radomir chewed Jean-Luc out. Jean-Luc insisted that he truly was there by chance, having had dinner with his uncle. Radomir didn't believe him.

Again Nevis felt shut out of these true-life dramas and conflicts, ones very like earlier events in his own life. He wondered at himself, that he still wished to figure in these kinds of events, still wanted to be a player, wanted to have these things happen to himself, although he had had his share of these so-necessary passions. It made him feel selfish. Radomir deserved his experiences, but still Nevis mourned that they were not with him.

On Saturday they raced about on errands all day and rewarded themselves with a lavish dinner at a nearby chateau hotel. On the chateau terrace, grand and beflowered, they were caught by a sudden and violently windy thunderstorm. In a flurry of blowing menus and tipping tables they dashed inside, carrying their glasses and wine in its bucket. They finished the very good wine they had carried inside, and as the storm abated drove home, tipsily. With the rain beating down on the old Peugeot, Radomir at the wheel talked about what he actually did in bed with the ever increasing list of lovers.

Nevis first told him that he preferred having love made to him face to face. He did make love to other men and enjoyed it but it was something like masturbation. Whereas having his lover in him was for him the true expression of love. He added, he didn't quite understand sex lives without sexual entry. He asked, "Do you just rub together?"

Radomir said there was rubbing and mutual masturbation and sucking, although wearing condoms made that less than really fun. With Phillipe the swimmer and his ex-priest lover they had "screwed around." And he said with women he was, of course, in them. He laughed and remembered the hit-and-run sex attack of the woman at the film laboratory who had dragged him home with her and "nailed" him.

Before they retired Nevis asked for a back rub and returned the favor. It was not at all the sexual temptation it had been in the past, although he thought he could feel Radomir's erection with his knee when he put it between his legs to steady himself. Radomir began talking about relatives in Phoenix, but Nevis thought he had a lot of information to digest and said good night.

~35~ The Ghost Lover

Sunday at breakfast as they ate croissants the famous ghost of the house came up. Now Radomir elaborated very fully on his encounters with the ghost. He said that as soon as he arrived at the country house one of the first things he had heard about was the ghost. Fritz, who had stayed in Nevis's house while renovating his own nearby, had told Radomir, "And of course there's the ghost."

Not long after, in the night, Radomir heard footsteps coming up the stairs. Getting up to look, no one was there.

Then in the night the ghost touched him. Radomir evidently shrieked and jumped. But the ghost continued to try to make his presence known. Radomir could feel the atmosphere of his being, and he had materialized to reveal a young man with long, dark hair to his shoulders, clean-shaven, wearing a white shirt. Shorter than Radomir. He was from the turn of the century, Radomir thought. Nevis the fashion expert wondered. That look was more the Romantic period from the early nineteenth century.

Radomir fell in love with his ghost. For almost that whole first year, of Nevis coming and going, friends visiting, renovating the house, going to Paris, Radomir had been obsessively in love with his spirit. Concealing the slightest hint from anyone, longing to get back to the country to be alone with the spirit again.

As he told Nevis this he moved uneasily about the kitchen. It obviously wasn't easy for him, and several times he said, "I really don't want to talk about this."

Radomir reminded Nevis about the fall in the bathroom as they were preparing to move to Paris at the end of that summer. He had looked up at Nevis from the floor and said, "I know, I know, nothing is by chance." But now his unwillingness to go had other dimensions. He thought the ghost had tried to keep him there.

When he returned to the country for weekends the spirit was still there until one day after Christmas. Then he was gone. Completely gone. Radomir was bereaved. It was soon after that he set out for Crete.

Nevis looked at the person before him, who in this terse little story had slashed apart their whole history together. All the time Nevis had been suffering, struggling in emotional chaos over Radomir, he'd accepted that in fact Radomir was sleeping with many other people, men and women. But now it was clear that more importantly the man he loved had been deeply involved somewhere in his own mind with the spirit of someone who no longer existed.

Radomir didn't say as much, but his desire to be with the spirit he loved must have edged him toward thoughts of death, to join the presence he loved wherever he was. Radomir said that when he told his experience to his spiritually inclined woman friend in New Mexico, the only person he ever confided in, she said, "He loved you enough to go away. He had things he had to do. And so do you."

When he told his parents later, those sweet, simple people seem to accept the story easily, as they did everything about Radomir. His mother said, "But he left traces. Now your hair is wavy. It was always straight before. And your eyes are gray-green, and they used to be brown."

Radomir was evidently shaken by his discussion of the ghost, but he went on to say, "When I went to Santa Fe while all this was happening, my friend had me hypnotized. While I was hypnotized they asked me what I was experiencing. I said I was at the chateau here at the edge of town. I was in uniform with two rows of buttons. I was talking to a woman with black hair in a blue dress with a kind of lacing on the front. She wore some kind of large ornament on the back of her hair. She was crying violently. We were in a corner ground-floor room of the chateau. A library with dark red, maroon wall coverings and draperies. I knew there was a man somewhere in the house, although he wasn't with us.

"I was telling the woman I was going away to the Spanish War. The hypnotist asked me if he knew who this woman was. I told her, 'Yes, Mr. Neeland.'" Nevis's last name.

The hypnotist had also had Radomir write down dates and phrases. The first one he wrote was 1823.

Nevis went to his library and found a French history. There *had* been a brief war with Spain in 1823.

Telling this to Radomir, he said, "Let's take a walk to the cemetery and see if there is a Comtesse de Bodard who fits into that time scale." They went in the rain under a single umbrella up the Rue de Paradis, but in the row of counts and countesses de Bodard none of the tombs went back so far. "There must be more graves somewhere. We will have to try to visit the chateau one day and also see if there is a red library there," Nevis said.

Nevis could accept that perhaps he had once been a French countess and Radomir his military lover. Perhaps the ghost was the Radomir of that time, trying to meet up with his present self. Perhaps everyone was revisiting the scene of their earlier mistakes and misdemeanors. Nevis didn't care very much.

Just before their train pulled into the Gare d'Austerlitz on their way back to Paris, Radomir said that the man he'd left in California so long ago when he first came to Europe had called him the previous week.

Nevis said, "He's not on your list of people you loved, and yet you saw him for a long time and lived with him."

"I was very fascinated with him. I don't know that I loved him," Radomir answered. "He could be very insensitive and dorky. Once I was crying in the car and he didn't even notice."

~36~ On Géricault

Do you know Géricault? The French painter? *The Raft of the Medusa* and all that? I've been following his career for some time. Something like keeping up with the news of an ex-lover. Except that this ex-lover died about 150 years ago. More maybe.

Géricault was a very sexy guy. He fell in love with his uncle's much younger wife and they had a tempestuous affair. It's interesting with artists; you can tell how tempestuous an affair was and what they did by looking at their art.

There is a wonderful drawing of a couple making love that I have to believe was modeled on Géricault himself and his mistress. He was a handsome guy with a strong body, quite a horseman, so one can easily imagine him as a dashing and virile lover.

In the drawing, white and black ink on a dark blue background, the man is kneeling, leaning backward with strong thighs and taut biceps. He is holding a woman who is sliding down his body, her legs extended backward like some great fish, or mermaid, caught at the crotch on the anchor of his cock.

The light and dark lines on the navy paper create the effect of bodies seen in moonlight. This is a couple plunged into the erotica of each other's bodies. It is hard to imagine that in the early nineteenth century, without the benefits of television's blue light or an electric lamp by the head of the bed, people actually tore their clothes off and got it on. Mad about each other's bodies. Mad about each other.

At an exhibition of nineteenth-century French sculpture at the Grand Palais I saw a small bronze done by Géricault. The same couple, this time both kneeling, he with his hand plunged deeply between her legs, feeling, feeling, feeling that crevice that soon he is going to plunge into.

Géricault was the kind of lover I want. That we all want. Strong of body. Passionate in nature. So crazy about us he wants to get *in* there and be one with us. *That's* a lover. That's how I always imagine Radomir would be if one ever got past all his defenses. If one ever could arouse any real interest.

Géricault's affair with his aunt was discovered. There was never any question of the woman leaving his uncle and going off with Géricault. The uncle simply took her to their country estate, Géricault was forbidden to see her, and I imagine she was reminded frequently by her husband what an absolute slut she was. She died after not too many years.

Géricault lived on a little longer than she did, but not much. He went to England to try to forget her. He went to the morgues to paint severed heads and lopped-off arms and legs, to harden himself against the inevitability of death.

When thrown from a horse and injured in the lower back he refused treatment. The wound festered, and slowly and painfully he laid in his bed and died. His artist friends mustered around, drew his portrait as he lay dying. And then he was gone. The young, handsome, sexy, talented guy was gone at thirty-three. He's the only artist I really mourn.

I've always said that I'm quite willing to not have any of Van Gogh's paintings in existence in exchange for his having been happy. I'm not big on the idea that creativity comes from suffering. Suffering is bad. Creativity is nice, but the world can live without it. What Radomir has put me through may have resulted in this book, but have I added greatly to the world's treasure trove of literature? Hardly. I would have much preferred to not have suffered.

~37~ A Visit to Sandusky

I must put all this down before I forget. I went to visit Radomir's parents in Sandusky. I always said if I was in that part of the Midwest I'd visit them, so I did. I don't know quite why. Yes, I do.

I couldn't get there except on a flight that arrived late. 10:30 p.m. They were sitting side by side in the waiting area when I got off the plane. They looked very much the same as they had in France over three years ago. His mother's hair was a lighter shade of reddish blonde. His father seemed slimmer, slighter, younger. Her name is Bernadette, but everyone calls her Brenda, for some reason. She was quite a chic lady at one time, and is still not unchic. She was a buyer at a major Chicago department store. I suppose at that time Bernadette was a pathetic, religious kind of name and Brenda rather glamorous.

His name is John. Just plain John. We hugged and they both kissed me. I'm a lot taller than they are. I didn't realize how much until they reached up to give me a kiss. They seemed really affectionate and a little nervous. Something in their manner was like parents greeting a child. I bring that out in people. They're only a few years older than I am but I mentally have placed them in another generation because of Radomir. And I usually deal with couples as though they are my parents or my children.

I'll never know what Bernadette and John knew about what had gone on or is going on with Radomir and me. So much less and so different than they suspect probably.

We had ham sandwiches before we went to bed. In the house where all the strange things had happened to Radomir. The house of the poltergeists. That was one reason I had to come. To see that house. A newish house, undistinguished. A strange floor plan and many levels on what isn't apparently a very hilly site. A stair goes up to the small bedrooms. A stair goes down to a library, study, TV room? Then down again to a basement and bedroom. Bedroom? Then up again to a back sunroom. There was *something* about all those levels.

My bedroom was small and faceless. The whole house had no feeling of having been much lived in, although they had brought up four sons in it. They probably had completely redecorated once the boys were all out.

The next day they took me to a small nearby town where my grandfather had once been the superintendent of the school and my mother had taught for him. He wasn't her father; she was later to marry one of his sons. I'd heard of this town often in childhood and wanted to see it. Masterbridge. A very early town for the Midwest, founded in 1829 when the area was still a territory. An important station on the Underground Railroad later, and there seemed to be many blacks living there. Like real people, not ghettoized.

Some large important houses. A decayed main street. Small. Brenda and John had never been there before, though it was only about half an hour away from their home. I knew it was so close only because Radomir had said that friends and he used to go there in high school. For what reason I don't remember.

The school where my grandfather taught was gone, but the library had pictures of it. It had been considered a fine building when built in the 1880s, and then was torn down in the 1950s. I'm sure the people of Masterbridge don't know why now. Just old, I suppose.

I imagined my mother walking those sidewalks, probably thinking of someone other than my father. She very likely lived with my grandparents as their son's near fiancee. I'll never know now why she was really there. Perhaps my grandfather fancied her. She was a lovely young woman.

We had a sort of awful lunch in Masterbridge. When we got back to Sandusky, Brenda suggested I might like to look at photographs. Brenda talks nonstop but she's canny. Without really bringing it to the top of her mind I think she sensed I was there to piece together what I could of Radomir when he lived there. John did, too, but I think they were in different zones. I don't think there was any complicity there.

Brenda had already pointed out a cubbyhole off Radomir's old room where she said they kept his books and some stuffed toys that had been his.

John pointed out a large drawing hung on the staircase of a very 1970s boy. Radomir had won a prize with it in school. I asked if it was a self-portrait and was told it wasn't. There were other paintings and art objects Radomir had made. He had done pottery sculpture that was not untalented, with something a little dark and violent about it. He had once brought home from California a piece for each of his brothers and his parents. They were symbolic, he had said, but refused to explain the symbolism. Brenda and John had a Pierrot clown seated in the splits. Something macabre hung over it, like Jack Nicholson as The Joker. It definitely wasn't cute. Certainly as a high school student he had been considered the artistic one of the sons.

Brenda first brought out large albums of old pictures, some duplicating a collection of old family pictures on the staircase landing. Brenda's mother when she married at sixteen. A soft-mouthed, babyish pretty girl, in a veil that fitted low over her brow as they did in the 1920s. Her bridesmaids looked older and wore very pretty chiffon dresses with skirts like petals. She had had an expensive wedding.

Her husband, Brenda's father, was handsome and obviously older. How much it was hard to say. He could have been in his late twenties or even late thirties.

Brenda said they always celebrated his birthday on July Fourth, but she never truly knew the year of his birth. John said someone in the family had once told him that his father-in-law was twenty-five years older than his bride.

There was another photograph on the staircase wall of the father as a younger man with a male friend. His best friend, now unknown. They were both good-looking. Their clothes were a style worn before World War I. There was an uncle in the photo book who had also married very late.

In the book, as well as on the wall, were photographs of John's parents as well. In their wedding portrait done in Yugoslavia Radomir's grandmother looked like a stunned doll. Another photograph of relatives in Yugoslavia showed a group of people in peasant costume wearing round hats, babushkas, and multilayered skirts.

Both Brenda and John's families were originally from Yugoslavia, and they met through the Yugoslavian community in Detroit. They weren't kids when they married. He was in his late thirties, she in her early thirties, when they started their family. In the albums were pictures of Brenda after she left school, looking cute and starletty in that early 1950s way. She had very dark hair then and that look of actresses like Peggy Ann Garner. Never a big star, but there was something there. One big picture was John when he was in the army. Cute. Very cute.

Brenda always looked chic in the pictures. The smart little dress. The immaculate hair. They were well put together, the women of her family. Her mother, though heavier, had that groomed look, too. Brenda never looked like the harried mother of four. I noticed there were no pictures of Brenda in her twenties. A definite gap there. John, also. Were they married to other people at one time? Or into heavy affairs. There were mysteries back there in their lives.

There were, of course, pictures of all the boys from babyhood on. In the upper hall was a row of all their baby portraits. Radomir was the last one, upturned smiling face, with a kewpie-doll curl on top. Immediately recognizable. All the boys were very cute, bright-eyed babies. But aren't all babies? I think not.

After I'd seen the big albums Brenda asked me if I wanted to see the snapshot albums, too, which I did. In these more of the pieces fit together. There were photos of Brenda's mother early in her marriage. She looked happy. A teenager having fun, even though a married lady. Both Brenda and her sister were born before their mother was twenty, I think. Then their mother became a portly lady, something like a stylish Russian commissar's wife. She was a clerk in the jewelry department of the same store where Brenda worked. Portly but soigné. Then she came to their home to die of cancer, when they had lived in the Detroit suburbs, before moving to Sandusky.

They had showed me the ornamental hand bell on the study mantel that one of the boys had bought with his own money as a child so his grandmother could signal from her bedroom if she needed help.

Brenda said she would ring just so the boys would run upstairs to keep her company. She was the grandmother who once told Radomir something very important when he was little and sitting with her. But now he can't remember it, although he knows if he remembers someday it will be truly important. Brenda also told me that when her mother was desperately ill she had to take her for radiation therapy every day, leaving Radomir with their neighbors. Finally the neighbor said to her, "You'd better talk to that son of yours. He thinks one of these days you're going to leave him and never come back." She was torn, not wanting to neglect either her mother or her child.

And there were pictures, pictures, pictures of Radomir. Somehow the three older boys seemed more of a team in the pictures, with him left out as the baby. In one he wore a little red coat and hat. "He always hated that hat," Brenda said. In another he slumps asleep over his father's shoulder in a little plaid jacket. And in a number of pictures he is a ring bearer in a wedding. About four, all in white. His sick grandmother said she would give him a dollar if the rings didn't fall off their cushion. He took it, although he confessed to her they weren't the real rings and had been sewn on so there could be no accident. In many pictures he has a slightly befogged and worn look around the eyes, as he must have been nearsighted and straining his eyes even then. At this wedding was a handsome young man. The four-year-old Radomir was very taken with him and wanted him to come home with him. "You're kind of young to be a friend," the man said. "I have older brothers," Radomir replied.

There was a photograph of Radomir as a teenager with a Beatles' haircut, like a helmet, hugging a white dog. And Radomir with his other grandmother, a prickly pickled-looking old lady. She had lived with them, not successfully, for several years when the children were teenagers. In the photographs one can see there was a bond between the sulky teenager and his grandmother.

Radomir in his prom picture has his arm around his little girlfriend. I mean literally little. He's not all that tall, and she was only up to his shoulder. I suppose they lost their virginity together.

There was a bigger picture of this period of the four boys together. Radomir is wearing an animal-print shirt under a suit. And there is also his graduation picture. His pictures of this period all have the look of a hot, dissolute teenager, with something definitely going on beneath the surface.

Then Radomir beside his aunt's pool in Phoenix. Other photographs of him leaping down snowdrifts in the Arizona mountains, falling back laughing, half-submerged in the snow. That was the trip he took as a birthday present from his hooker roommate/girlfriend. A faint "bad seed" air hangs over him in these pictures. How much do his parents know of his life at that period? Plenty, I guess. He was thinner, hungrier looking then. The sex toy of many, as he put it. Only later did he get hunkier looking.

And pictures when I knew him but that I'd never seen. One on Crete where he stands beside a sign for a nightclub he's painted. He's wearing brief shorts, looking so husky and long-legged I had to ask to make sure it was him.

Later there were pictures of Radomir at the family Christmases and holidays where he is the visitor from California or France. He's always there, always pleasant, but somehow usually a bit apart. There is something of the good sport about his manner.

The pictures, a few, where his lover Linton, the ex-priest, visited them have very much that atmosphere. There, at ease, but somehow distant. Linton is good-looking but not exceptional.

There was one oddly poignant picture of Radomir looking back over his shoulder on a sidewalk in front of a brick building. "That was taken in front of Linton's sister's building in Chicago," Brenda said. "They stayed with her." She, too, seemed to feel the picture meant something, though neither of us could say exactly what.

We talked about Radomir's name. He had been brought up as Ronald Don Pool. Their family name had been Pulkanovic but had been changed. The children were all brought up with the name Pool, and his brothers were known by that name. Only he had decided in California to return to his grandfather's name. I was surprised when Brenda told me that he had chosen the name Radomir himself, and that his legal name was now Radomir Ronald Pulkanovic. I thought back over all those pictures and realized that they were almost all of Ron Pool. Ronnie Pool. Ronald Pool. His parents dutifully called him

Radomir when they talked of him to me. But I started referring to him as Ronald and they obviously preferred it. How could they not? They were quite amazing in their ability to graciously follow their youngest son into a new personality and not feel resentful. I liked thinking of him as Ronald Pool. It made a lot more sense with all those pictures of a high school student in Sandusky, a little bisexual sexpot in Phoenix and Los Angeles. Ronnie Pool. What's that song? "All About Ronnie?"

Brenda fixed an elaborate dinner for just the three of us. None of the brothers or their wives could come to dinner, although one brother was promised for afterward. At dinner John talked a little bit about the paranormal experiences Radomir/Ronald had in the house. He remembered waking one night to a smoke-filled bedroom and going downstairs to find Radomir/Ronald and a friend trying to burn a Ouija board in the fireplace with the damper closed. They had evidently just had some very scary news, and when John kiddingly mentioned the incident years later, Radomir pleaded with him to never get another board. Brenda said that one night when they had a lot of guests she had slept in the basement bedroom and been disquieted by the memories of the presence down there. "But finally I just turned my back to the door and went to sleep," she declared. John added that he had asked Radomir how a house that had been built for their family to occupy could be haunted, and Radomir told him he believed it was built on an Indian cemetery and they had disturbed their resting place. They both seemed to neither believe nor disbelieve that a spectral presence was there. In a solid Midwestern way they seemed to accept things as long as it didn't seriously inconvenience them.

Radomir's father also talked a little bit about his war experiences and the buddies he never particularly wanted to see again. In the albums there had been pictures of a very handsome blond brother who was lost in the war as a pilot. The one thing in their home with great distinction was a framed collection of his brother's medals with a small oil painting of his brother in the center. It had great emotional weight, although John didn't express any great loss at his brother's death. He told me of one of his army buddies having sought him out a few years ago, even though when they had separated after the war they had all agreed to let their acquaintanceships evaporate. "He keeps inviting us to visit them in Alabama," he said, "but I just don't want to go."

"It's not so far." I ventured, "You've taken longer trips."

"It's not that," he replied. "I just don't want to see him again."

Earlier in the day he and I had been leaning against the kitchen counter talking. He looked up at me and then suddenly walked off across the kitchen in a youthful way that made it clear what he must have been like as a young man. It wasn't exactly flirtatious, but rather like the memory of what being flirtatious was all about. Radomir had wondered if one of the reasons his father no longer wanted to see the old espionage and assassination team from his war days in South America was that there had been some romantic attachment, complicating the memories even further.

After dinner Radomir's next older brother stopped in with his three children. An attractive man who surprised me by actually seeming to want to meet me, and not dutifully responding to his parents' phone call. His smallest child, a rambunctious two-year-old, had his head shaved to call a halt to his pulling his curls so much he pulled them out. The family thought he resembled a tiny Buddhist monk. A tiny, tough Buddhist monk. He resembled Radomir's early photographs and chased his older brother sturdily around the living room. When his brother sat down in an easy chair he clambered quickly up to squeeze in behind him as though they were riding a motorcycle together. He brought to life in front of me what Radomir must have been like as a child. The rollicking, fun-loving, roll-about, knockabout style was certainly the same.

I had to leave very early the next morning, and Brenda and John were up at six o'clock to take me to the airport. Real troupers, even though they were leaving even earlier the next morning for Mexico to vacation. In the dark of dawn in front of the deserted Sandusky airport we hugged and kissed again. An unusual pair, they seemed to realize and understand a great deal. I wonder if they sit and talk about what they know, or just share the understanding.

~38~ Ronald Pool

On my way back to France I remembered two things. His father had told me how Radomir/Ronald had completely decorated his room when he lived alone with them as a teenager. Murals on the walls, violent colors. And now the room is an innocuous pink with fluffy curtains.

Brenda had said when they first moved to Sandusky Radomir/Ronald had wept every morning and hadn't wanted to leave his mother and go to kindergarten. She'd felt terrible every morning pushing him out the front door to wait for the bus. His teacher had realized he was having a tough time being separated from his mother and set him to drawing pictures of everything he saw in the classroom, which distracted him. Even today, it is Radomir/Ronald who draws the little cartoon signs they put up around his office to tell the staff of new regulations or coming events.

It also occurred to me, which I hadn't thought of at all at the time, that perhaps Brenda and John were edgy because of all those times when I had called desperate to find the fleeing Radomir and they had pretended they had not heard from him and didn't know where he was. Maybe not. Maybe they had forgotten those days, too.

In the morning arriving in Paris by plane, a large red sun emerging from the horizon, the same sun that had just set a few hours before miles out over the Atlantic from New York, I felt the world was rolling too fast. That I stand too tall upon it, like the Little Prince on his tiny globe.

As I got off the plane I said good-bye to the steward. I had noticed when he placed the tray in front of me that he had good-looking hands. Tan, well modeled, with some fine, black hairs on them. Often when I see men's hands, good-looking or not, I imagine them pulling at their penis. It isn't a sex fantasy, but a reality, however difficult to imagine in some cases.

When I returned to France Radomir/Ronald was still in a distant mood. He then wrote a long and rather intelligent letter explaining that he felt I had slipped back into the mode of loving him and that it was based on a fantasy and in fact there had never been any reason to think I could be in love with him.

That night, not really asleep but not really awake either, my mind began to examine the phrase "Ronald Pool, The Trickster." Somehow my mind was grappling with the idea that in fact the Radomir I was so obsessed with in fact was not Radomir at all, but Ronald Pool. This person was Ronald Pool. There was no Radomir Pulkanovic. There never had been. That person was a chimera, dreamed up in California by a kid from Sandusky. The person I dropped in to see at his office was Ronald Pool. And he was right. There was no Radomir for me to love. It was like a movie image.

Can I hang onto this idea? Now after my visit to Sandusky, I begin to see the fix I'm in. In some way I think Brenda and John were trying to help me and let me know all they could so I could rescue myself. If any evil spirit rose up out of the bowels of their home, it was gone now, perhaps hovering around their son Ronald, who now called himself Radomir. Something very Central European informed their actions. They didn't like it or dislike it; they were only observing it.

~39~ Can We Talk About Obsession?

Finally, my relationship with Radomir was all about obsession. Can obsession be called love? Or is what most people call real love just a form of obsession, to lesser or greater degrees? Whatever it is, it isn't just a new fragrance from Calvin Klein. And it certainly isn't a million laughs.

Very recently Radomir sent me a document he'd written titled "The Missing Facts." It was designed to fill me in on any missing details in his checkered sexual history. A lot of it I knew from those conversations we had had sitting on beaches and over wine with candles flickering.

But there were things I didn't know about. Another opportunity to scratch that itch, so painful but so necessary. Isn't there another side to this obsession, too? Doesn't Radomir have a kind of obsessive need to tell me all these things? I'm not sure whether this is some kind of need to inflict pain on me; I know on any number of occasions he has told people how much he hates me. Or is it some kind of need to unburden himself and try to find some answer to his ricocheting back and forth between men and women without finding any safe landing places?

He said in his letter that when he lived in Denver he didn't consider himself "promiscuous" because he had five or six both male and female "regulars" with whom he slept. He referred to himself as their "toy." He often likes to refer to himself in a childlike way. On Crete he said that he had even tanned his "little tooshie."

Of his life in Los Angeles with the lady who awarded kisses and prizes at the Indianapolis Motor Speedway, he said that cocaine was a standard accessory. With his look-alike roommate he would get high and then zip through gay clubs, dancing and hugging and turning everyone on and departing suddenly. They called that "wrecking 'em."

There never is any concern about AIDS in anything Radomir writes, and in fact I don't think I have any concern for myself about it. I told him once that if he slept with me and gave me AIDS I would prefer to die than to stay behind without him. He told me that he thought I was crazy. Yet it was true and is still true.

I remember the first time I saw Radomir, slouching toward us at the airport in his leather jacket and jeans. My immediate reaction was "studlet hustler." How accurate we are sometimes.

With the great love of my life from the 1960s my immediate reaction upon first meeting him was that he was insane. Ten years later I came to the same conclusion. Could I have saved myself a lot of trouble? Or was it the trouble I was looking for? Same story with Radomir.

He admitted in his letter to me that in California he used imaginary "girlfriends" to cover up a lot of his sexual carryings-on. When pinned down he would conjure up an imaginary girl back home to the degree that he actually did begin an affair with a young woman from his hometown who was visiting California.

This was the first time he experienced something like "love" and also the first time he thought of fleeing to Europe and "starting over again." This rang a bell for me. Perhaps this had all been about restarting his life. With a woman or a man? It was this indecision that led to his reprising the whole scenario in Paris.

This is not good, I told myself when I finished reading Radomir's fact sheet. I don't see any light at the end of the tunnel. A long-ago friend used to say, "If there's no solution it isn't a problem. It's just a fact." And there was no solution that I could see. Both Radomir and I could go on indefinitely with me longing for him and him telling me about all the people he was sleeping with. We were obviously seeking some kind of answer by doing this, but neither of us knew the questions.

I called Radomir in Paris from my deck in Miami Beach.

"I think we have to cut off all communication," I told him. There wasn't any reply. This is perhaps what he has been longing to hear for some years. "I have to go cold turkey. If I don't hear from you or see you or know anything about you maybe I can get interested in somebody else and get myself out of this situation."

When he spoke Radomir was calm and even kind. He said he understood that I had to do something. He sounded neither relieved or unrelieved. I had probably never meant a great deal to Radomir. It was only the exotic and bizarre nature of our relationship that had appealed to him.

I felt the ghostly presence of many others standing in the line to take my place in the life of Radomir Pulkanovic, who was himself a kind of ghostly presence for Ronald Pool. I said good-bye, hung up, and called Don Amour, my husky sailor friend. I was going to need distraction.

~40~ Letters from Lo De Coy

Lo De Coy wrote both Nevis and Radomir from Guatemala, where she had returned to pursue a career as a photographer. Busily photographing babies and weddings, she found time and distance to review her years in Paris, which prompted her to write letters to many of the people she had known there.

In her letter to Nevis she wrote:

Dear Nevis,

I call you by your first name, though we never met, because I feel I know you very well. Perhaps not as a friend, but certainly as someone with whom I am very familiar.

Radomir Pulkanovic so often spoke of you, and although his comments were in the most part negative, I did not perceive you that way. I felt you were someone caught in a moment of destiny. Someone who managed to preserve his dignity despite events which must have often been difficult for you.

Here in Guatemala one cannot but be very aware of destiny. The native Indians consider themselves still to be victims of an invasion.

Just to live in Guatemala is difficult as one is forced to move emotionally from one century to another regularly. With the Indians one is in the simple but violent world of the Mayans. With the people who fancy they are running the country one is in a nineteenth-century world of privilege and prevarication.

Beneath it all is some spiderlike web of connection, a connection I think you would sense and perhaps understand more than myself.

I always envied Radomir's connection to you and your inexhaustible love for him. With parents like mine, obviously this is a kind of love I have never known. Impossible as it would have been, I would have liked to have been loved by you like that. I think it is rare. People call this kind of love obsession. I would think to be obsessively loved is a kind of good fortune. But I would, wouldn't I?

Radomir once told me that he had a friend who referred to you as "the man who creates destinies for others." I'm sorry I missed knowing you personally and perhaps having had my own destiny molded by your deft and loving hands. Could I end this letter by saying,

Love,

Loretta De Coy

Nevis read her letter and started planning a trip to Guatemala. Where the hell was it? Just south of Mexico, it seemed. Not even as far as from Miami to New York.

Lo's letter to Radomir was somewhat different. She obviously felt less affection for him than she had for the unknown Nevis.

Dear Radomir,

What rhymes with Rad? Bad, sad, glad? All of these things may well be you, my friend of Paris days.

I've just written a letter to your, what should I call him? Certainly, friend Nevis.

Lost as I am here in Guatemala City with many photographs to do of very similar brides and identical babies. I use the same lighting on all of them and they are very content.

My work here is not so demanding of my time and talent that I do not have much time to think of you, Radomir. Although all is calm here now, there has been much conflict with the rebels as you know.

This endless conflict generation after generation has a relationship of some kind with you I believe, Radomir, and your conflicted life with Nevis. There was something there that ran deep, the two of you twisting and turning in the wind of the past. Not understanding what the Gods had planned for you, who knows how long ago? I think Nevis understood this better than you did. And was more willing to suffer to see where it would lead. Or was unable to free himself. Although I guess he finally did. Perhaps he shouldn't have. Perhaps he just could no longer handle the pain.

I only write this because I have a kind of envy of the love he had for you. My parents, as you know, regard their children as property. Love is not something they have known, I think. And I wonder what runs beneath the world we see day by day?

Is my English good enough to communicate what I am thinking? I wish you all the best in the life you now have, even though it is unknown to me. You have already lived a life that I will probably never know. I can only hope that one day I may find myself hopelessly in love with someone or that someone will be hopelessly in love with me. I think I will know how to conduct myself having lived it a bit through you.

The girl from Guatemala,

Lo-Lo

Radomir sent this letter to Nevis without an accompanying note.

~41~ A Few Last Words from Radomir

It's me, Ronald Pool. Radomir Pulkanovic. However you may want to think of me. I finally got my shit together. It took a while, but I did start over in Europe. I am a homosexual. That decision has been made.

Of course Nevis and I are talking again and we see each other several times a year when he comes to Paris. The last time he was here he said, "All those years ago, what did you use for masturbation fantasies? Men or women?"

"Men," I said. "That should have told me something, shouldn't it?"

I had a French lover for several years, who was very handsome and loved to be affectionate in public but much less so in private.

I had a Russian lover for several years who was very handsome but thought of himself as some kind of princeling swept in from the steppes. I could service him but I never fucked him. Not even once. And he didn't me, either. He didn't like that kind of thing. That, too, wound up in the trash heap.

Now I'm planning to spend the rest of my life with a good-looking Englishman. We've been together for almost five years and we still don't bore each other. Sexually or any other way.

Julian and I were in Miami Beach not too long ago. Nevis wasn't there, but we had lunch with his sister, who also lives there. At the end of the meal she turned to Julian and said, "You look very much as my brother Nevis did when we were much younger."

I told Nevis this when we met next and he said, "I know. My sister told me. Do we want to discuss this any further?"

I said, "I don't."

Nevis said, "Neither do I."

~42~ My Last-Minute Thoughts

It's been hard weaning myself away from Radomir. Refusing to see him, refusing to think about him, I even have thought of not returning to France. The one thing I would miss if I left France is the quality of the coinage, the thickness and the heaviness. I'd miss that feeling of extra-living . . . those late violet evenings in good weather that last until almost eleven in the summertime.

But I can't go on like this dreaming of hard-ons I haven't seen for many, many years. Thinking of lovers that, even if they are living, no longer have any power to move me.

It was a clear, sunny morning in Miami and we were whirling along one of the vertiginous highways that soar about the old city, circling the clutch of towers in downtown. I don't know where we were going. Perhaps Vizcaya. Or Parrot Jungle. Or Monkey Jungle. Not Butterfly World, that's way up to the north. My nephew was driving. My nephew Willem. There was something about the clear sunshine, the old wooden houses down below, my legs in their shorts in front of me on the car seat that made me think of California long ago. When I would be in a car with a young man in the morning sun, heading down the coast highway to Carmel or across the Golden Gate Bridge toward Tiburon.

And I felt anguish. I felt the excitement and the hope and the future of those long ago years and at the same time I felt the knowledge that those years are now long past. I have lived out the hope; I have lived into the future; I have been with those men as they aged from handsome abstractions into worried realities. There had been nothing bad about my life unless you want to call reality bad. Now I know where those dreams lead, what becomes of that excitement. I felt a pang. And yet, and yet. If Mel calls from Chicago tonight, I might have a little flash of those feelings again. We might plan a cross-country trip. Chicago—San Francisco. On blue roads. No highways. Cheap motels. Stuckey's candy. Rodeos in Wyoming. Over the Donner Pass. Mornings in some cheesy wooden Victorian hotel in San Francisco. I could kind of go for it.

I seem to have been refreshed by the agony and the anxiety and feel younger than I used to be. I know I've been a fool over this whole Radomir mess. But it's over now and you must forgive me because I was older then.

ABOUT THE AUTHOR

The Millionaire of Love is **David Leddick's** fifth novel. His other books include a number of photography books on the subject of the male nude that he has edited, an art history of the 1930s titled *Intimate Companions,* and a nonfiction work on gay men who married women titled *The Secret Lives of Married Men*. He has been a dancer, naval officer, advertising creative director, and a director of television commercials. He recently returned to the stage as a cabaret performer with a new one-man musical based on the life of Quentin Crisp called *Quentin and I*. He lives in Miami Beach, Paris, and Montevideo, Uruguay.